RESISTANCE OF LOVE

The Strong Family Saga
Book Two

Ros Rendle

SAPERE
BOOKS

RESISTANCE OF LOVE

Published by Sapere Books.

20 Windermere Drive, Leeds, England, LS17 7UZ,
United Kingdom

saperebooks.com

ISBN: 978-1-80055-433-7

For Sid, a good friend, who gave me information for this book. He never did believe he was a hero, but he was.

ACKNOWLEDGEMENTS

My husband, Scott, is always supportive, not least because writing takes over from housework quite often! He is always willing to help with researching hard to find facts, too, and we have been known to travel quite some distance to verify those small details which ensure accuracy, for example when I couldn't remember the exact layout of the long gallery at the Chateau de Chenonceau which formed part of the escape route.

Sapere Books have a very talented team of editors and publicists. They also engender a great friendship ethic between their authors. I'm truly lucky to be part of that family, so it's with huge thanks to them for the success of this series of books.

PART 1: DELPHI COMES HOME

CHAPTER 1

1927, on board the Jervis Bay

Now they had left sight of land, Delphi could see how the next thirty days or so might be. Surely this was the right decision. After all these years, she had been jittery about making the move, but having got this far she persuaded herself it was a good result. She should take Flora to meet her family, even if it meant travelling halfway around the world. It was only right, wasn't it? Flora had been persistent with her questions for a while now and she, as her mother, had to face facts. Perhaps her child's restless warring with those around her was part of her quest to know more of her roots.

Maybe I need to tell her more about her father, Delphi thought. *But it has all been so delicate and painful. How do I tell her we were not married, that she is a bastard, with all the shame that involves?*

As she lay back in the deck lounger, Delphi stretched her arms wide and took a deep breath. Her home in Australia for the last ten years suddenly seemed remote. The die had been cast when she had received that last letter from Papa saying how ill Rose had been. He had been very persuasive and had even sent her the money for the fare. She had supposed it was time to go and make her peace back there, after all this time. She still had Flora, though, the evidence of the so-called sin she had committed. She hadn't regretted one moment of it, despite the difficulties. Breathing out slowly, she allowed the sun to seep into her soul. She closed her eyes. Yes, this had to be the right thing to do, surely.

"May I sit here?"

Delphi became aware of a shadow across her face. She opened her eyes and there was the older lady she'd seen on boarding. She wore a rather old-fashioned long flowered dress.

"Oh, I'm sorry, my dear. I'm blocking out your sun. May I take this lounger?"

"Yes, by all means. Please do," Delphi answered.

"We met when we boarded, although I don't expect you remember. You had your hands full with the little girl. Is it your little sister you're travelling with?" Without pausing for a response, she continued, "We must have cabins close to each other. I mean, there're only fourteen of us in first. I've not seen you during the last couple of days. I was laid low with seasickness. Oh, I've never felt so ill. I do feel a bit better today, though. I thought I'd make the effort. So … here I am."

Delphi was bewildered, unsure about which part of this diatribe to make comment.

"Listen to me rabbiting on and never a pause for breath. I'm not letting you get a word in edgeways." There was much puffing and heaving as the lady sat down, arranged her flowing skirt and delved into a capacious tapestry bag for her knitting.

"That's a pretty colour wool," Delphi said to be polite. After all, they were going to be very close neighbours for some weeks, and there was no one else to whom she had really spoken. There was a middle-aged married couple who didn't seem too friendly, and a few older men who looked as if they had formal business to attend to. She and Flora had taken their first few meals in their cabin.

"It's for my granddaughter. I should have it finished by the time we dock back in the old country. Where's your little sister, then?"

"She'll be lying on her bunk, reading. She's always got her nose in a book. She's had to entertain herself all her life, so

11

she's very good at it. I think she'll run out of things to read long before we reach England." There was a pause. "I do have two sisters." Delphi frowned at the thought of that meeting to come. "But Flora's my daughter, not my sister."

"Oh, I'm sorry, I didn't mean to be… You don't look old enough. How old is she, then? Nine? Ten? She's very pretty with her long dark hair. Takes after her mum, I can see."

"She's ten. Her name's Georgina, but we call her Flora. It's a long story." She smiled. "My husband's name was George, but he was killed on the Somme in 1916." The little lie tripped off her tongue as it had for the last ten years. In fact, she had said it so often it seemed true, and if George, her dear George, had lived…

Delphi wriggled in her chair and closed her eyes again. She could see jazzy swirls of colour through her lids and the warmth seeped in to relax her spirit at long last. The click-clack of knitting needles was a relentless but soothing metronome, and she began to feel sleepy. The ship rode a gentle swell. She might have dozed off, but then she felt a shadow pass between her and the sun again and she squinted up.

She couldn't quite see who it was standing there against the glare, but she wasn't pleased. Delphi became aware that she was frowning up at this stranger. Brushing her hair away, she tried to relax her forehead and put on a bit of a show, just as she would have done in the old days. Some habits had never quite disappeared.

"Good day, ladies," he said and touched his forelock. "It's a grand day for sitting out."

"Hello to you, young man," said Delphi's companion, saving her from speaking. "I don't believe we've been introduced. I'm Mrs Shearer and this is … I'm sorry, dear, I don't even know your name."

"It's Delphi. Delphi Dight."

"And you're travelling with your little girl, Flora. Isn't that right?"

"Mmm."

"And I am Rainier, Rainier Harman. I don't believe I've had the pleasure yet. I didn't see you dining, even."

"I've not felt like eating anything these last couple of days. I've felt too ill," Mrs Shearer said.

"Poor you." The young man pulled a wry expression. "Have you been ill too, Mrs Dight? We've not had the delight of your company either."

Delphi answered with coolness. *He seems a bit smooth*, she thought. "No, I've been fine. I chose to eat in my cabin with my daughter."

"Well, enjoy the sunshine, ladies. I hope we meet later."

By now Delphi's gaze had become more accustomed to the bright sun, but she only saw the man's broad shoulders and black hair curling on his collar as he retreated. *He has a very strange accent*, she thought.

She huffed as she lay back again and tried to relax. Now, though, she was feeling restless. Pulling at the back of the lounger, she sat more upright and looked out to sea. There were still a few birds following the ship, but not many. She watched them idly as they tossed and swooped like pieces of white paper. Otherwise, the blue swell seemed vast, and she with her worries and concerns suddenly felt small. Glancing across at her companion, she took in Mrs Shearer's substantial shape but also saw that her skin was soft and downy. She had a mouth that was wide and generous, and her bright blue eyes almost disappeared when she smiled. She was a comfortable companion, Delphi decided. The older lady must have become aware of the scrutiny as she looked across at Delphi with a sparkle of wit.

"He's very attractive for a casual little fling." She gave a wicked grin. "Too young for me, though. More your age, I should say."

Delphi frowned at her. "I'm not in the running for any shipboard romance, that's for sure. There will only ever be one love for me, and sadly he is no longer here," she replied with an air of wistfulness. "I have Flora to consider, too."

"Oh no, of course not, my dear. No harm in dreaming, though." She winked across the narrow space between them.

Delphi shook her head and laughed. "I can see you are incorrigible and a force to be reckoned with, Mrs Shearer."

"You better call me Bea, if we are to be friends and neighbours. It's Beatrice, of course, but that sounds far too serious."

"Thank you, Bea."

Flora appeared and introductions were made. She plonked herself down on the edge of Delphi's lounger. "A very nice man just asked what I was reading," she said, waving her book around. "He said he has some books that I might borrow. He's going to France. That's where his folks are from, he said."

"We'll see what sort of books he's offering before we agree to that," Delphi said, and Flora huffed at her.

I wonder if that was Rainier Harman. That must be why he speaks as he does, she thought. *It's a weird mix of a French and Australian accent.* She let out her breath. *I don't know why I'm even bothering to think about it.*

"I've read enough for the time being," Flora said. "What shall we do? They have deck games down there." She nodded towards the rear of the ship. Then, putting her head on one side, her green eyes looked up at her mother through long lashes.

Delphi laughed at her. "You can stop looking at me like that, my girl. I was the master of wheedling things with a look like that, so it won't work with me."

"Can you knit?" Bea Shearer held out her work for Flora to see.

"No," she answered with a frown and peered at the cardigan that was emerging. "It looks very complicated."

"No, it's really easy. Would you like me to show you how it's done? I've some spare needles in my bag."

So it was that Flora was occupied and Delphi was not when Rainier Harman came strolling by again. He invited Delphi to walk along the deck with him, and she accepted in order not to seem rude.

"I was wondering, Mrs Dight, if you and your daughter would care to join my table at dinner tonight," Rainier offered.

"Well, um…" She cast around her mind for an excuse. "Flora and I are happy to eat in our cabin," she said. "She's at an impressionable age and needs close supervision." Delphi could see further chasms of trouble between herself and Flora if the child started to form incorrect ideas again. When Delphi had gone out to dinner with a local man, there had been hell to pay upon her return and for several days after. Delphi had not repeated the experiment.

"I'm sure, but it's a long voyage, and it was just a friendly suggestion."

Delphi felt mean and guilty for her response. He was trying to be gallant and affable. That was all. Bea Shearer's earlier flippant remarks had coloured her judgement. There was nothing flirtatious here, simply a good-natured gesture. "Yes, of course. We should like to join you. Thank you, and it's

Delphi. Short for Delphinium, but I hate that. My two sisters and I were all given flower names. The others are Rose and Iris, but we call her Izzy."

They wandered on.

"Was it you who offered to lend Flora a book?"

"Yes. I have a few adventure stories that have travelled with me over the years. I have an ancient copy of Stevenson's *The Black Arrow*. I imagine she would devour it at her age. I had it as a boy, and it's been with me ever since."

"It must have special meaning for you if you've had it that long," Delphi said.

"It's more the inscription in the front. My dad wrote it for me. It says 'Remember, my dear boy, that loyalty and duty are not always the same thing, but honour remains constant.' I know his words by heart I've read them so many times." He smiled to himself.

"That's very profound."

"It became significant along the Chemin des Dames in 1914, and especially in Ypres. My lungs have not been quite the same since then, so loyalty was tested to the full."

Delphi looked at him for several seconds. "How old were you in 1914?"

"I was 17 and full of ideals about duty then. We learned," he finished and shrugged.

"Yes, we all did. So, you went to war before you were old enough, too." Delphi's thoughts strayed to her late brother, Hector, before she continued. "She would love to read it, but only if you're sure. It sounds very precious."

"It has been, but I'm going home now. Time to move on."

"Me too," she said. It slipped out, and she could have slapped herself for allowing that. "Where is home?" she asked quickly before he could quiz her about her own motives for returning to her family.

"My family home is a place in France. The nearest towns you might have heard of would be Amboise or Tours, of course, but my home is just south of there. We have vineyards and my father passed away recently. I've been studying wine production in Western Australia, so it's time to return."

"I think you'll miss him. It sounds as if you were close."

"We were, in many ways, if not in miles."

"Why did you go so far away to study?" Delphi's curiosity was getting the better of her.

"I needed to get away; to have a change after the war; to travel and see life in a better way. Australia has some of the oldest grape varieties in the world. Many of Europe's established vineyards were destroyed by disease in the 1800s, you know. So, they had to import vines from Australia. Australia has some of the leading research centres in the world, too."

"I know it's a major grower of vines, of course, but I lived on a ranch, so that was very different." Here she was again, giving information about herself. She quickly moved on. "So, you'll be disembarking at St Nazaire, then?"

"That's right."

They stopped walking and Delphi rested her arms on the rails, staring out to sea. The waves were a constant, rising and drawing away, scattering the light across their surface. Her mind drifted to the future and to seeing her sister Rose again after all these years. Would she have forgiven Delphi yet? Surely she would. Wouldn't she? It had all turned out alright. She wondered how it would pan out now, though. There were so many unknowns. Her whole future was debatable, but first she must see Rose, and Michael too, of course. A shout from the group playing deck quoits brought her back.

"You were deep in thought there," Rainier said.

"Yes," Delphi answered. She did not elaborate but turned to retrace her steps.

Rainier watched her slim retreating figure before catching her up with a few long strides. "You're an enigma," he said.

She didn't respond.

"I've told you quite a bit about myself, but you've managed to evade all my openings. What are you hiding or … what are you afraid of?" He asked with sudden insight.

"Me? I'm afraid of very little." She flashed a brilliant smile in his direction and skipped a little turn in front of him, her dark chestnut hair swinging out from her shoulders. Suddenly she was flirting, tilting her head and looking up at him with flashing green eyes. This was a completely different woman from the one at the railings. Now she was lively and sparkling. Her wide, generous mouth laughed at him while she danced around. He wasn't fooled by this show of carelessness, but he was enchanted and prepared to play along. This voyage could be fun with the little diversion of a beautiful woman along the way. No ties, no seriousness. She seemed just the distraction to make time pass pleasantly and quickly. There was the slight complication of her daughter Flora, but she was of an age to amuse herself and would be in bed early enough to make the evenings an entertaining game until the cat caught his little mouse. Not that this one was a mouse. Oh no, he could see that.

"You're a minx," he said, and dimples appeared at the side of his wide mouth as he smiled, exposing strong, even, white teeth.

With that, they returned to Bea Shearer and Flora, who had mastered the basics of knitting. She held up an uneven, raggedy-looking strip with such pleasure that both Delphi and Rainier exclaimed their genuine pleasure at her achievement.

"That will make a fine scarf, or a little skirt for one of your dolls," he said, and her frown dispersed a little.

"Thank you. I know Mummy will say it's good whatever it looks like, but if you think so too…" she said innocently.

"Oh, I do indeed. By the way, your mother says you may borrow one of my books," Rainier added.

"Oh, bees' knees," Flora said in the latest slang.

"Calm down," Delphi said, and Flora shrugged her shoulders and tossed her head.

"Might she come and collect it now?" Rainier raised his eyebrows at Delphi.

"You leave that with me, Flora," said Bea, indicating the knitting. She winked at Delphi. "I'll just catch that dropped stitch. You all run along, and I'll see you later."

"We'll walk that way together, then," Delphi said as she picked up her own book from the lounger.

As they arrived at the cabins, Delphi waited by their door while Rainier collected the book and gave it to Flora.

"What time would you like to go for dinner?"

They made arrangements.

"Are we eating in the restaurant tonight?" Flora asked excitedly. "Oh, goody. I could wear my green dress at last, the one Gramps and Granny bought for me before we left." She turned to explain to Rainier. "We lived with them, didn't we, Mummy?"

"Come along now, that's enough chatter." Delphi took her arm gently and guided her towards their door.

"Mummy!" Flora shook her off.

Rainier stood watching as she opened the door of their cabin. *I bet she turns before going in*, he thought.

Sure enough, her eyes met his. He saw her breast heave with a sharp intake of breath as she realised he was still watching her. A smile twinkled across his face.

He imagined her thoughts as she disappeared, probably regretting giving him the satisfaction and being annoyed with herself. Her resistance was intriguing, and he looked forward to the evening.

CHAPTER 2

Delphi watched Flora prance and skip ahead of them as they lurched their way along the ship's passageway to the officers' mess where the first-class cabin occupants ate. She could be so innocent and childlike one minute and tempestuous the next.

It was the first time Delphi and Flora had been in here. The door was open, but Rainier stood back to let them enter before him.

"All the tables are stuck to the floor," Flora said. "They've all got ledges around. Is that so things don't roll off?"

"Yes, that's right," Rainier answered. "You can imagine in rough weather things will slide around quite a bit."

"Including us." Flora laughed.

"Absolutely. We found it strange walking along to here just now and the sea's quite calm."

A member of the crew came forward to show them to their seats, pulling one out for Delphi and spreading a crisp white napkin across her knees before helping her to tuck herself under the table. Rainier did the same for Flora.

"There you are, ma'am," he said.

She wriggled and preened. Delphi smiled across the table at him, appreciating that he was making this first dinner in the mess special for her daughter.

"You're looking particularly lovely tonight," he said to the child. "That shade of green suits you, and you're tall so the fashion is very becoming. You, Delphi, look stunning."

Delphi felt a warmth rise up her neck and was annoyed with herself, but it had been a long time since she had been out with a man, if this could be called 'out', and she was relieved that Flora was enjoying Rainier's company too.

As she had on the deck earlier, she recognised her old recklessness bubbling up. She'd had this feeling in adolescence, and it had ultimately been her undoing. She squashed it down. She had to be aware of Flora, who was more demanding than most of her age. Glancing at her daughter now, a rush of love swept over her. Flora, unaware of her mother's gaze, broke her bread roll, trying to look grown-up and worldly.

When Delphi dragged her eyes away and looked across the table, Rainier was staring at her intently. She turned her head quickly to look out of the porthole next to her. When she returned her gaze to Rainier, which she could not resist, he was still looking at her.

To hide her confusion, she put her head coquettishly on one side and said, "So, Rainier, tell me … tell me of the life you will lead when you return home." She relaxed, now on safer territory again.

"The house is old, very old. It's been in my family for a couple of hundred years. There's only about ten hectares of vines, but we produce mainly white wine from the Chenin grape, although we call it pineau blanc, and sauvignon blanc too. It's thriving."

"We better drink white tonight, then," Delphi said.

The first course, little pieces of fish in a delicious sauce with small toasts and garnish on the side, came and went. Conversation was light, like the wine. The main course was chicken goujons and so the alcohol was a perfect match, even though the choice was limited aboard ship.

While they ate, Rainier was the perfect host and asked Flora what hobbies she enjoyed and what her favourite subjects at school were. He studiously avoided questions about why they had lived in Australia or where they were heading and for what reason. Delphi was relieved and grateful.

"Good evening, dears," said Bea Shearer as she swayed into the mess. "I thought I'd give in here a try since I feel so much better. I think I've found my sea legs at last."

Rainier stood. "Will you join us?" he asked gallantly.

"Oh no, but that's very kind. You're well along the way and I shall hold you up. I'll sit over there." She tottered across the room, holding a table edge here and a chair back there to steady herself. Her copious bosom heaved as she took a deep breath and collapsed into the seat held out for her by the steward. She waved across at them and smiled.

As Flora finished her dessert, Delphi and Rainier sat quietly with their coffee. Bea came back across to their table.

"I'm not having dessert or coffee. Why don't I take Flora to her bed? I could read to her, and you folks can have a gentle stroll on deck before saying goodnight." She winked at Delphi.

"Oh, you don't need to do that," Delphi said, suddenly feeling trapped.

"That would be grand," Flora said. "I've started the book Mr Harman gave me, *The Black Arrow*. Do you know it?"

"My goodness me, yes. It's quite exciting."

Flora pushed her chair back. "That's alright, isn't it, Mummy?" Delphi couldn't believe that Flora was being so flexible, but despite her pleasure in this she gave a tight smile. She didn't need to be left in this position with Rainier Harman.

"Go on then, sweetie. Teeth and bed in good order. Love you," she added when she saw a worried look flit across Flora's face. She must have picked up on Delphi's unease.

She watched her child and the older lady, who clutched Flora's arm as they lurched across the floor.

"It's a very long time since I was on board a ship," Delphi said. "I hope we don't have too much rough weather this voyage."

Rainier rose and helped her stand. She preceded him from the mess but staggered herself as the ship rode a particularly big wave. He caught her before she hit the bulkhead too hard and kept his arm under hers as they headed outside. She felt his warmth seeping through her.

While there were only a small number of first-class passengers, there were more than seven hundred third-class passengers aboard, so the deck was busy since it was a fine night. Gone were the days of segregation to the extent of the famous and infamous ships of the White Star Line.

"It's busy here. Let's go up one."

"We'd have been third class if Papa had not sent me the money for the ticket. I wouldn't have minded sharing a cabin with someone like Bea."

Rainier guided Delphi to the quieter area and they leaned on the railing. Despite the fading light, the sun cast hues of pink and palest orange and pearl across the horizon. The sea rose and fell, and the ship rolled with it. The wind had died as it often does in the early evening, and all was calm, including Delphi's raging thoughts for once. Perhaps it was the wine.

"So, will you tell me?"

"Tell you what?" Delphi pretended not to know to what he referred.

"Where you're going and why. Where you are running from."

"I'm not running away, definitely not that," she said.

He stood leaning on the railing next to her and said nothing.

"Please smoke if you wish," Delphi said.

"I don't smoke," he answered. "Not since the war. I had a brush with some gas, but fortunately it wasn't bad. It's just left me with a patch on my lung, so I have to be a bit careful." He chuckled. "Hey, you've got me talking about myself again. Tell me something about you. Anything. A scrap of information which helps me to know you better."

She sighed. "Very well. I was happy in Australia. I lived with my husband's parents and had Flora there with them." The little lie tripped from her mouth again. "I'm going home to see my family again. My sister, Rose, has been very ill with TB. My mother was never strong after my brother was killed during the war, so Papa only has my younger sister now. It's another reason to return.

"I see. Australia was a long way for you to go to have a child. Tell me, please, what happened to your husband?" He spoke so that Delphi hardly heard him.

She said nothing for a long while, and Rainier stood beside her patiently until he wondered whether she had heard his question. "George was killed. On the Somme. My brother-in-law was his best friend and they were together, except Michael survived."

"You must have been very young."

"Yes, well, it was war, wasn't it? Things happen."

He looked at her quizzically, but she said no more. "Have you not been home in all this time?"

"No. My sister and I had a major falling out. Still, she's been so ill, and Papa was very persuasive. Flora needs to meet her family too. She's been asking. Things have not been easy for her and she rebels quite often. I think she must be in a muddle about who she is and where she belongs."

"Your in-laws will miss you back in Oz."

"My father-in-law died last year, and my mother-in-law will go and live with her daughter, so she'll be fine. I think she'll sell up the ranch. It's too much now, anyway; managing all the hands and the finances. She'll miss Flora in some ways, but probably not in others."

"Anyone would miss Flora. She's a credit to you."

Delphi looked up into his eyes and allowed herself to smile. "She's been particularly amenable to you. She can be a little demon if she doesn't like someone."

She saw him regarding her, and by the deck lights she noticed the crinkles at the corners of his warm brown eyes as he smiled back. A tremble somewhere deep inside surprised her and she felt wobbly. His shoulders were broad, and he was tall. His hair curling onto his collar was unfashionably long, but it suited him well. She caught a whiff of lemon and something else cleanly honest and earthy from his clothing. She recognised her feelings but resolutely quashed them. Flora needed consideration. He would disappear from her life in three or four weeks. She was independent and had been for more than nine years. What she didn't need was a romance, never mind a short-term affair. She knew where that could lead. Although George had been the one love of her life, he'd caused her major upheaval and yes, she did still miss him desperately. She did *not* need a man.

"So, Delphi Dight, exciting times ahead for both of us," Rainier said, lightening the mood. "Would you like a nightcap before we part? Don't panic. I saw the look in your eyes just then. I have a bottle of exceptionally good whisky in my room which I shall fetch here. I have no wish to compromise you. I think you may be a girl who would appreciate a man's drink, though." He winked at her and laughed.

She relaxed again. "Thank you. That would be lovely."

Returning with the bottle and two glasses, Rainier stood in the shadows for a moment and watched her. She was certainly a complex baggage, but her lithe figure sheathed in the silk of her evening dress was very alluring. She had high cheekbones and slanting eyes and her long dark hair was different to the bobbed haircut that was currently in fashion.

She threw back her head as he watched, the better to take the evening breeze, he supposed, and her long neck was pale and inviting. He'd said he had no wish to compromise her, but he did. God, how he did. He felt himself grow stiff, so he waited a moment longer. Apart from anything else, she was a challenge and that he admired. She had a past, the detail of which he could only guess, but it certainly did not deter him.

He cleared his throat, which had become tight, and moved towards her, thankful for the darkness that had descended.

"Shall we find a seat?" he asked.

They moved together and he poured for her. She sat sideways on a lounger in the shadow of the bulkhead and out of the stiffening breeze.

"Here's to our future." They clinked glasses.

CHAPTER 3

Delphi and Rainier shared many such evenings while Bea kept an eye on Flora, either reading to her or helping with the ever-growing knitting. Delphi became more confident in her friendship with Rainier and felt less need to be false and flirtatious. She learned of his home life in France and in turn she told him of her adolescence in England and a little about each of her sisters and their parents. She didn't tell him about George. As far as he and the rest of the world were concerned, they had been married, albeit for a short time, and he had been killed when she was already expecting his child. Australia was far enough away from all she knew for that to work.

This afternoon they stood on the games deck. They had laughed such a lot. Rainier played the fool for Flora's benefit, running around, balancing the quoit on his head and pretending he couldn't find it; using the shuffle stick as a wooden leg and acting like a pirate. Delphi had watched and wondered at a man who was so unafraid of making himself appear absurd for a ten-year-old and appreciating the fact.

"I think the weather's on the turn," Delphi said, looking out at the ridge of cloud approaching and feeling the wind across her face.

"One more game of shuffleboard?" Flora had the pleading look that Delphi knew so well.

"Just one, then. It'll be time to get ready for dinner soon."

Delphi looked forward to dinners in the mess. The habit of sitting with Rainier and seeing the appreciative look in his eyes was appealing after so many years of living miles from civilisation like a nun. She felt powerful and confident. She liked Rainier's eyes following her; dark brown and soulful one moment and sparkling with vitality the next. She appreciated his physique too. His shoulders were broad, and his hips were narrow. Often his shirt came untucked from the back of his trousers, but still he managed to look suave and handsome. Well, she thought so anyway.

They finished their game and collected the pucks, moving to stow their sticks in the box. The sea became more choppy by the minute and the cloud cover was flat and grey. Wind blew Delphi's hair around her face and she pushed it back from her eyes. She shivered in the stiff breeze. Gazing across the wide sea to port, she saw the waves' white tops and an uneven heaviness about it all.

They needed to balance carefully as they went back to their cabins. Rainier's arm came around Delphi on more than one occasion to steady her.

"You come between us, Flora, and we can steady you." Delphi manoeuvred across.

"I'm fine. This is fun. It's a bit like being at that funfair we went to. Do you remember?" She skipped ahead.

That night, Delphi was awoken by Flora.

"Mummy, I feel sick."

Delphi leaped up, pushing her hair from her bleary-eyed face. She guided Flora into the bathroom, where the child made it just in time to lean over the washbasin before she heaved up her dinner.

The ship pitched up and down and rolled from side to side. Delphi hung on to the handle beside the basin and steadied Flora at the same time.

"I don't like it. I'm scared," said Flora. Her face was pasty and pale, and her neck was damp. Wisps of hair clung to her cheeks.

"Nothing to be scared about," Delphi said, grabbing the tin wastepaper basket on her way back to the bunk as she guided Flora. Her own stomach was rising and falling with the motion, but she didn't feel sick.

There was a crashing sound from nearby.

"That sounded like it came from Bea's cabin," she said to Flora. "I hope she's alright."

"Mummy, don't leave me," came a pitiful cry from the bunk.

"I'm not going anywhere, sweetie. Hush now. Don't cry." She stroked her daughter's sweaty hairline. "I'm going to get a damp flannel, that's all."

Delphi hurried to the bathroom, reeling across the floor from one side to the other. She managed to avoid all manner of things that had fallen off the side and were rolling about. A dribble of salt water ran from the porthole-casing as a wave crashed against it and the ship shuddered. Each time the vessel went bow down, there was an immense banging and juddering that was, indeed, very frightening.

"Mummy!" Flora called, and Delphi made her way back.

The night wore on as Flora alternated between retching and moaning. Delphi's heart was thumping, and her stomach was tense.

Slowly, the porthole took on a lighter shade as the day dawned grim and grey, but still the wild sea crashed against it. Flora dozed at last, but Delphi could not.

There was a tentative knock at the door. She staggered across to open it and peered through the crack, clutching her dressing gown across her rumpled nightdress.

It was Rainier. He took in her pale face and her wide green eyes. His heart went out to her as he saw the worry and discomfort etched there. "You look done in," he said. "Are you ill?"

"No, but Flora is. I've been up all night, so I'm a bit raggedy around the edges."

"Is there anything I can do? You look so weary."

"Is Bea alright? Do you know? I heard such a crash earlier, but I couldn't leave Flora."

"I went in and helped her up. She fell against the desk on her way to the bathroom. She'll have a huge bruise, I think, but nothing's broken. I sat with her for a while. She's been very ill too, but she's quieter now, so I said I'd check on you. All's fine, so if there's…"

The ship lurched again in a different direction. Delphi clung to the door and it shot open. She was flung back and dropped the front of her dressing gown as she struggled to remain upright, grabbing at the door with both hands.

Rainier stepped forward. He placed one strong arm around Delphi for support and at the same time pulled her dressing gown across to protect her modesty. Although his eyes strayed and he gasped, he managed not to betray his interest more than that. He had seen enough to know that, although she was lithe, she was full-breasted and very desirable. However, at that moment all he wanted was for her to be safe and content again.

He guided her to a chair and sat her down. She was soft and compliant. Brushing her hair from her face, he turned to the bunk where Flora was stirring again.

"Mummy," she murmured.

"Shh, she's here but she's really tired. I think you better have some water, but not a great gulp." He put his arm behind Flora to help raise her head. As he held the cup, he let her take a sip.

"I'm thirsty," she whispered.

"I know, but take several small mouthfuls rather than a lot at once. Your tummy will be tender."

He turned to look at Delphi for confirmation of what he was doing, but she sat in the chair with her eyes closed. He didn't know if she had fallen asleep, but he took the flannel and indicated to Flora that he was going into the bathroom to refresh it.

On returning, Flora started heaving again, but nothing much came up. He wiped her face and lay her down again.

"Thank you," she murmured.

He pulled the other chair to the bedside and sat, happy to be of assistance. Looking across at Delphi again, he wondered what her life had been like. He had learned that she had lived with her in-laws in Australia, and it appeared there had been no other man on the scene. She was capable yet vulnerable; independent yet frightened of any advancement he might have tried in those early days.

He was aware that he must be falling in love. He had not felt this way before. Women were for enjoyment and fun, nothing too serious or anchoring. As he watched her, he felt tenderness and desire. He wanted her body, but he yearned for her soul. These thoughts startled him.

He put his head in his hands. Why this? Why now? He had to disembark at St Nazaire. His family duty awaited and could not be postponed.

He had put duty above loyalty in 1914. There had been a heavy price to pay then. Had he to do the same again now?

He knew the answer.

CHAPTER 4

The night of the balloon dance was imminent.

"It's going to be so exciting." Flora could hardly sit still. "Are you looking forward to it too?"

"I certainly am," Delphi said.

"I'm so glad I can go, even if it's only for a short while. Tell me again about the balloons."

"It's only what I've heard, but I believe there will be hundreds all over the floor and decorating the walls, tied to the lamp brackets." Delphi had very mixed feelings. It would be a great diversion. The voyage had become tedious in many ways with lazy days, stormy interludes, deck games. But the evenings had been charged with sexual tension from which Delphi had tried to distance herself, but she'd found it hard. "We've been at sea for so long, now, the dance'll be fun," she said.

"The only thing is…" Flora hesitated. "It means Rainier will be leaving the ship in a couple of days. I'll miss him. Will you miss him, Mummy?"

Delphi became breezy and brittle in her response. "Of course, but he has a big responsibility awaiting him, so we must be pleased for him. It won't be long after that until we dock too, and we'll be ready for our next adventure. Now, let's plan what we shall wear."

When they entered the grand salon the next night, the lights were settling a soft lambent hue on everything. It transformed the room into a land of magic. Glasses caught the sparkle; the furniture was burnished to a rich deep shine; the floor was covered in a thousand balloons singing of every tone and shade imaginable.

Flora stood in the doorway and clasped her hands together.

Rainier spotted Delphi and her daughter as soon as they stood framed in the doorway. The magical radiance reflected on them both.

They are captivating, magnificent, he thought. Flora looked like a smaller version of her mother. She wore green and innocence shone from her smiling face.

In her peacock-blue gown, Delphi seemed to whisper across the room to him. He was overwhelmed and could do nothing but stand and gape. She had her hair piled up, emphasising her long neck. That white skin had affected him so. Her figure, silhouetted, aroused him afresh. All else faded to silence, until there was only the two of them facing each other.

Then Flora left her mother and came floating towards him through the balloons. He put his arms out to give her a hug, and she snuggled into him with confidence. As she lifted her head, she looked at him and said, "This is the best night ever, in the whole world."

"Yes, it is," he said, smiling down at her. Taking Flora's hand, Rainier moved towards Delphi and reached out. She placed her hand in his, and together the three of them crossed the room to take a seat.

"I've never danced among so many balloons before," Delphi said as Rainier held her for a quickstep and they did a spin turn in the corner. It wasn't the easiest thing to do in such a confined space, and there was the occasional bang as a balloon was trodden by an eager dancer. There were far more men than women among the first-class passengers and senior crew, so not many were dancing.

"They're all the rage, apparently. The first officer told me," Rainier shouted in her ear. What with the noise of chatter and the loud music, it was difficult to talk normally. He shuffled around the room with Flora, and once or twice with Bea. The older lady and the child sat together now and watched Rainier and Delphi, who made a striking couple, both being tall and handsome.

"It's like dancing in a dry mist of colour." Delphi lifted her left hand from his shoulder and held her skirt as they spun again.

"Or among soft globes of enchantment." He looked down at her and smiled.

"You're quite the poet."

"When I'm inspired." He smiled again.

The next dance was a waltz, and without asking if she'd had enough, he glided her back and forth and around and around. He pressed his hand on the small of her back and as she turned her head to the left, he felt the whole length of her body close to his.

"Oh, Delphi," he murmured into her hair, but he didn't know if she'd heard him.

The music ended and they pulled apart. Rainier took her hand to guide her back to Bea and Flora, who sat around the low table they had commandeered at the beginning of the evening.

"What a handsome couple you make," Bea said.

"You do look lovely when you dance, Mummy."

"Thank you," Delphi said.

She was distracted by the First Officer, who asked for the next dance, and then another gentleman claimed her. She had to refuse the third because she was gasping for a drink. She needed to be with her daughter. And with Rainier.

Rainier had watched as others had spun her round or tried to hold her close. He was troubled, and he knew exactly why.

Two days later, Delphi and Flora shared the air of expectancy among the crew and the passengers. France had been in sight for quite some time, and now they were heading up the mighty River Loire into the busy port of St Nazaire.

The passengers who were not disembarking leaned on the railings to watch the activities of the bank slide by.

"What's that?" Flora pointed at a skeleton hull away to the side.

"Apparently it's a new ship being built. That's the SS *Île de France*, miss," said a passing sailor.

"Where's Rainier, Mummy? He's missing all this."

"He'll be packing the last of his things, darling." Delphi put her arm around her child. She felt in need of comfort.

They were travelling slowly now. They passed a large building with a tall chimney belching smoke. Delphi could easily see the time on the clock, telling her that sadness was imminent.

As they manoeuvred and turned, someone said, "There's *le Pont Tournant*. It's not old but the bridge swings open to let water traffic through."

"Will we be going through there?" Flora turned her face up to Delphi.

"No, we shan't be going that way."

Rainier arrived by her side. He had some hand luggage with him, reminding her of his departure. This must be borne with fortitude. She had suffered worse in the past, but at this moment she was close to weeping. She hadn't felt like this for nearly ten years and hadn't believed she would ever again until recently.

The business of tying up alongside the quay seemed to take forever. There was clanking and shouting of orders. Bumping and shuddering sent waves of nausea through Delphi, and she became light-headed.

I want to tell him things. I want to share my feelings, but it's no good now. I can't share the circumstances of Flora's birth. He'll know what I was, what I am, what Rose said I was. Society doesn't forgive that, and neither will he. It's better this way ... but, oh, how it hurts.

Tears were very close. She'd almost committed the same sin after the dance the other night, but had managed to hold herself back.

Her thoughts were interrupted as she sensed Rainier's approach. Highly aware of his every breath, his every movement by her side, she gritted her teeth as she felt his arm steal around her waist.

"Oh Delphi, this is awful. You know how I feel," he said at last.

"I do know."

"I have my duty to perform, and you have something you need to complete too, I think."

"Yes."

"And still you have not confided everything," he said, giving a small, bitter laugh.

"Rainier, I can't. Not here, probably not ever."

"This is goodbye, then, my dearest. Will you walk with me to the top of the gangplank?"

"Bea, will you watch Flora for me?" She knew there was a pleading in her eyes.

"Of course. You go along. We'll watch from here."

"Thank you so much. I shan't be long and then, Flora, we can wave bye-bye from up here together."

Rainier gave Flora a quick hug and shook Bea's hand warmly before kissing her soft plump cheek. She had tears in her eyes.

"I hate goodbyes. Go on with you, and God speed, my dear boy."

Together, Rainier and Delphi pushed through the crowds amassed between the railings and the bulkhead towards the gangplank, which was now firmly in place.

The dreaded moment had arrived; he had to go. He dropped his bag and enfolded her, then kissed her full on the lips with passion and longing. Before she realised and appreciated the full impact, he grabbed his holdall and left.

Delphi watched his tall retreating frame. She took a step forward and put out her arm.

Just once he turned, and then he was gone from her life.

CHAPTER 5

Delphi and Flora climbed into her father's car outside the train station with trepidation, and Izzy followed. In a short time, she would be seeing her sister Rose for the first time in ten years. The thought was unsettling to say the least. Izzy had been too young to really know what had gone on, and it had not had any effect on her anyway, although she clearly knew the cause of her banishment now. Others in the household would know of her disgrace, of course, but not of the row between her older sister and herself or the reason for it.

"We'll go home," her father said. "We'll get you settled in. Izzy has been dying to see you again, haven't you? She came home from Berlin just for this."

I wonder if that is true, Delphi thought. *Papa will have told her to return. Still, she's older now. Perhaps she's forgotten how horrid I could be to her when we were young.* She glanced across at her sister. Was that smile genuine? As she sat there next to Flora, she was transported back. The smell of pipe tobacco and Papa's toilet water had not changed. She suddenly felt all her childhood insecurities again.

"As for Dora…" Her father continued, seemingly unaware of the turmoil she felt. "She has hardly been able to contain her impatience. She stays in her room for most of the time and copes with the mending and suchlike, since we employed a new cook. She really is too old for the full workload. I think she enjoys the peace, but if she ventures down to the kitchen she tends to interfere with things and the new maid, Betty, gets quite short with her. You've sorted out more than one row, Izzy."

"Yes, Papa."

The memories and the news of such changes robbed Delphi of her composure, and Izzy sounded snappy. She forced down her feelings.

"You will resume your little charity groups, won't you, Izzy?" Papa said.

Poor Izzy, Delphi thought. *That all sounds very dull. The fate of the youngest sister: to be left at home to tend to her widower father.*

Flora had sat almost silently until now. Delphi knew she was shy of this other grandpa, who she had never met. "And Aunt Rose? How is Aunt Rose doing, and how is Uncle Michael managing the school without her?" Flora plucked up the courage to ask the question that Delphi had put off asking.

"Rose has been very poorly, as you know, but I do believe she's on the mend. She looks like a shadow, though. I think you'll see quite a difference in her, Delphi." Papa was concentrating on the road ahead, but he glanced over his shoulder at his daughter. "You must be brave and school your face not to let your shock show, my dear. Flora, you won't mind staying with Dora when we go to visit, will you? They won't allow children into the sanatorium." He drove on in silence and did not address the second part of Flora's question.

Delphi patted Flora's hands, which were held together tightly in her lap. She could wait no longer. "And the school?"

"Oh, Michael's employed a senior mistress while Rose is recuperating. That great mausoleum of a place is very draining both financially and in every other way, I believe. He doesn't say a lot, not to me, anyway. I have a feeling his father has been helping a bit. The bills must be extraordinary just for heating the place. Since the Duke of Norfolk entrusted the building, I think there's an agreement that he'll continue with maintenance for the time being. The roof alone must cost a fortune to keep watertight."

"Why on earth did they take such a place?" asked Delphi.

"Well, you'll see eventually. It is beautiful and has all the facilities they need to develop the school into the sort of place that will command high fees. It's been improving very nicely, but then this blow of Rose's illness and all that worry has influenced everything. Still, the parents of the pupils seem very loyal, so I suppose that's some sort of testament to how they feel about the whole setup."

Delphi said no more. She wanted to confide her nervousness about seeing Rose again, but not in front of her daughter. Again, she glanced at Izzy who sat gazing out of the window, so it was impossible to gauge her thoughts although she had smiled at Flora and made a consoling remark when the child spoke of missing her Australian grandparents.

"So, what about you, young lady?" Flora's grandpa stretched his neck to see her in his driving mirror. "Big changes, eh? How was that long voyage?"

"It was fine, thank you. Rainier lent me some books and we played deck games. I didn't like the storms, though."

"She was very seasick, I'm afraid, weren't you?" Delphi turned to her daughter.

"And who is Rainier?"

"He was a very nice friend on the ship," Flora answered.

"Was he your age?" Grandpa Strong asked.

Flora giggled. "Oh, no. He was Mummy's friend."

He looked back at Delphi again. "Oh, I see," he said.

Delphi could not hold his gaze, or that of Izzy who stared at her.

When Delphi looked properly at her sister after they had entered the house, she would not have known her. Izzy had grown into a woman, and was quite a beauty. She had Rose's fine hair, but her colouring was that of Delphi. Whilst she did not have the high cheekbones and slanting eyes that were Delphi's alone, she had the same heart-shaped face, giving her a pretty elfin look.

"Delphi, welcome home." Izzy hugged her elder sister with enthusiasm, dismissing Delphi's own anxiety that Izzy might be resenting her return after so long. She always did have a sweet nature.

"It's good to be back."

"You have a definite twang to your accent now." She turned and put her hand on Flora's arm. "It's so good to have you here."

Dora enveloped Delphi. "My darling child. It's very good to see you." Then the elderly retainer enfolded Flora, and the child all but disappeared into her ample bosom. "Little Flora, you are most welcome. I've been so looking forward to meeting you." She turned to Delphi. "A child in the house again. What could be better?"

"Welcome, Mrs Dight. Pleased to meet you and you Miss Dight," said Betty. "Let me get you some lemonade. You must be tired and thirsty."

Dora harrumphed at that, but Izzy asked her to join them all in the salon, so she was mollified.

CHAPTER 6

The following day, Papa drove Delphi to the sanatorium. He led her to the conservatory, holding the door for her as she passed him. It was hot and steamy, and smelled not unpleasantly of damp moss, but as she moved forward, she felt a breeze and realised that huge vents above were open, as were the double doors at one end.

And there she was. Rose. Her elder sister sat on her own, reading a book with a slant of sun striking the floor beside her.

She always was studious and so clever, thought Delphi. *That was a problem too. I was jealous of the opportunities she had. But then that was my fault. I know that now. I could have gone to college too if I'd wanted, but I was childish, resentful and flighty. I should have stuck to my studies as Rose did.*

Delphi stood for a moment, partly shielded by a large fern. She watched and took a moment to process what she saw. Rose, always small, looked shrunken in the capacious wicker seat. Her flyaway hair was neat, of course, but her glasses kept slipping down, and she pushed them up again as she read.

Then Delphi felt the doctor's hand on her arm, and she turned her face to him. He smiled and nodded his encouragement.

He knows my feelings. He seems to understand my turmoil.

She looked again into his dark eyes and thought of Rainier. If only he was here with her now. He would know how she felt too. She should have told him everything when she'd had the opportunity. He may have understood even her most heinous sin. He had been to war. He knew what it was like and how rich emotions were back then. And now it was too late. He was gone from her life. He had responsibilities and so did she. She closed her eyes momentarily and took a deep breath.

"Rose, my dear," she said as she stepped out from the shelter of the greenery.

Rose looked up and smiled. There was her sister, the Rose she knew, though tired and frail. There were dark circles beneath her eyes, but a light from within shone out. She closed her book and struggled out of her chair. "Doctor Brown, Benjamin, says I am no longer contagious." She opened her arms. "Oh, Delphi, my dear sister. How we have missed you."

Delphi went forward and received the benediction of Rose's kiss on her cheek.

"We have much to talk about," Rose said, "but for now it's enough that you're here and I'm getting better. We have lots of time to get to know each other all over again."

"There's so much I need to say to you, Rose."

"I know. I too, but as I say, we have plenty of time."

She was always seeing the good in people, always looking for the reasons behind my bad behaviour, Delphi thought. *She always tried to forgive, but it didn't serve her well to be self-effacing all the time.*

"Let's just enjoy being together. I do want to know all about Flora. I'm so looking forward to meeting her. Papa, thank you for coming to see me again." Rose accepted his kiss on her forehead. "Delphi, come and sit here next to me, and we'll ask a special favour and see if we can have tea early." She rang a little bell, and someone appeared to see what she needed.

Rose patted the cushion next to her and Delphi sat.

She still has such elegance and beauty. I wonder if Michael will see that too, she thought with unease.

"You are well looked after here, it seems," Delphi said.

"Oh yes, it's all amazing. I'm very well looked after. So, how old is Flora now? She must be ten, surely. Does she look like you or more like her father? He had such distinctive colouring."

"Yes, she's ten, and she has George's features but not his red hair or brown eyes. People say she looks like me. She's very pleased to be here and to meet all her family. She'll miss her Australian grandma, but I fear she has my adventurous spirit."

Rose noticed how Delphi was avoiding eye contact. She placed her hand on her sister's arm. "Delphi, I'm truly so pleased that you're here," she said, and was happier when Delphi's eyes at last met her own. "You must take her to see the school. She will need to attend somewhere. You might consider placing her at Kingshaven, and Michael would love to meet her and to see you again too."

Why am I forcing them together? Especially when I can't be there to witness it, Rose thought. *I need confirmation that all is over and in the past, I think.*

"Oh, there's plenty of time for all that." Delphi smiled at her sister. "You're right, though. Eventually Flora will have to go to school somewhere. How is it going there?"

"Before all this, things were doing very well. Bedales, Frensham Heights and we at Kingshaven are developing quite a name for being forward-thinking and the new face of co-educational education. Our policies are claiming attention in some of the highest places. Having the Duke of Norfolk on the board helps our cause, of course. Wait until you see the place, Delphi. It's magnificent."

"It all sounds fascinating," Delphi said.

"You must visit the chapel. My painting hangs above the altar. It's one of my best works. I've called it 'Not by Might nor by Power, but by my Spirit'." Her voice shone with her enthusiasm.

"That sounds like you, dearest," Delphi said.

"It's allegorical, of course."

"That sounds like you, too," Delphi said but then added, "I didn't mean to be rude with that remark."

"Please, don't fret. All is in the past." Rose picked at her skirt and returned the subject to the school. "The grounds are perfect for outdoor lessons. We have a pageant with dance, prose and poetry every year. Parents come for each Speech Day and they have been very complimentary. They've been supportive too during this bout of trouble, but it's still a worry for Michael. The bank is always knocking at the door." Her eyes glittered behind her spectacles.

"You mustn't exhaust yourself, Rose, my dear," her papa said. "All will still be there for you."

"Yes. It's just that I do so miss it."

"Michael will keep it safe. This new senior mistress seems to be up to it as well. She has embraced the philosophy of the place and I gather the parents like her."

"Michael must miss you," Delphi said. "It won't be long now, will it? Before you can leave here, I mean."

"I do feel much better." Rose sat back in her chair, though, and suddenly seemed tired.

"We'll go," Papa said. "We do not wish to tire you too much."

"Come again soon, Delphi."

"I will." Delphi bent to kiss her sister's forehead, having risen from the seat at Papa's prompting.

"And do go to visit Michael and take Flora to meet him," Rose said again.

Right on cue, the doctor reappeared. "Visits little and often are the best thing. She still gets weary easily." He smiled at Rose and then accompanied Delphi and Mr Strong as they left the way they had come in.

Delphi turned to the doctor at the front door. "Thank you."

He smiled at her and his dark eyes made her heart swoop.

"She seems so frail, Dr Harman."

"It's Doctor Brown," he said.

"Oh, yes, I'm so sorry. I was reminded of someone else." She shook her head.

"She's been very, very ill, but she's on the mend. A few weeks and she'll be able to go home. We are concentrating now on building up her strength with fresh air and good, nourishing food. We don't want her to succumb to this or anything else while her system is so depleted."

"She worries about her husband and the school," Mr Strong said.

"Yes, I think you're correct, and that's not good for her either. We try to keep her calm so that she's not fretting. Mind you, her husband has had a fright too. When he visited last time, he was very tired when I saw him, but he managed to distract her. Will you be visiting him, Mrs Dight?"

"I'm sure she will," Mr Strong answered for Delphi while she tried to master her thoughts.

"Yes, yes, I shall, and I'll give him my sister's love, of course." Delphi was still in turmoil. *Fancy calling the doctor by the name of Harman. What an idiot! What was I thinking?*

With that, they left.

Doctor Brown returned to his patient. He said to Rose, "You mustn't overdo things. I'm going to listen to your heart." He took a stethoscope from his pocket. "Mmm," he said. "It's fine, but you must take it easy now. I think this visit has wearied you, although from what you have told me I imagine it was made worse with worry."

"You're right," Rose admitted. "I've been worrying about my sister visiting my husband." She smiled and shrugged. "I've been here long enough for you to know my entire life history, it seems."

"All part of the cure and as we said, it's all confidential too. Your sister told me she would give your husband your love. Worrying is not good for you."

Rose nodded. It was all very well of Papa to have brought Delphi home. She understood that it was for the best of reasons, but she had felt safe and confident with her on the other side of the world. She and Michael had made a good life, and although they had no children of their own yet, a source of disappointment for them both, she knew he loved her.

Give him my love, please, dear sister, but not your own, Rose thought.

CHAPTER 7

The visit to Rose's and Michael's school was organised, and Flora was sitting next to Delphi as the car rolled up the long and impressive drive. She would need a place to study for a while anyway, although Delphi was far from sure Michael and Rose would want her at their school. After all, they knew the circumstances of her conception and birth. That was the trouble with returning home. It was fine in Australia. Everyone believed that she had married George and were sympathetic to her for her loss. There was still such a stigma attached to having a child out of wedlock. However, she regretted none of it.

Now, Delphi was pleased to have the excuse and distraction of showing Flora everything when she met Michael for the first time in so many years. How could she forget the fool she had made of herself with him when she was a girl? She grew warm at the memory.

The car tyres scattered gravel as they braked outside the front of the building and Delphi stepped out. She put her hand to her hat to hold it in place as she craned her head back to stare up at the roof line, where grey gargoyles glared down at her ominously. Turning to take Flora's hand and glancing across at her papa, they mounted the long flight of steps towards the heavy front door. By the time they stood before it, her legs were aching. Papa pulled the bell handle and they waited.

"It'll be alright," he said, sensing her unease.

She took a deep breath.

They were shown into a large and formal drawing room, with settees set at right angles to the great fireplace, which was laid but not lit. Other chairs were scattered beyond.

"Can I get you anything, ma'am, sir?" the housemaid enquired.

They declined and she left, saying, "The headmaster won't be long."

Delphi perched on the edge of a seat. She glanced at Flora, who was looking around with eyes wide and eyebrows raised. This was so vastly different from what she was used to. Even her Grandpapa Strong's house was not this big. Delphi noted the grand piano with its lid open and music in place. The brocade that cloaked the windows was thick, but she saw it was also becoming threadbare, although the brass tiebacks were ornate and polished to a high shine. The rug beneath her feet had also seen better days, but she could tell it had once been very costly.

There were footsteps outside the room on the marble floor, echoing around the great hall through which they had come. The sounds came closer. Then the handle turned and the door opened. There was Michael.

Delphi had not seen him since before those fateful events of 1917, and she still burned with embarrassment at her foolish proposal to him before that. She remembered her childish infatuation because now she knew it was just that, but she also understood the devastation it had caused Rose. She was still truly ashamed of her deception back then.

He stood before her now, tall and just as handsome, although slightly heavier. His blond hair cascaded across his forehead, hiding the scar she remembered. As he approached, she could see streaks of grey among the fairness and lines on his face that had not been there all those years ago.

"Delphi, you are as beautiful as ever." He stretched out his hands to hers. As she took them, she marvelled at how the brain can play tricks. She'd remembered him as he had been and was surprised by the passing of time. He had called her beautiful. Was she still attractive? Rainier had thought so.

Michael did not stir her heart as he once had, although he'd never moved her as George had. For him she had been delirious, mad. She was wise enough to know that back then, before she had met George, flirting with Michael had been a perverse pleasure she'd taken in upsetting her sister, a power-play that she'd needed to win. And now she had met Rainier, so different with his black hair and flashing dark eyes. Oh, Lord, how her soul cried out. Her love for Rainier was mature, considered and deep. It was not a flush of youthful infatuation, nor was it cast from desperate times and desires heightened by fear. She tried to imagine him striding between the rows of vines in France, the sun shining upon his head, but she couldn't.

Why did she always have to mess up her life and that of others around her? But if she *had* shared all this history, Rainier would probably have run a mile anyway. Her own mother had been ashamed of her. When she had felt the full force of Rose's anger, which was so out of character, it had been utterly devastating. Delphi should have had greater resistance, but she had never regretted one moment of Flora's being.

She dragged her mind back to the present. As Michael let her hands go, he turned to Flora. "It's a pleasure to meet you, young lady. I can't believe I have a niece of your age. You are very like your mother."

Delphi could see her daughter was as charmed by Michael as she had been as an adolescent, with his dimpled cheek, broad grin and his compelling stature.

"Would you like to look around the school?" He turned to Mr Strong. "You're welcome to come too, of course, but you're more familiar with things. Shall I ring for tea?"

"I'm fine here, lad. You go. We might have tea when you all return," Mr Strong replied.

The dining room was in the fine tradition of the hunting lodge this place had once been. "What an experience for your students," Delphi said.

The dormitories each held beds for six. "There's a senior in with each group. They have that curtained area at the end," Michael explained. "We're definitely part of the progressive movement. We have a liberal ethos and a relaxed attitude, but we also promote responsibility and leadership, reasoning and explanation rather than bossiness and hectoring. That's why we focus upon dance, art and crafts, and music too. We're encouraging freedom of thought."

As they emerged into the grounds, Flora skipped ahead to look at the fountain and its pond. Delphi watched her daughter's yellow dress spreading like melted butter as she sat on the low wall. Her trailing fingers created ripples and the sun scattered its bright diamonds around them.

"When we started out, Rose and I were determined to follow John Badley's example at Bedales and ensure co-education here. We want to get away from the unwholesome behaviour that can occur in a single sex school. We know co-education isn't widely adopted in England because of fear of sexual mistakes." Michael looked sideways at Delphi and stopped walking. He turned to face her. "Delphi, I want you to understand that we hold no sense of blame for Flora's birth. Those days of the war were extraordinary. George was my dearest friend. He needed your comfort to fulfil his duty."

"Thank you, Michael. That means such a great deal to me. She's my world."

"Have you considered schooling for her?"

"Yes, but I thought you would not want her here at Kingshaven. From what you have just said, however, I might have misjudged you."

"Oh, Delphi, I think you have. Rose and I would welcome Flora here, and you too, should you need a home."

Delphi laughed. "Papa isn't going to want us forever, I'm sure of that. He has Izzy to look after him, and I'm not certain he would want more female clutter these days, but we couldn't simply scavenge from you either."

"What if we could come to some sort of business arrangement?"

"What do you mean?" Delphi glanced across at Flora, who was still preoccupied with the water.

"We…" He hesitated. "You must say if you think it wouldn't work." He looked down at her and seemed awkward.

"I can't give an opinion unless you tell me." She smiled at him, feeling at ease at last.

"We need someone to take control of the kitchens. I don't mean slaving at the stove." He rushed on. "I mean to control the thing, plan the menus, and order the necessary stocks, food and equipment. The senior mistress has been doing it, and before that, Rose did, but it's too much. We need someone with the skills and understanding. It would be small fry for you after what you did in France in the Women's Legion." He finally paused for breath.

Delphi was taken aback and said nothing while she thought through the possibilities.

"You would be part of the senior team here. It's a critical role, not some Cinderella position." He paused again. "Please do consider it. Rose and I talked for simply ages about it. Have I offended you in some way? Please do say something. Rose is as keen as I am. I'm sorry. I have offended you, haven't I? It wasn't meant that way." He looked at his feet and then placed his hand on her arm. "I'm sorry," he said again.

CHAPTER 8

That night, Delphi had so much to think about she couldn't sleep. Tossing about wasn't helping. She grew hot, and in her restlessness the covers were getting tangled. Swinging her legs out of bed, she went and stood by the window. The moon was full and cast a glow over the grass to the trees beyond. It was so clear and bright their shadows were long across the lawn, their branches a muddled filigree web.

That's how I feel, she thought, *confused. Do I want to set roots down here? How would I feel, living in such close contact with Michael and Rose? How does Rose really feel about that? If only I had heard from Rainier. Clearly it was only a shipboard romance. He would have written if he felt more. How stupid I've been to harbour hopes. Flora needs stability, and the school seems to offer that to us both. I would have a purpose if I took over the organisation of the kitchens at the school, and Flora would receive an education and make friends.*

She gave an enormous sigh. Why was life always so complicated?

The next morning, Delphi was heavy-eyed and lacked enthusiasm for the day ahead. She had a letter to write, and then perhaps she and Flora would take a walk and get out from under her papa's feet. Izzy seemed to need no help either.

Before going downstairs, she sat at her little desk and wrote to Michael to accept his offer. Sealing it in the envelope and addressing it, she felt slightly better. At least she had decided.

"Mummy, I thought you were never coming down." Flora greeted her, looking lively and sounding alert. "Grandpa Strong said I shouldn't disturb you, that you were tired, but there's so much to go and see."

"Sorry, sweetie, I didn't sleep too well, but I'm here now. Just let me have a cup of coffee and we'll get started on some adventure, shall we? I have a letter to post as well."

"There's a letter here on the plate for you. Who do you think it might be from?" Delphi's heart gave a leap, and then Flora continued. "I don't think it's Granny. It's got an English stamp."

Delphi glanced at the letter lying on the salver at the bottom of the stairs. Memories of other letters lying there long ago flashed through her mind. She picked this one up with apathy and glanced at the back. No address or indication there.

It's not from Rainier anyway, she thought. *That just makes my decision more valid.* She felt for the newly written letter in her pocket.

"Have you eaten yet?"

"I had breakfast ages ago," Flora replied. "Who do think that's from?" She nodded at the envelope in her mother's hand.

"Do me a favour, darling, and go and ask if I might have coffee. Then come through to the dining room with me. I'll open it there."

Flora hopped and skipped along with the excitement and anticipation of the young.

Once they were seated, Delphi opened the envelope and said, "Oh, it's from Bea Shearer." She started to read. "Ah, she's heard from Rainier. He's getting settled into his new home and sorting out the vineyard and production issues. She speaks of her new grandchild, too."

"Rainier hasn't written to us," Flora said and looked disappointed.

"No, well, he's far too busy. He'd know that Mrs Shearer would pass along any news, I'm sure."

"Does she say what her grandchild is called? Is it a boy or a girl?"

"You always want to know everything, little Miss Sticky Beak." Delphi laughed and tweaked Flora's nose.

"Grandad Dight used to call me that," Flora said.

"When I was young, Papa used to call me little Miss Nosey Parker. It means the same thing. Anyway, the baby is a boy and he's called John, apparently."

"Can we go and see her and the new baby?"

"I'm sure we could arrange that at some point, but not now. Let me get on, and then we can go out for a walk. Shall we go into the town and explore there, or shall we go across the fields?"

"Oh, across the fields, definitely," Flora said.

"I'll show you down the lane where my sisters and I used to go when I was young," Delphi said. "There's the little local shop and post office that way. I wonder if the same lady still works there."

As they went, Delphi set Flora the task of collecting something for each letter of the alphabet. She was soon busy scavenging in the hedgerows for flowers and other things to pop into her little basket. In between exclaiming, praising and helping, Delphi had the space to consider the other news in Bea's letter; the news she hadn't shared with her daughter.

"J is such a tricky letter," Flora said, interrupting her mother's thoughts.

"Sorry?"

"Mummy! The letter J. I'm stuck on that one." Flora sounded exasperated.

"Juice. Find a berry or something like that," Delphi suggested.

Flora skipped ahead again, the skirt of her dress swinging with the joy of being outside in the country.

So, he was asking after us, she thought. *Bea referred to 'you both', though, not to just me. He's probably being polite. I really can't read much into that. I shouldn't anyway. And what if he really did come over to visit, as she suggests he might? He still doesn't know the truth of Flora's birth.*

Her thoughts flowed up and down in similar vein until Flora interrupted again.

Having posted her letter to Michael, she was feeling more positive about their future. She had to make another new start, and this was as good a way as any. She would prove herself to Rose and all would be well.

When Delphi and Flora returned from their walk, a further surprise awaited.

A letter had arrived by the second post while they were out. Delphi didn't recognise this writing either, but she recognised the images and the words *poste* and *République Française* on the stamp. After all, she had spent many months in France herself, albeit a long time ago.

She became breathless and her knees wobbled. She felt dizzy. She realised all the longing she had supressed was flinging itself around her head. Flora had run off to show Dora her collection basket, so Delphi grabbed the letter from the salver on the table and collapsed onto the stairs as her heart thumped in her ears.

Eventually, as her shaking subsided, she sped up the steps to her room. Shutting the door, she leaned against it and ripped open the letter. Then she started shaking again. The letter was short, but when she reread it, she knew she had to share everything with Rainier.

My dearest darling Delphi, mon amour, mon coeur,

I must call you that because it's true; you have my heart and I am incomplete. I miss you. I thought when we said goodbye that would be the end of it, but I cannot leave it. I am being swallowed by this great empty hole.

I know there is something you held back from me, but I miss you so much I don't care what it is. It cannot be so terrible that I would not love you anyway.

My duties here on the estate prevent me from coming to see you immediately, but I hope and pray that as soon as I am able you will allow me to visit. My life is so bland. Please write to me soon and tell me how you feel. If I am making a fool of myself, I shall understand, but in my soul I think you miss me too.

I am yours,
Rainier.

Delphi, not prone to tears, staggered to her bed and curled up and cried. She cried for all the lost moments, for her own cowardliness, for all the missed opportunities and her own stupidity in not trusting his good judgement.

Eventually, when she was all cried out, she sat up. Looking in the mirror, she saw her eyes were red and they stung. She felt exhausted with emotion. Taking up her brush, she passed it through her hair, contemplating all that she had read and all that she was feeling. In the end, the repetitive motion began to soothe her spirit. She replaced the hairbrush and took paper and pen from her writing box. This was not going to be easy, and it was important to get it right. She sat and thought for a long while before writing the first words: *My dearest Rainier, I must tell you something and if you detest me after, I shall understand. It concerns Flora and the circumstances of her conception and her birth…* Then she screwed it up and threw it in the bin.

CHAPTER 9

Beside herself with emotion, it wasn't until later in the day that Delphi remembered the letter that was already winging its way to the school, with her acceptance of the job that Michael and Rose had offered.

"I really have to go and see Rose first thing in the morning, Papa." Delphi had knocked on her father's study door and was now seated in front of him. She explained her dilemma.

"From what I understand, Rose and Michael would welcome any help you can give. Nothing is certain for you in any other camp, my dear. Take their offer and see what happens. If you want to leave in the future and take up elsewhere, then of course you can do that, but in the meantime you and Flora will have security and a home. Flora will have an education which will serve her well."

"Thank you for your wise counsel." Delphi stood and leaned in to kiss her papa on the cheek. She smelled his tobacco, and the roughness of his face transported her back to when she was little more than a child with a whole new life beginning to engulf her.

They had never been demonstrative. Her papa was from an era when things were not expressed, and before she went to Australia, life generally was more formal. That summer, though, had changed her life forever. Rose had shouted her innermost feelings at her and her mama had hardly spoken to her. She had gone to Australia with George's parents and Flora had been born.

Delphi did go to see Rose, but not for a couple of days. If she was going to take the place offered, the urgency was diminished. After all, her papa was correct. There were no promises of anything elsewhere.

She needed to be open in her dealings, and she craved her sister's respect. She needed to talk, just the two of them, so that she could cement her apology for past wrongs and be reassured that all was left behind.

Again, she headed to the conservatory at the sanatorium, but this morning the sun had disappeared, and the sky was a heavy grey.

Perfect, thought Delphi. *Just what this conversation needs.*

When she arrived, there were others present. It wasn't conducive to a private, possibly emotional, conversation.

"There's a small sitting room. Come on, let's go there," Rose said, leading the way.

"You always were the sensitive one," Delphi said, and then regretted it when Rose looked back over her shoulder but said nothing. It sounded like a criticism, and it wasn't meant to be. Delphi sighed. She seemed to be sighing a lot lately.

"I'm coming home next week," Rose said. "I shall have to be careful, but I'm fretting about my absence. Doctor Brown had a long conversation with us and has finally agreed to let me go." She closed the door behind them and went to sit down in the little room. They chatted inconsequentially for several minutes. Neither was willing to commit, it seemed.

"So, Michael has put to you our proposition, and he tells me you have accepted." There seemed to be some coolness about her sister, and Delphi was overcome with misgivings all over again.

"Look, Rose, if you think it would cause problems, me being there…"

"No, we discussed it at length. It seems the perfect solution for all of us."

"I'm not sure how long I will be there. I've met someone."

"Oh…?" Rose's voice ascended in a question, and for the first time Delphi saw the glimmer of a smile.

She shared all that had happened between her and Rainier. "I must explain to you, too, Rose. The lies I told you about Michael and…"

"Hush, Delphi. We were children."

"But…"

"I know, but it worked out in the end. Michael and I are very happy. I do believe he has loved me well. We all grew up. The war changed everything."

"It did. I loved George to the exclusion of all else. Now I've met Rainier. I don't know what will happen there, but working with you and Michael will be a wonderful opportunity for me, and especially for Flora. Yet again, I owe you much."

"No, you don't. You're my sister, and we will gain as much if not more from having you there taking a great weight from our shoulders." Rose stood. "Come here."

Delphi moved towards her sister and they enfolded each other. Rose felt like air, she was so tiny and thin. Tears came, and even though Delphi raised her eyes to the ceiling to prevent a tell-tale cascade, the moisture slid down her cheeks.

"We will be a good team," Rose said as she stood back, and the smile this time reached her eyes.

The following week was madness. Delphi visited the school again and tried to familiarise herself with all that she would need to do. She wrote copious notes and made lists until her fingers ached. As Michael had intimated, it was a big task, but it did not match up to the size of her responsibilities in France when she'd been feeding hundreds of troops.

The little flat that she and Flora had been given was fine for their needs, but it still needed a thorough spring clean, and Delphi wanted to rearrange the furniture to make it more like her own home. Flora would sleep in the dorm with others of her age, but she would come here at the weekends when many of the others also went home.

After having spoken to Rose, she planned to take Flora up to Manchester on the train to buy her new school uniform.

"We have tried to build a good reputation, and so the best upmarket establishment must be associated with Kingshaven. It caused a little uproar in the family when Michael announced to his father that we had commissioned Kendal Milne and Faulkner instead of the family department store. The one we have chosen is known as the Harrods of the North, though. That's the level at which we are beginning to operate." Rose spoke with pride.

"It must certainly have helped to have the Duke's patronage, even though he no longer owns the premises as such," Delphi said. "It's a magnificent building. You have come far, Rose."

Her sister laughed. "We certainly have when I think how Michael started in the garage at the cottage with no more than five children from the village."

Until they moved into the school, every day Delphi looked at the salver at the bottom of the stairs, despite her resolve not to. She had finally plucked up her courage and posted a letter she had written to Rainier, explaining some of her past but still only hinting at Flora's birth. Each morning, she felt crushing disappointment. While there was no letter from Rainier, she imagined the disgust he must be feeling at her revelations.

She immersed herself in her new work. Dressed in a white smothering overall and with her neat, newly bobbed hair covered, she busied herself for long hours. Her staff needed some further training to match her exacting standards, and menus needed updating.

"I think I might write a book," she said to Rose one day. "A cookery book, but one which will also be a training manual for young people. What do you think?"

"Are we not keeping you busy enough?"

"You are. It's just a vague thought at the moment." She smiled at her sister. "How do you think Flora is doing? It's all very different for her. I've tried to keep out of it as much as possible and let her find her own feet. She doesn't say much."

"So many parents say the same thing when they ask their youngsters what they have done. Children seem to find it hard work to recount everything. I've been keeping a special eye on her. How could I not? She's beginning to settle."

"She has talked a lot about Edith. They seem to be making friends."

"Edith hasn't been here long either, so it's a friendship of convenience, but I think they may become really good friends. They complement each other."

Flora joined her mother at the breakfast table. It was small and tucked into the bay window but overlooked the front drive and the fountain. The sun beamed in, and the room was light and fresh since Delphi had smiled at the handyman and got him to add a fresh coat of paint above the dado rail and across the ceiling.

Ever open in her dealings, Flora said, "I like it here. My English family are very kind. I do miss Granny Dight, of course." Delphi knew she had added this last phrase because she thought she ought to. "We had dance outside yesterday. Miss Healey told Edith and I that we did very well. There's going to be a pageant. Everyone's going to be in it. I don't think we'll get speaking parts or anything because we're so new, but I don't mind. It sounds like great fun. Frightfully *mezzo-brow*, one of the seniors said."

Delphi smiled at her enthusiasm.

"I don't even know what that means, but it will be ever so good," Flora continued. "Miss Healey said we would move through the ages from the Stone Age to The Gifts of Science. There'll be dressing up and dancing and poetry. We started to learn figure marching. We really had to think hard. It was quite tricky. Edith said…" She flowed on.

Delphi listened and nodded and added a comment here and there.

"Aunt Rose said… Can I call her that? When I'm in school, I say Mrs Redfern."

Delphi nodded.

"Aunt Rose is lovely and kind. She always smiles, and when Joseph was unkind to Peter Moore, she said we had to understand why he did that and not just be cross with him. We don't see Uncle Michael so much, but everyone likes him. He takes us for worship each morning, of course. He's much funnier than when we went to the services on the ship. When we sing in the chapel, it echoes all around and sounds lovely. Mummy, did you hear me?"

"Sorry, darling. I was miles away, but only for that bit."

"What were you thinking about?"

"I was remembering the SS *Jervis Bay*. You mentioned the ship, and it set me thinking."

"We haven't heard from Rainier, have we? I hoped we might."

"Mmm, me too," Delphi agreed. "Right, we have the whole day. What would you like to do?" She stood and began to busy herself clearing the table, so Flora got up to help.

CHAPTER 10

Dear Delphi, and Flora, too, (of course),

I hope this finds you well and happy. Your last letter was full of news and it was lovely to hear how Flora is settling into her new school. You sound very busy yourself with so much to organise.

My grandson is growing quickly and Sophie, my daughter, takes him out in his pram every day for the fresh air. I often go too and, in fact, am sitting on a bench in the shade of a tree in the park to write this to you while they continue a circuit.

Now, the reason I'm writing is a delicate one. I was sworn to secrecy, but as I haven't yet responded to that I think it would be alright to bend the rules a little. The thing is, a mutual friend from the good ship Jervis Bay is thinking of visiting me. I suspect that is a ploy and that this person will visit elsewhere in England whilst here.

There, really, I have told you nothing. I thought you might like to know and be a little prepared. I'm not sure when this will be.

The person in question is particularly busy now. On the farm place there are many workers who need to get back into good habits, and the crop itself needed much trimming and improvement in many ways, I hear. It seems at this time of year the vines grow rapidly, and unwanted shoots must be kept to a minimum or the fruit will not flourish. Whoops. I've said too much.

Ah, John needs changing apparently, and Sophie says we must go. I'll finish this and get it off to you, my dear. If I hear more news of our friend, I shall be sure to let you know as soon as I can.

Best wishes to you both.

Your good friend,

Bea

The letter had been forwarded to Delphi at the school by Izzy, as had other letters that had arrived, although there were few. She'd had nothing from Rainier.

Delphi plonked herself down on a chair and re-read it. She wouldn't say anything to Flora about this, not yet. It may come to nothing, anyway. A hundred questions buzzed around her brain. Why had he not written to her? Was he just going to see Bea and avoid her? She wouldn't blame him for that. Why would he come all that way to see an old lady and not come to see her, though? Again, she wondered why he hadn't been in contact with her. She thought the worst. *He won't come here. I better get on and forget all this nonsense.*

She stuffed the letter in her pocket and decided to burn it when the fire was lit this evening. No need to excite Flora with news of something that wasn't going to happen.

Flora and Edith had just emerged from their English class, clutching school copies of Charles Kingsley's *The Water Babies*.

"Let's head down the bank to the oak tree," Edith said. "I really want to know what Tom thinks when he sees himself all grubby in Ellie's mirror."

"Me too," Flora said. "Do you think they'll fall in love?"

"It's not really that kind of story, I don't think. Anyway, Miss Pryce wouldn't let us read that sort of book. Too racy for her." They giggled as they ran.

Flopping down on the coarse grass beneath the ancient tree, Flora said, "We've only got about half an hour. It's a bit spiky here anyway." She brushed the twigs and old acorns from under her. "I'd really like to read *The Thirty-Nine Steps*. It's by someone called John Buchan. My mother was reading it. It's about spies in Scotland. She said it was really exciting. I'd like to be a spy."

"Oh, yes, me too," Edith agreed. "Do you know what a spy does?"

"Not really, but it sounds daring." She opened her book.

A short while passed and Edith leaped up. "I can hear voices. It must be the seniors coming out. We'll be late and get a right wigging. Come on."

They ran for it across the field and arrived just as the last of the class were walking into their next lesson.

"You look a bit hot, girls. I hope you haven't been running around school, that's not creating the correct ambience for your morality lesson," the teacher said.

"Oh, no, Miss," said Flora.

"It's Miss Pryce, Flora."

"Sorry, Miss Pryce." Flora glanced at Edith and grinned. "I'd love to spy on her," she whispered as they took their seats. "That would be a tale to tell. I'm sure she has a secret life and she's not as prim as she makes out."

"You have something to add to the conversation, Flora?"

"No, Miss Pryce."

Delphi entered the salon after tea was finished and she had set the two kitchen maids on clearing up and washing the dishes.

"I think Flora's becoming more confident," Rose said.

"Oh?" Delphi sat down opposite her sister.

"Don't frown," Rose said. "It's a minor matter, but I thought you'd like to know. She was caught passing notes in class and when the teacher asked her to read it out, she flatly refused. I think she was playing to the audience a little, so she has been awarded a detention."

"Oh dear," Delphi said. "Sorry. That doesn't seem like her. She can be bold but not usually rude."

"She wasn't rude at all. She refused to hand over the paper with extreme politeness. Actually, just between us, I think the teacher asked for it."

"Who was it?"

"Miss Pryce, but please don't say anything to her. I've had a word with her about how she might have handled it differently."

"I'll have words with Flora. I think you're right, though. She's finding her feet, as you say, and gaining independence that she's not had before."

"A different kind, I imagine," Rose said.

"You're right. She used to roam for miles and ride on her own around the station, but she always had the security of the family each evening, and the hands would often see her around when they were out seeing to the sheep. Crikey, I hope she's not going off the rails."

"You sounded so Australian when you said that." Rose laughed. "She'll be fine. In my experience, and I have seen it many times, children will try out behaviours, but they almost always revert to form and follow family values."

"I hope so. I'll speak to her anyway," Delphi said.

Delphi had settled into her new role comfortably. Menus and ordering were simple for the numbers concerned, and her book-keeping skills resurfaced with comparative ease. She liked the staff. She saw little of Michael but when she did, things were easy between them, and Rose was affectionate and natural. Flora continued to be lively. From time to time she overstepped the mark a little, but did nothing too bad.

Then they had a visitor.

Constantly mindful of Bea's last letter, Delphi ripped off her white cap and overall. Running her hands through her hair as she hurried along the corridor, she wondered who it could be.

Arriving in the great hall, by the front door she found her younger sister, Izzy. Her heart plummeted. Not the one who she wished to see particularly, although pleasant enough. Delphi had not seen much of her younger sister since returning from Australia, and was a little puzzled that she had come calling.

"Hello, Izzy," Delphi said, rallying her spirits and moving to kiss the arrival. "This is a lovely surprise. We don't often see you here, I believe. Is Papa alright? There aren't any problems, are there?"

"No, no, nothing like that," Izzy said as she removed her coat but kept on her hat.

"Put it on the chair." Delphi pointed.

"I wasn't exactly passing, but I had my ladies' German group. We were discussing the rise of this man Hitler and how he says that Germany is steadily slipping towards communism because of the economic problems, like bankruptcies and higher unemployment. People over there are borrowing more and more. It's a bit worrying."

"I was reading something about it the other day," Delphi said. "You always were interested in the country, even as a girl."

"More so since I've lived there. Papa wanted me home because Rose was ill, and you were coming and... It's complicated."

Delphi knew they had never been close. Was Izzy resentful and blaming her for having to give up her German friends? "Would you go again?"

"Like a shot. I've lots of friends there."

"So, what brings you here today?" Delphi was uncomfortable and sought the mundane. Had she really affected so many people's lives with that reckless act so long ago?

"There was a telephone call for you. I took it and said I would pass the message along."

"Oh? Who was it?"

"This fellow Rainier that you seem to have set your cap at."

"Izzy, for goodness' sake, get on with it. I haven't 'set my cap', as you say. We met, we were friends, that's all. So, what was the message?"

"He wanted to know if he could speak to you, so I told him you were no longer living there."

"What did he say to that?" This was so frustrating.

"I gave him the number and the address of the school. He asked me to tell you he had rung. That's it."

"That's all? Did he say where he was ringing from?"

"No."

"Didn't he say anything else at all?" Delphi was becoming increasingly annoyed with her sister.

"No, that was it. Now, if you want to thank me for making this special trip to inform you, then please do. You can be so grumpy and ungrateful still. I'll go and see Rose."

"Oh, Izzy, I'm sorry." Delphi breathed out her tension and was contrite. She and Izzy had never got along as children. That was why Rose had had to share a bedroom with their youngest sibling and Delphi had had one of her own. "It was very kind of you. I don't deserve you. I'm just tense about the whole thing. Come along, let's go together to find Rose. I'll arrange some tea for all of us."

She linked her arm through that of her sister and they went in search of the one who had always been the peacekeeper.

CHAPTER 11

Delphi's mind was everywhere but on her work over the next week. Luckily it was all so easy that it didn't take much concentration, and the kitchen staff were beginning to function at a higher level and to think for themselves. The ordering of supplies was her responsibility alone, however. Fortunately, the grocer was perceptive and when he received an order for a hundred times one hundredweight sacks of potatoes instead of ten, he rang the school and asked for clarification.

Rose followed up the telephone call by searching out Delphi in her little office off the kitchen. "Is everything alright? I looked around the kitchen as I came through, but it was only a glance. Everything seems as neat and orderly as it should be, but you seem distracted, dearest."

"Yes, fine. Why do you ask?" Delphi felt a frisson of worry. "Have I done something wrong?"

Rose explained the telephone call. "It seems so unlike you not to double check. Is this business with Flora worrying you?" Yet again Flora had been in trouble, only this time it had been more serious.

"To be honest, Rose, it's that and the information that came from Izzy about Rainier telephoning. I just don't know where I stand. I had set my mind on never seeing him again. It was just a fleeting friendship. I never divulged the real issue of Flora's father. It was my sin and mine to live with. That telephone message set it all off again, but there has been nothing since, and now this business with Flora is upsetting me. I'm not sure how to handle it. If I interfere too much, she'll start to resent me, but I can't ignore it. She's been a difficult child at times, but she's never caused me to worry like this."

"The worst thing for children is to be ignored. Maybe she feels your distance and turmoil. I know we don't want to give credence to silly behaviour by making too much of it, but on this occasion her safety was at stake. She and I spoke, as I told you, but maybe she's craving your attention. It's the first time she's not had it all now she's not living with you in the same way. She's lost the attention of grandparents too."

"You're right. It's all my fault."

"That's not what I meant at all. It's no one's fault. It's the way things have developed, and she must come to terms with the changes. You can't keep her that close forever."

"I'll speak to her tomorrow when she comes home to our flat," Delphi said.

Something else to worry about, she thought.

Having grovelled down the telephone to the grocer, she made herself a cup of tea and went to sit in her office, where she planned what to say to the recalcitrant Flora.

Delphi was determined to be reasonable and understanding. "I'm not going to be cross with you. I know you've already spoken about it with Aunt Rose." That was the way she had planned it the day before. "I just need to understand. Why on earth were you on the roof in the middle of the night?" She was aware that her voice was already rising.

"I had a wager with the other girls in the dorm."

"A wager? What about?"

"We were talking about spies, like in your book. You know, *The Thirty-Nine Steps*. It sounds such a good book. I do wish you'd let me read it."

"You're deviating, Flora." Delphi made her voice sound firm.

"Miss Pryce has been such a dragon."

"That doesn't explain why you were doing such a madcap, stupid thing."

"You said you weren't going to be cross," Flora reminded her, and tears looked in danger of appearing.

"No." Delphi took a huge intake of breath. "No, you're right. Carry on. What was the wager?"

"I was saying I wanted to be a spy when I grow up. It was a private conversation with Edith, but one of the other girls was listening in and started making fun. We had a bit of an argument. She told me I was childish and stupid and knew nothing about spying, so I told her I did." Flora hung her head.

"And do you?" Delphi was tempted to smile but managed to hold it in.

"Not really, but I told her I did and that I could prove it. I know it was bragging, but she was being so annoying."

"What happened then?"

"I said I could find out what colour nightie Miss Pryce wears."

"What? You risked everything to find that out? I don't believe it. This is ridiculous." All of Delphi's restraint and mirth vanished. "I can't believe you would be so stupid. How did you get up onto the roof, anyway? And what were you going to do from there? All I can say is it's just as well the caretaker heard you and shone his torch up. For goodness' sake, Flora."

"Don't shout at me," she wailed.

"How did you get up there? I think I need to know that, at least."

"There's a window in the attic and the catch has stuck, so it doesn't close properly. I climbed out onto the roof and scrambled along to the parapet and jumped down onto the flat bit above the teachers' wing."

"You could have been killed, you foolish child! At the very least you could have injured yourself badly." Then she had another thought. "You could have knocked slates off, and they might have landed on Mr Swift's head while he did his rounds and killed him instead."

Flora looked horrified. "I didn't think." The tears started to fall.

"Oh Flora!"

"I'll never live this down. They'll all know I failed, and they'll laugh at me even more. I already get teased because I sound different and I don't have a father."

"I beg your pardon?" Delphi had the force taken from her voice. "What did you say? You don't have a father? You do, darling child. You do. He was killed fighting for what he believed in, fighting for this country, miles from his own home." Her own eyes stung at what Flora had said, as well as the thought she could have lost her too. "Come here." She enfolded her child and they both wept, their heavy tears binding them together. "Tell Aunt Rose if you are being teased. Tell me and I'll give them extra lumpy mashed potatoes." They both laughed. "Don't hold anything back from me. We'll sort it out together."

"I'll manage it," Flora said between post crying gulps. "If I can't be a spy, perhaps I'll be like Mary in *The Secret Garden*. Well, not rude like she is at the beginning, but I'll discover a secret hiding place and meet a sad boy and make him better."

"You have too much imagination. I hesitate to say you read too much, but..." Delphi tweaked Flora's nose. "Shall we go outside for a while and get some fresh air? Let's wash our faces."

Flora nodded.

Having donned cardigans against the cool breeze, Flora, no longer quite so subdued, ran ahead down the stairs. Delphi could hear voices as she began to descend.

Someone to have a look around, perhaps a parent, she thought.

Being in front, Flora saw who it was before Delphi. She suddenly let out a great shout. "Mummy, come and see who's here! Come quickly."

CHAPTER 12

Rainier stood in the hall, looking awkward, with his hat twirling round and round in his hands. Delphi stood stock-still halfway down the stairs, taking in the sight of his dark hair and broad-shouldered physique. She could think of nothing to say for several moments. As he heard her descent, he took a step forward and then stopped, looking up at her. Then Flora flung herself at him, forcing him to take his eyes off Delphi and to gaze at the top of her daughter's shining dark hair. Flora put her arms around his waist. Although now eleven, she did not have the inhibitions of a child brought up in England and saw nothing wrong in greeting a dear friend thus, even though it had been months since they had seen each other. He tousled her head.

"Hello, bright young thing," he said.

Delphi was hampered by her sudden shyness.

Just then, Rose came through from the kitchens. "Ah, there you are," she said. "I was looking for you. This gentleman has come a long way to see you, I believe. Flora, I was looking for you too. I really need your help with my wool winding, if you wouldn't mind."

"Aunt Rose, I'd really rather talk with Rainier."

"I know, my dear, but if you help me now, when Mr Harman and your mummy are ready they could have tea in our sitting room, and you could come too. We have Madeira cake, so it would be a special treat, and you will be such a great help to me."

With the bribery and attention, Flora went happily enough with her aunt and Delphi descended the rest of the stairs and went to greet Rainier, having had some moments to collect herself.

As he held out both his hands, she had little option but to take them. He leaned towards her and kissed her, first on her left cheek and then on her right. She took a breath and smelled the familiar scent of lemons as his roughened cheek brushed hers. She was transported back to the ship and their time together. Her knees trembled and there was a quiver deep within her.

"I've missed you so," he said, his accented English arousing complex emotions.

She'd missed him too, but there were issues about which he was only partly aware. What would he say? Perhaps she need not divulge all her secrets. She could continue to pretend that Flora's father had died after they were married. She had to think of Flora too, didn't she? She didn't want her forever tainted in his eyes. The lie she and George's parents had used so often had almost become fact; almost, but not quite. She knew the truth, and so did Rose and Michael. What sort of a life would she have based upon untruths and deception?

"Why are you frowning? I'd hoped you'd be pleased to see me," Rainier said. He rubbed his thumb across her forehead to erase the lines that had formed. "Now I'm wondering if I have misremembered our feelings."

"No, no, you haven't, but ... but there are things I must tell you and after that you may wish to leave, and I shall understand." Delphi pulled her shawl across her and folded her arms, hunching forward in a protective stance.

"Oh, Delphi, my dearest, I have wondered for so long what could be so terrible that you cannot share it with me. I knew back on the ship that there was a barrier between us, and yet I was also sure you had feelings for me."

Delphi looked over her shoulder. They stood in the large hallway, which was connected to several corridors. There could be prying eyes and flapping ears. "Let's go outside and walk. I shall try hard to be open and honest," she said.

She led him across the lawns towards the beech trees. There was always peace and security among their tall grey trunks. They must have seen many things and shared many secrets, these great ancient giants. The golden bed of leaves discarded by the branches in early spring when the fresh shoots pushed them off the twigs lay beneath their feet, crunching and swishing as they walked, and the cups of nuts cracked. This wood was so different to the one about which she now told Rainier. There, the rhododendron bushes and carpet of soft green had been such a blessed relief for George, compared with the mud, blood and horror of war.

"He was so frightened to go back and face what must be endured. Yet he knew he must. That was true bravery, knowing what lay ahead."

"I understand all that," Rainier said in a quiet undertone.

"Of course you do. You were in just that position on another front," Delphi said.

"I am in the right place to understand how it was for him, and I can guess how difficult it was for you, too."

"He needed something to take with him. I wanted to give him a memory full of love. We loved each other in the fullest sense and completely. Afterwards he told me we would marry as soon as possible, and I believe he meant it. It was said after, not before. It was no false promise. Flora was the result, although he never knew that. He died at Flers and was buried there. Later, his grave must have been blown apart as the front moved back and forth and the bombardments were ruthless. He was never found. This great new memorial they are starting to build in France, the one designed by Sir Edwin Lutyens, they say his name will be there as one of the missing."

Rainier was silent. He was silent for what, to Delphi, seemed a long time. She glanced up briefly to observe his features and tried to gauge his emotions about her revelation. She was tempted to gabble on to fill the emptiness but managed to refrain. This was a shock to him, she could tell. She stopped walking and turned to leave him. That was it. She had been honest and open, which was necessary if they were to proceed with any kind of trusting relationship, but if it was too much for him, she understood. Her sister had screamed abuse at her, which was uncharacteristic of Rose, although to be fair that was more about the lies she had told regarding Michael. She had been a selfish youth, she thought as she walked away. There was no way he could want her.

"It's to be the largest Commonwealth Memorial to the Missing in the world," Rainier said to her retreating figure.

Delphi stopped but did not turn, because tears were streaming down her lovely face.

"Perhaps we will go there one day, together, and find his name and lay some flowers in his memory," he continued.

At that, she turned. Her shawl fell to the ground as she ran to him. His arms enfolded her, and she sobbed into his shoulder, all her pent-up fear slowly washing away as she wept. "I've been so frightened … of how you would feel … about Flora, never mind despising … me for what … I did." Loud gulping sobs punctuated her words.

"People who were not there will not understand. They were dreadful, horrific times and people behave differently when under such extreme pressure. What you did, you did for the most caring of reasons. If things had been different, we would not have met. You would not have gone to Australia. You would not have been on the ship. How could I not be grateful for your history, every moment of it?"

Delphi looked up at Rainier and saw tears in his eyes too. He chuckled and she recognised his self-consciousness.

"What a pair we are," he said, wiping his eyes with the back of his hand whilst still holding her with the other. "I imagined all kinds of things, but I didn't guess this. There are many worse things that people do. Your actions do not count among them." With that, he tilted her chin and brought his mouth to hers in a long and gentle kiss. "Come along," he said. "We better go back for that tea and cake."

"So, you are not disgusted by me? You won't assume I shall lie here in these woods for you?"

"Oh, Delphi, do you think so little of me?"

"No, I don't. I'm sorry."

"Come here." He drew her to him again and silenced her with more kisses, which were eager and hard. "We really had better go back, now," he said. "Maybe we will tell them we are to be married, if you will have me, that is. I'm a poor wretch with an ancient vineyard in the middle of nowhere and I work long hours, but I want to marry you, Delphi Dight. Will you come to me in France? Will Flora be happy to have me as her second-best papa?"

"She never knew her first, but you better ask her yourself. As for me, I should love to be Madame Harman. I love you, Rainier."

She had said those words, finally. She knew George would be happy for her, and so she was at peace at last.

PART 2: DELPHI AND FLORA IN FRANCE

CHAPTER 13

Spring, 1932

The first time they travelled to the home of Flora's aunt and uncle near the town of Thorelière, fifteen-year-old Flora was still little more than a child. Despite previous invitations, Rainier had been busy at his own vineyard in the Champagne region and time had passed.

"It smells lovely," Flora said. "I think it must be all those tiny flowers along the banks. I remember all the French names you taught me, Rainier, when we came to live at your home in France,."

He smiled at her with the bright light of his affection. "The years are speeding by," he replied. "Mmm, you thought the spring cinquefoil a French name, and yet we call it…"

She interrupted her stepfather. "*Fleurs de potentille de printemps.*" She laughed. "What a mouthful for such a tiny yellow flower."

As they turned the bend in the lane, there was the house. Rainier stopped the horse and Flora became aware of the glance he gave Delphi across the top of her head. Flora's mouth dropped open as she took in all before them.

The building was tall and grey with terracotta tiles and shutters of blue that had paled in the strong sunlight. The blooms of wisteria lent a soft lushness to the property.

As they arrived in the courtyard, Rainier's family came out to greet them. His brother, Jean, shook hands with Rainier and introduced his wife, Francine, to Delphi and Flora. She kissed them and welcomed them. Then Jean put his hand on his son's shoulder.

"This is Luca," he said. "He must be about your age, Flora." After receiving a gentle shove from Jean, a tall gangly lad with dark hair like Rainier's and flashing black eyes stepped forward to kiss her on each cheek.

"Don't think you're going to worm your way in here," he hissed in her ear before moving back to greet the adults.

Flora was shocked. She had been looking forward to meeting this branch of her adopted family, and here was her step-cousin being spiteful. She was angry but regarded him coolly. No way would he see her hurt. Then, on reflection and despite his attitude, somewhere deep in her young subconscious she had a strange premonition that this place was to be of immense importance to her.

CHAPTER 14

June 1940

"Flora, in the name of … whatever, hurry up. You haven't got time to do all this. They'll be here soon. You were there when Marcelle telephoned, and that was a quarter of an hour ago. I told you, they're coming." Delphi's voice rose in panic.

"I'm going to get the car out," Rainier shouted from below.

"Whatever are you doing? Come. Now." Delphi turned to leave.

"I just…"

"No!"

Flora, at nearly twenty-three, was certainly no longer an infant but would always be her child. Delphi knew she shouldn't be chiding her so, but worry was making her snappy.

The crunch of tyres on the gravel outside the window wormed into Delphi's head, causing her further dread. She heaved the old leather suitcase into which she had rapidly flung some things. God only knew if what she'd grabbed was appropriate.

She struggled down the steps from the *porte d'entrée* onto the driveway.

No moon, she thought, glancing up. *At least the sky is on our side.*

Delphi's heart pounded in her ears. She felt breathless and a bit sick. The weight of her thoughts and her suitcase were equally awkward and heavy on this hell-black night. An image of the ship's gangplank flashed into her mind. How different carrying this bulk had been back then when she and Flora had left the ship with Rainier as they joined him, twelve years ago.

Glorious, exciting, sun-singing years, they had been. And now this. Pétain, the Lion of France, feathering his nest and cosying up to the Nazis when he'd fought Germany so valiantly the last time. The last time, oh, damnation! That was the war to end them all, and it had been hell.

Was it because, still English at heart, she saw things differently to many of her local French friends regarding this new Free Zone?

She strained to listen. Silence. No sound of vehicles yet. No tank tracks rolling. *It won't be long, though*, she thought.

"Flora, please…"

Her daughter pounded down the steps behind her with an overflowing bag. Rainier came around the corner of the house to meet them. He took the case from Delphi without a word. She couldn't see him clearly but imagined his beloved face, grim and sad to be leaving his family home. Who would tend the vines now? Who would remember to trim the shoots and who would be bothered anyway? The estate workers might continue in a half-hearted way, but there would be no one to chivvy them along and nobody with whom to celebrate another successful harvest in the autumn.

Tears stung her eyes as she ran back to get coats from the cupboard. She grabbed a headscarf that she had carelessly flung down only yesterday. That would have to do. They couldn't waste any more time. Oh, there was so much that she was leaving; so many memories and treasures.

"Delphi, sit in there." Rainier indicated the driver's seat. "Flora, we must push it to the end of the drive. We can't risk Pierre or any of the other workers hearing us leave. It's for their safety as well as ours."

Getting the car rolling was difficult, but, once going, Delphi steered as best she could in the dark. She wound the window down the easier to see the grass verge and she strained to listen for the approach of the enemy. It was hard to hear above the noise they made, despite trying to be quiet. The crunch of the tyres, each footstep seemed to echo. If they didn't get away now, they would never arrive in the new *Zone Libre*, and living under occupation wasn't in Rainier's nature. They speculated that France might fall, but they had never expected it to happen so soon, and so rapidly.

Delphi tensed at the wheel and took a sharp breath. What was that? She made out a distant rumbling and the sound of metal on metal screeching across the once peaceful countryside.

No. Oh no. Hurry. We must hurry. What if we are caught like this? In the middle of the night. It's so obvious we are running away.

"Should I start the motor? Is that them coming? I'm sure it is." She forced herself to a whisper, although she wanted to shout.

"We mustn't lose our heads. We have some time." Rainier puffed. His lungs, never good since Ypres, struggled with the exertion of pushing the car.

"Rainier, I'm scared," Flora whispered.

"It's alright, *ma petite*. We'll be fine. Not much further, and we'll be far enough from the cottages."

Delphi had never been so frightened. This was the desperate, stomach-churning terror of an advancing enemy. What if they didn't get away before the Germans arrived? Would they be shot or even raped? There had been such awful rumours recently. In her youth, Delphi would not have been so afraid.

Perhaps it's because I have a child. I have a full and happy life here, or I have had. I don't want to lose it. I hate this change. A new wave of panic flowed through her, heightening her senses and curdling her stomach. Blood pounded in her ears, or was it the thunder of military lorries in the distance?

"Surely we can start it now?" Delphi called softly with her head out of the window. "We have to get going. They'll be coming down the hill soon."

Rainier and Flora stopped pushing. Delphi opened the driver's door and twisted in the seat to leap out so that her husband could climb in behind the wheel.

"Look," she nodded at the treeline. There, a definite illumination was confidently waving up into the sky. "How dare they shine their lights so arrogantly? Aren't there Allied aeroplanes to be afraid of?" Delphi asked.

"Evidently not," Rainier answered. "Come, my love, let's go." Without looking back at the solid shades of the house behind them, he got into the driver's seat.

Delphi held the door as Flora collapsed into the seat. She ducked her head and shuddered as the door closed with what seemed a deafening bang. But no lights appeared at any cottage windows, and she took her place next to her husband as he started the engine.

"I'm not putting the headlights on. We'll have to go slowly and hope for the best," Rainier said as he turned the handle to wind up the window.

The car seemed dangerously loud. As they snaked their way up the hill and climbed out of the village, Delphi realised her shoulders were tense with anticipation of all that lay ahead, as well as with grief for what they'd left behind. She took a deep breath and made herself relax for Flora's sake, and so that she could concentrate on the road ahead to help Rainier.

Near the top of the steep incline, just before they descended to the start of the next, Rainier pulled over and slowed down, turning his head. Delphi looked back too. They could just see the outline of several buildings, some long and low, others squat and square among the trees. The church steeple sat in the centre of the village, pointing up to the heavens like a sword. As they watched in silence, Rainier took Delphi's hand and raised it to his lips. Headlights appeared around a distant corner and began to crawl down the road, like the eyes of an alien insect.

He won't be content to sit out the war in his nephew's house, Delphi thought with dread. *Flora has been at peace here, too. Rainier has given her a secure home after her years of being at war with herself. What will life hold for her now?*

Delphi covered Rainier's hand with her own, and they turned back to face the route ahead — the road to Thorelière.

CHAPTER 15

Rainier had arranged for them to travel to the house near Thorelière that was now his nephew's, south of the river Cher and not far from the Château of Chenonceau. It was situated just inside the Free Zone and was not too distant from their own home. He had spent time there in his youth and the family had visited often, so they knew many local people and he was respected. Delphi knew this was all so desperately sad for him. Behind them lay memories of his long-gone parents and another brother killed serving his country. They had been close as they'd grown up, hiding amongst the vines and scaling rocks and streams. The childhood gems of experience were ingrained in his soul, and they'd had to leave it all.

Thorelière was not home, although Flora loved aspects of it dearly despite Luca's continuing animosity over the years. She'd learned to live with that. Rainier's middle brother, Jean and his wife, had long since died, too, and Luca ran the place now. However, on their arrival they discovered things were different from their last visit many months ago.

An elderly man sat in the shade of the oak tree in the courtyard, even though an early morning mist clung to the bottom of the valley. A thin cigarette with a soggy-looking end hung from the corner of his mouth. "Ah, my boy," the farm labourer said as Rainier approached him.

"François, we've made it by the skin of our teeth. The Germans arrived as we left."

"I'm glad to see you. Eh, it's all so different. Luca is busy elsewhere all the time and hardly seems to be here. What am I to do? I'm too tired for all this." He waved his arm to indicate the whole property.

"What do you mean, hardly here?" Rainier pushed his hand through his hair. He was exhausted.

Flora and Delphi joined him and the obligatory kissing, three on alternate cheeks, interrupted the conversation.

"What's he up to?"

François shrugged. "I don't like to ask. He leaves me with all this to take care of. I'm glad to see you. How do I manage? He was always such a good boy for helping, but now… These few weeks and everything's changed."

"It's not good in the north. We're so pleased to be here."

"Eh, these bliddy Boche." The old man spat into the dust. "I'm too old. I've seen it all before. God help us."

Flora pulled back the curtain the following morning, and as she looked down into the courtyard, Luca emerged from the barn opposite and disappeared momentarily beneath the branches of the oak tree. Curiosity got the better of her and she stayed to observe him from the privacy of her bedroom. His face was hidden from this height, but she saw his shiny black hair. His shirt gleamed white, and his sleeves were rolled up to reveal strong, brown forearms. Carrying a bucket and a three-pronged hoe over his shoulder, he headed off in the direction of the vines.

She couldn't help admiring his neat backside as his retreating figure crossed the space beneath her window. He was damned lucky that working this place had kept him from joining up or, worse, being taken as a worker for the Nazis. As he strode out of sight, his boots kicked at stones as he turned the corner.

Why does he have to be so mean and foul-tempered? I shall never forget his first words to me all those years ago, and he's made it clear since then that I should have no right inheriting half of this eventually because Rainier has legally adopted me. But if it's his birthright, he doesn't seem to care that much for it all anyway. He certainly doesn't work hard here, according to François. I'm sure I heard him coming in during the early hours. Lazy bastard.

Later, when Rainier and Luca came for lunch, Delphi called for François as she carried a large pot of stew outside. Flora put the plates and glasses on the table. A light breeze blew the oilcloth, but the table clips held it in place. Rainier poured the wine from a flagon he had filled directly from the barrel. As Flora swilled it around her mouth, she tasted the young but fruity wine on the edges of her tongue. It was cold from the marble slab in the pantry and was certainly the cheapest option.

The men took large gulps and Flora watched Luca's Adam's apple bob as he tipped his head back and swallowed, clearly savouring the freshness of it. Dark hair clung to the sweat on his forehead, and curled down onto his collar.

With a gusty sigh, he said, "Ah, I was ready for that."

As he replaced his glass on the table, his black eyes met Flora's, but he didn't smile. She looked away quickly.

"Pass that down, Flora, you're in a daydream," her mother said, giving her a plate of stew. "How's it going out there?" Delphi looked across at the men.

"We're getting on well with the *griffage*. The soil's good but still needs aeration," Rainier said.

"Ah, I saw you disappearing this morning with the hoe," Flora said, looking at Luca. Then she regretted admitting that she had been spying. Luca turned to his uncle Rainier, pointedly ignoring her. She glared at the back of his head.

"It's hard work," Luca said, "but the seasons turn. Late spring's always back-breaking, but hopefully we'll reap the rewards later."

"Yes, I think it could be a good crop if the weather holds up, although it takes a lot more than that." Rainier raised his glass in salutation.

"Let's hope so. There was early and rapid flowering, this year." Luca held up his own glass before taking another drink.

Luca appeared just after lunch one day later that week. Flora saw him arrive as she scattered grain for the chickens in the courtyard. He looked ragged, dishevelled. There was a dark shadow around his chin. Flora regarded him with mixed emotions. He was good-looking, there was no denying that, with his black hair, curly and wild. Height gave his broad physique strength.

She spoke to him with disdain, since he ignored her presence. "Hello to you too, Luca. You look a wreck. What have you been up to?"

"Men's business." He turned away from her.

"It's men's business to guide your workers." Following him across the courtyard towards the house, she said, "Why are you being so rude? You always resented me being here when we visited. You should do something to help François occasionally, instead of rollicking off having a good time."

He strode towards her. "And you've no idea. I don't need nagging and certainly not from you." He was so close his breath brushed her forehead as he spat out the words. Her chest tightened as, against her will, her body realised his warmth. "Grow up and leave me alone." As he disappeared into the gloom of the house, he left her angry and frustrated. Physically attracted as she was to him, she entirely disliked his attitude. If anything, over the years that had worsened towards her.

Over the next few weeks they got into some semblance of a routine. Sometimes François stretched his legs as far as the local bar for a beer and a chinwag with the other old boys, but that was all. He was in bed by eight in the evening, and although he arose with the dawn, he was usually to be found under the oak tree in the courtyard, smoking. Rainier had taken over the vineyard and it was a welcome relief to the old man.

For Rainier, it was as simple as it could be, so familiar was he with the working of all the equipment. The workers accepted his easy ways and helped as they should. When Luca appeared, it was not for long. Delphi kept house and for her, too, the changes from what she did back at home had not been great, apart from looking after François. Flora knew she had been, by nature, brave and fearless, even reckless in her youth. She had heard of her mother's utter soul-wrenching sadness when George, Flora's father, had been killed on the Somme, not knowing about his offspring and not having had time to marry her. She could only imagine the exhilarating disquiet of uncharted events when Delphi had travelled all the way to Australia with his parents to have his child. Now, Flora understood her mother was content with her life and loved Rainier to distraction.

For Flora, it was different. She railed against her present circumstances and almost wished she had returned to England when war had first been declared. In the end, she'd decided to stay. Being part French now, or as good as, her main allegiance lay here with her mother and stepfather, who loved her like his own. It was more than ten years since she had lived in England, and while she had been back to visit, it was no longer her home.

"I miss Edith," she said to Delphi one morning.

"Mmm, the two of you were like sisters, living at the school."

"We did have such fun and adventures." They had met as often as times allowed since then. "Here, there's no work other than playing second fiddle to you in household affairs. I have no network of girl-friends either. At home, when I worked in the solicitor's office, I had responsibility."

"You're sounding sorry for yourself this morning," Delphi said. "You know why we came here, though."

"Yes. It was the best option. I know that."

Flora was restless and uncomfortable with a foreboding that did not sit well with the tickle of significance that she had sensed upon her first arrival at this place when she was young.

"At least this new government are traditionalist. They're returning to conservative culture and religion because they're afraid of the growing communist factions," Rainier said at breakfast some weeks later. He held his copy of *Le Nouvelliste*, which he'd managed to pick up in the town the previous week. It was Catholic by nature and supported the Vichy regime. "It's hard to get a decent newspaper anywhere these days," he said as he re-folded it and tossed it down.

"Fine if you like to put down women and dismiss democracy," Flora said with a degree of bitterness and a spark of her old rebelliousness.

"Flora, Rainier didn't mean that." Delphi was unused to taking the role of mediator between her husband and her daughter.

"I hope you're not turning into a collaborationist," Flora said.

"Flora, don't you dare suggest that." Her mother's tone was shocked.

"It's alright, darling." Rainier took his wife's hand. "It's good that she's thinking about things. No, I'm certainly not that, Flora. More perhaps a *Pétainiste*," he said. "He was a great leader during the last great show, and now he's trying to tread a fine line and keep us out of trouble in this Free Zone. Better him than the red menace in the east."

"Who's this de Gaulle fellow in England? They're saying he's rallying people to resist the Vichy Government and the Germans being here," Flora said. Then she changed the subject. "And do you know what? Amélie Lebrun's brother and his family came here from Malines only last week. I was surprised to meet him in the town, but then so many people seem to have come to the *Zone Libre*. Do you remember them? He said he saw a troop of British prisoners being marched east right past our old house. They were soldiers and airmen in full uniform except for their tin helmets. They were made to wear all sorts of hats as if they had looted them, but it was to make fools of them. They had bowler hats, women's bonnets, berets, plumes and feathers, all kinds of ridiculous-looking things. They looked laughable, he said. That's no way for even Nazis to treat prisoners of war."

"Watch what you say, child. It's fine in this house, but be careful in the town."

"There you are, then," Flora replied to Rainier. "We can't even express an opinion openly."

"Is Amélie's brother living here now, then?" Delphi stood behind Rainier and placed her hands on her husband's shoulders.

"Yes. They've moved into a house that a family named Lévi left when they disappeared in the night last month. It seems no one's wise about where they went, but they have evidently gone for good." Flora stood with her plate and cup and moved to the sink to help her mother with the dishes.

"We'll have to agree to differ, then." She turned to Rainier as she spoke.

"It's early days for us here," he said. "Many things are changing in France. Let's see what happens."

CHAPTER 16

June 1941

Flora was in the kitchen when she heard the men return from the field. She knew they would be hot and dusty and that after returning their tools to the barn they would go to the pump outside and get rid of the worst of the day's sweat and grime before coming indoors. Hot water was at a premium, so baths were reserved for weekends.

At the sink, she decided she would just wash the cups. She grudgingly admitted to herself that curiosity was part of the reason for her task at this precise moment.

She watched the two men take off their shirts. Rainier, she had seen countless times, but it was not him in whom she was interested. Luca ... despite his irate nature, she didn't tire of seeing.

Used to heavy work, his stomach was firm with defined muscles. His torso was paler than his forearms, but his trousers hung low, revealing dark hair on his stomach. She could only imagine where that led. Watching the water running in rivulets from his hair and body, she felt a frisson of pleasure to which she was becoming accustomed. As he shook his head, a thousand droplets caught the sun and a rainbow appeared just for a moment. Turning hastily and hotly guilty, she busied herself looking for a cloth to dry the cups.

"Would you both like a coffee?" Her voice sounded overly bright to her own ears as they entered the kitchen's gloom, so she turned and put the kettle back on the hob.

"I'm certainly ready for that," Rainier said. "Thank you, my lovely girl." He gave her a warm smile and touched her arm as she returned to the table.

"I'm going out," Luca said and left the kitchen without further words or glances.

"He's so rude," Flora ranted at her father. "There's no need for him to be like that. A 'thank you' wouldn't have hurt, instead of sounding so grumpy."

Rainier smiled at her and invited her for a hug.

Her mother arrived just then. "Flora, there's always this ironing to do if you want something to keep you busy," she said, but stopped as she listened to Rainier.

"That word 'grumpy' makes you sound like a child again, my sweet," Rainier said, a smile taking any sting from his words. "He's had much to take on board with all of us coming to live here. He has a very strong sense of duty to his property and his country, which is admirable, don't you think? And I'm sure he has other things on his mind too."

"What other things?" Flora pulled her head back and looked up into his face before he released her.

"Oh, this and that. He really has a tunnel vision of what he needs to do or not do," he said.

Flora frowned but asked no more. His words puzzled her.

"The men were talking of the current situation today. I can't help thinking that Pétain is trying to get France back on track with this government. He has to be admired for that." Rainier sipped his coffee.

"In what way?" Delphi folded some clothes she had retrieved from the line outside.

"Well, the way France was going was sinking us all."

"How do you mean?"

"The American film industry being allowed to supersede our own. We have a very competent set-up. Then there's all this cubism and surrealism in the arts. It's corrupting society; self-indulgent city dwellers." He paused. "The new women and their independent views." He grinned and winked at Delphi.

"What do you mean by that?" Flora took the bait of the tease, as he knew she would.

"Ignore him, Flora," her mother said. "He's goading you."

With a backwards look at him, Flora picked up a pile of clothes to press but heard her mother speaking as she left the kitchen and headed for the stairs.

Delphi said, "What was all that about?"

"I think she's finding living under the same roof as Luca quite, um … challenging." Rainier's voice was deep and melodious.

"It's not easy for any of us."

"No, it's not," he said. "Luca is behaving strangely too."

"I heard that mail is still getting through to England. I'm going to write to Edith again. It's such a long time since we spoke, and I haven't had replies to any of my previous letters." Flora came up behind her mother, who stood at the sink, staring out into the courtyard. She put her arms around her.

Delphi turned within the circle, comforting to both. "That's a good idea, darling. The censor will read it, though."

"I'll be careful. It'll just be girlish chatter," Flora said. With that, she left for her bedroom.

I miss Edith so. We used to have such fun at school, although I did get into some scrapes. There was that business of spying on Miss Pryce. Crikey, I was such an idiot.

As she sat at the desk, she chewed the end of the pencil, not unsure of what to say but how to say it. The censor would read it and she didn't want to get anyone into trouble. She really needed to share what was going on, though. There was nobody in the whole world who would understand as Edith would.

Dearest Edith,

Here we are, still in my cousin's house. Life here is dull. I told you I had to leave my job as M. Bonheur's secretary. I enjoyed working there. I learned a lot about the law, and he was such an old fusty fellow but really kind. Now I do ironing and feeding chickens. It's so meaningless.

My cousin — well, obviously we aren't blood related, as you'll remember — is so uncouth, but he does have a great body!!! He'd probably like you, but he detests me. He thinks I'm going to steal half his birthright (this vineyard) but it's my entitlement too since Rainier adopted me.

Anyway, dearest friend, do you remember that book that got us, well, me, into such trouble at school? The one by John Buchan, set in Scotland? I'm going to use those skills to keep my eye on him. He must be a good ally to our Protectors here.

I don't know if you are able to write back, but you are in my thoughts. I miss our girlish giggles and hope when this lot is over, we will be together again. I'll tell you how I get on with my 'Hannay' activities.

God bless us both,

Flora.

Rainier sat at the table, reading a newspaper. "I'm sure it's suited Herr Hitler to allow us to continue with our own government."

Luca scowled. "Be careful what you say in my presence, Uncle. That man is a monster."

"Don't worry, Luca. All I meant was that he doesn't want to make greater enemies of us. Quite possibly the French turning against him more would not have suited his purpose at all. We could very well have continued the fight by sending troops to North Africa and caused much trouble there. As it is, we narrowly missed this new government being based in Morocco."

The scowl was still evident on Luca's face when Flora entered the kitchen.

"Oh, I see what you mean. Yes, that's true," he said, and she saw him relax. "If that had been the case there would be total occupation here and all the agonies of that, but this is an uneasy peace and I don't trust it."

"There were valid alternatives to this armistice, uneasy as it may be, like I said."

Flora stood at the sink, her back to the men, and although she was making a pretence of tidying, she listened to every word.

"I heard that Pétain and his crowd are trying to operate from Paris again, instead of working out of hotel bedrooms and dining rooms in Vichy," Luca said. "Like that's going to happen." She pictured his face with a sarcastic expression on it, but she didn't turn around. "They would rather collaborate with these Nazis and secure their position wherever. That town has been a shock to look at for decades, with its faded Napoleon III splendour. It's tried to be something it's not with all those neo-gothic buildings, and it certainly isn't anything now."

"Does it gall you that you had to remain here instead of going off to fight?"

"If I had gone, I would be one of those two million prisoners of war they're talking about, most likely. No, I'm serving my country. There are different ways of doing things," Luca said.

"That's enigmatic."

Luca pushed back the chair and stood without further comment. He left the room to go outside.

Flora turned and leaned against the sink. "What is he up to?"

Rainier closed the newspaper. "Up to?"

"I'm not sure I trust him. There's all that talk of serving his country, but in what way? He's hardly ever here looking after the vineyards. He leaves all the work to you and the others, then makes a fuss about us being here. He definitely doesn't like me, anyway." She sounded petulant.

"I really don't think that's the case," Rainier said.

"He certainly gives me that impression. And where does he go all the time?" She lowered her voice. "You don't think he's a friend to the enemy, do you? What if he's giving all our secrets away?"

"We don't own any secrets." Rainier chuckled. "Don't be a goose."

"He could be meeting Nazi sympathisers and feathering his own nest that way, because he certainly isn't supporting you here."

"I really don't believe that."

"Rainier, you are gullible sometimes," Flora said with an air of worldliness.

He smiled at her mildly.

That night as she was preparing for bed, she was sure there were footsteps in the courtyard. Blowing out the candle, she peeped around the edge of the curtain. At first, she saw nothing and was about to turn away.

Then, there he was, slinking along the side of the barn. Was he entering it? Why was he hugging the wall like that? If he was going to fetch something, he would have walked straight across the yard. His movements encouraged her to keep watching.

I could follow him. Don't be empty-headed, idiot. It's nearly dark. What if he caught you? She shivered. *Where's he off to now?*

Flora watched as Luca made his way out from the lea of the building and scooted across the lane towards the hedge and away.

CHAPTER 17

Luca looked over his shoulder yet again as he moved with caution towards the barn of his friend Antoine's family. The moon was waning, but the night was still bright. Eleven o'clock and dusk had fallen fast. Now it was not difficult to see, but he could also be seen. Luca had been careful as he hustled along close to the hedgerows. He'd stopped to listen on several occasions. Once, the repeated mechanical noises of an old bicycle and someone whistling were not far away. Probably only a farmhand returning from the local bar, and he had turned off before they could meet. Luca waited until he was certain the lane was empty.

On arriving at the barn, he knocked three times and then just once more on the wood before he snuck in through the small door to the right of the main opening. Closing it quietly, he stood for a moment while his eyes grew accustomed to the shade within.

The sweet smell of haybales wafted over him, and he felt the crunch of dried mud and straw beneath his feet as he crept forward.

"Luca, is that you?" A whisper soft as the waving corn in the field opposite came to him.

"Yes, it's me."

"You're the last. Over here. We're in the back room. No one will see the candlelight from there."

Luca moved with a hand outstretched until he gained his bearings. It had been a while since they'd met here, and he was uncertain of the distance to the wall.

"You're a bit late," Antoine said in a forced whisper, to guide his friend. They shook hands as he entered the little room. A dim light flickered from a single candle in a jar. Its position on an upturned wooden box cast dark shadows across the faces of the men who sat around, deepening their eye sockets and diminishing their sun-reddened colour. The coarse blue fabric of their overalls, like a uniform, was dusty and broad hands rested on knees as they leaned towards the centre of their group.

"Uncle was talking to me about the crop and my aunt wanted me to take a coffee before turning in. I'm not sure that my cousin didn't watch me from her window as I left the house. She was trying to hide behind the curtain, but I saw it moving."

"Your cousin? Is this the step-cousin you told us about? The pretty one?"

"Yes, her."

"You said she was spirited. I hope she didn't follow you."

"No, I'm sure of that. There was only one person. It was probably fat old Franc. I'm sure it was him riding home. He was whistling, the old fool. Half drunk, too, I imagine, but he didn't see me." Luca greeted the other two men there before him, shaking hands with each and clapping one on the shoulder as he did so.

Antoine poured the small glasses of pastis for all four of them. The liquid turned cloudy as his friend added the splash of water from a bottle he produced.

The men clinked glasses in the time-honoured way. No business could be discussed until all traditions were complete, even in these desperate times.

"*Santé*," they each whispered.

"What we need is someone inside the *mairie*. That new fellow, André Duclos, must get to see stuff since he was appointed by the Germans," Antoine said.

"Strongly recommended by them, anyway," Luca added.

"That secretary of his can't be trusted, though. She's too staid and frightened of her own shadow. Someone to look at any official papers that are sent his way would be so helpful. Anything at all would be useful at this stage." Antoine took a gulp of his drink.

"We don't have any kind of plan yet, do we?" Luca stated. "We're like headless chickens. What we need is to discover what they're up to so we can formulate a purpose."

"Troop movements would be good. We could disrupt those, somehow, I'm sure," said Hubert, a burly youth with curly red hair and freckles. Luca knew him from school days.

A young skinny lad was almost bouncing with eagerness. "We're not that far from the train lines from Tours. What if we could blow them up?"

"We've got to be realistic, Thibault. Calm down," Antoine said and clicked his tongue while the burly red-haired man sighed.

The boy looked crestfallen and glanced at Luca for his view.

"They're right, Thibault. We don't have the equipment for that kind of thing."

The lad nodded. "Of course, Luca, sorry." He soon perked up when someone else spoke.

The current position and numbers of the enemy seen were discussed.

"How are we ever to get hold of a radio and the crystals to make it work? Contacting others who might be trying to disrupt things should perhaps be a priority," Antoine suggested.

"Or even England. De Gaulle's encouraging activities from over there, like we want to do."

A discussion on how to find a radio transmitter, ever their favourite topic, continued for some time.

Eventually, the group broke up with only Antoine and Luca remaining. Antoine filled their glasses again.

"Thibault will be a liability. We need to ditch him. *Connard.*" Antoine gave the international sign for arsehole.

"He's immature, but we don't want to upset him and turn him against us. But we certainly don't need him at every meeting, I agree. The boy's not realistic and too excitable." Luca took a gulp of his drink. "*Merde!* We have no real idea of where to go or what to do."

"It's early days. We'll get a plan together and do our bit to disrupt these bastards. So, this family of yours," Antoine said, changing the subject. "They don't suspect you?"

"Flora thinks I'm a lazy bastard and continues to tell me so. She's clever, though, and as I told you, she's unafraid."

Antoine nodded.

"My uncle is still at the stage of believing, like most of the others, that Pétain and his government are not all bad and saved France from total occupation and licentiousness. He'll learn. These Boche simply cannot be trusted. Look at what happened in Czechoslovakia. Unbelievable. And I'm sure we haven't heard the whole story by a long way."

"Lots of people are returning after this great exodus we've been having. Will your family go?"

"The Germans moved into his old home and are using it as a headquarters in that area. He was horrified, I can tell you. The family owned that place for a couple of hundred years. The house is one of the largest properties, so I suppose that's why they've taken it. I hope the workers are continuing with the vineyard. It shook him up considerably. Mind you, it's gone partway to him seeing what's really going on and that the new government are collaborating rather than resisting. That speech that De Gaulle transmitted from London on the 18th of June last year made him sit up and think differently, too." He took another drink. "There must be other cells like ours all over the place. Having more information at this stage has got to be important."

Finishing his pastis, Antoine held up the bottle again and raised his eyebrows in an unspoken offer.

"No, I must be off. It's late already. I better put in a day's work tomorrow too."

"Go carefully, my friend. Especially back at your place. We don't really know how things go with this family of yours. You need to watch your back. Keep your eye on that cousin." He leered at Luca, giving extra meaning to his words.

"Enough, Antoine," Luca said. "Flora's attractive, but I've got too much on my mind for that. I'll watch her, though."

As Luca entered his own courtyard again, he stood for a moment and looked up at the window from where he was sure he had been observed earlier. There was no sign of movement.

He imagined his step-cousin in her bed, her dark hair across the pillow and her full-breasted body lying under just a sheet, displaying her outline. He took a deep breath.

Why did they come here, getting in the way? Why, oh why did Uncle Rainier take Flora on in an official manner? He didn't have to make her adoption legal. Now she'll be entitled to half of all this when her parents pass on, and it's mine. Okay, so I'm taking a back seat now, but I've worked bloody hard since Mama and then Papa died.

Luca shook his head, let out his breath with a gust and continued silently towards the door at the side of the house. All thoughts of Flora in bed departed.

CHAPTER 18

June 1942

The family rose early, as habit dictated. The men had left for the fields to continue their back-breaking task of scratching out the weeds from between the vines. During this, the main growing season, things went wild in no time. Side shoots had to be trimmed so that all the goodness drove into the tiny clusters of forming grapes and not into the leaves, as well.

"If you're going to the market in Thorelière, you'll have to get there early to buy the best bargains," Delphi said to her daughter.

"Rainier was taking me, but he's gone off to the fields."

"He said he'll be back, so are you ready? He's only gone to collect something. Luca is there too. Rainier said he needed to let Luca have some time without him always directing the men, so he'll be here to take you."

"Hmm, working this morning. That makes a change," Flora said.

"He has a lot on his mind, I expect." Delphi tried to placate her daughter.

"Like what? Drink and girls?"

"Rainier's said several times, it's difficult for him with us all landing here. Things have changed significantly for him."

"He's lucky Rainier is doing so much on his behalf, if you ask me. I'm sure he was out again last night. Probably sneaking off to the bar again."

Just then, Rainier appeared. "Shall we go? I need to get a new handle for this hoe. It's snapped clean in half."

They left the courtyard in the trap with the old brown mare pulling it. Luca came from the field as they passed. Rainier raised his hand, but Flora sat impervious to any greetings there might be.

The sun's rays pierced her shoulders like spears as they trundled along in the cart. Flora was glad to have her straw hat. The cheerful flowers that adorned it had made her smile when she'd looked at herself in the cheval mirror before leaving. The horse swished the flies with its tail and seemed happy enough as it trotted. A lark shot up from the other side of the hedge, its staccato song in contrast with the soft sibilance of the wafting wheat.

"That's always such a glorious sound," she said. Then she nodded at the field. "The barley is almost ready for the harvest."

"Yes, it's the first. This wheat will be a while yet," Rainier answered. "I'd rather be handling grapes than that, though. Dusty, messy stuff."

"Is Luca up to something?" Flora turned to her stepfather.

"What sort of something?"

"Collaborating." There, she'd said it.

"Mmm, collaborating. I hadn't thought so," Rainier said, looking back at her. "There's nothing really for him to tell, is there?"

"No, I suppose not, but I'm sure there are more ways of being treacherous than telling secrets." Flora sat silently for quite a while.

"He seems so tight-lipped with us, well, me, anyway. He's hardly around and I'm positive I've seen him sneaking off late at night. He just looked … furtive. That's the word for it."

Rainier had gone off to buy what he needed. Flora carried her basket full of vegetables over her arm. Tomatoes were plentiful now, so she was also balancing a shallow wooden tray filled with them. The atmosphere was not strained or awkward. In fact, you could believe no war was happening and no enemy occupation had taken place not so far away in northern France. Food was abundant in the country areas, unlike in the Occupied Zone, if rumours were to be believed. Even a town the size of Thorelière had a thriving market on Thursday mornings. Meat was scarce, however. Rumour had it that much was purloined and shipped off to feed German troops in the north, but nothing definite. The tentacles of collaboration insidiously crept everywhere under the surface, it seemed to Flora.

Rainier and Flora had agreed to meet at the *tabac* for a coffee before heading home. She was five minutes early and didn't want to go in alone, as a young woman. She stood between the *tabac* and the *boulangerie* and took in the scene before her. A trader called as he held up the best lettuces. There was bulbous fennel with its feathery tops and a tray of lovely asparagus tips, which lay all white and pale pink in bundles tied with string. Baskets of new apricots from the south somewhere, and cherries, more local, appeared on the stalls now the weather was warmer.

Every so often she caught a whiff of garlic and onion and bacon as the huge pans of creamy, cheesy *tartiflette* were heated and served to the patrons of the market. Her mouth became moist with the aroma.

If only I'd brought a bowl, I could have bought some to take home. It smells so wonderful.

She waited, shifting from one foot to the other. A car drew up. Three *gendarmes* got out and she watched with interest. The older man seemed to be familiar to many in the crowd outside the *boulangerie*, where a queue had formed to buy M Durand's delicious loaves of mixed grain flours. Her tummy rumbled with the sweet aroma from there, too. Several people greeted the arrival and he nodded at them, but he avoided meeting their gazes.

He looks embarrassed, thought Flora as she stood idly and took it all in.

Straightening her back, she became more alert. She puzzled for a further moment. Then she saw the two much younger men. Their uniforms were new with shiny buttons and clean braid around their *kepis*, which they sported on their heads with arrogance. They had a swagger as they walked behind the older man. Flora knew several stations had opened recently, and there were many new recruits.

"Hey, you, wait!" One of the new-looking recruits with a fresh face and blond hair shouted as he raised his arm and pointed.

All heads turned to the unfolding events.

Flora's eyes swivelled in the direction the young man indicated, as did everyone else's. Further along the street, a youth in grubby blue overalls and a cap pushed a rickety bicycle with a large box on the back. He was moving away from her as she stood and waited for Rainier.

All three *gendarmes* started running. Unaccountably a basket of turnips from someone in the bread queue fell in their path and one of them stumbled, falling flat and banging his head. Flora's eyes followed his *kepi* as it rolled and ended up in the road. His companion stopped running, knelt on the ground, and pulling out a pistol he aimed at the youth, who struggled to mount his bicycle.

No! Flora was stunned.

The load on the back must have been heavy. The bicycle became unbalanced. The lad tried to get on it to make good an escape. A shot resounded as the young *gendarme* fired in the air. People ducked or flattened themselves against walls. Three further shots resonated, and the sound echoed off the buildings in quick succession.

Women screamed. More crouched down. Flora pressed herself against the building. She dropped her basket and shielded her head with her arms. As she peeped towards the youth who had fallen beside his transport, a pool of something dark and viscous oozed across the path. Then she felt strong hands grab her and steer her unceremoniously inside the *tabac*.

Flora's stomach churned. Her knees trembled. She sank onto the nearest empty chair. Rainier pulled another close to her and held her. The owner rushed to the window and stood peering out, standing up on his toes to look over the heads of men and women outside.

"He's been shot," he said needlessly. "*Merde*, he's been shot in the back. I cannot believe it. Who was he? What was all that about? People are crowding round."

Rainier left Flora and crossed to look, too. "Women who were in the queue waiting for bread, shoppers with baskets full of groceries," he said, "they're all on the pathway to see whatever they can. The policemen are shoving them aside." He turned to Flora as he recounted all that was happening.

Men who had been in the *tabac* having an early beer or a coffee hurried to gather round the scene outside.

"Get back, all of you. Disperse. Go about your business. This fellow is a felon. He deserved what he got. He is an enemy of your Protectors." Flora heard shouting through the door left open by the departed men.

The young policeman who had fallen staggered to his feet and waved his arms expansively at the crowd.

Rainier moved to the bar. "Hey there." He called the tender. "Two small brandies and two coffees, *m'sieur*." Rainier took them to Flora and put his arm around her shoulder again while she downed the brandy and stopped shaking.

An ambulance with its tinny siren arrived shortly after. Once they heard it retreating again, Rainier said, "Come along, *ma petite*. Let's get home as quickly as we can."

He helped her up and together they left their hiding place. Unbelievably, Flora's basket still lay outside with the vegetables tumbled across the pavement. The tomatoes had rolled into the road, but Rainier gathered them all up and they headed to the garage where he had left the horse and trap.

As they rumbled home, Rainier continued to put his arm around Flora's shoulders. She couldn't get the image from her mind. The huddled figure of the youth and the dark pool that came from his lifeless form were more shocking than anything she had ever seen before. Despite the day, still hot, Flora shivered.

"Why would they do that?"

Rainier looked at her before he answered. "I don't understand it," he said. "They must have thought he was doing something very wrong."

"He was no thief, I'm sure of it," she said. "That box on the back was too cumbersome for him to be stealing. He could never have got away quickly enough."

"Perhaps that box had something to do with it," Rainier said.

"What do you mean?"

"Oh, I don't …" he said. "I'm talking rubbish. Let's get home and give these things to your mama."

That huddled body with the dark stain, thought Flora. *That huddled body with…*

The ostinato of her thoughts kept rhythm with the wheels of the trap all the way home.

CHAPTER 19

Prevaricating, Rainier took a deep breath as he and Luca headed back to the fields after lunch. He'd been meaning to ask Luca something and now seemed the best opportunity. There were several minutes before they reached the row of vines on which they were working, where the other men would be gathering to help.

"Did I see you in town the other day? When there was that awful incident of the boy being shot?"

"Don't think so, no," Luca answered.

"Someone grabbed the box as the bike fell over and that person handed it on while the crowd gathered. The police had to push through. There were several moments before they arrived."

Luca shook his head. "We need to press on. That row from this morning needs finishing, and the next one down the hill to the gate."

"Yes, of course, as you say."

There was an uneasy working relationship between Luca and his Uncle Rainier. The older man was very aware that Luca had been running the place for a couple of years, but he was so often absent, and Rainier had so much more experience and knowledge. This was treading a fine line.

Coming back to the house later, Rainier could not abstain from pursuing the subject from earlier. "What do you suppose was in that box? Apparently, it was very heavy and cumbersome."

"I really couldn't say … since I wasn't on the scene."

"During the last war, I worked with radios that were big and heavy in wooden boxes like that. They must be considered an asset round here, and no one would want them in the hands of the wrong people, our Protectors, for example, should someone be caught with one."

"Dangerous talk, Uncle. Be careful. People might get the wrong impression of you. Hey, Frederic!" He hailed one of the workers and strode off.

Later that night, Luca sat on an upturned wooden box and waited in the back of the barn for Antoine and Hubert. They had not told the excitable Thibault of their meeting.

They arrived. "What do we do with it?" Antoine spoke as they stood around the box. "*Merde*, Luca, you were either very brave or very foolhardy to whip this out from under their noses."

"*Fils de pute*," Hubert swore.

"Yes, he certainly is one lucky son of a bitch," Antoine agreed.

"Not luck, my friend," said Luca, "well, not for that young fellow who copped the shot. In the back, too. There was an opportunity not to be missed. No way would I leave it to those traitors. The crowd forming so quickly was a bonus, though, and if the *allée* hadn't been right next to us I should have had nowhere to take it."

"So where did you go after that?" Antoine was full of admiration and his excitement showed in his voice.

"It was bloody awkward, I can tell you, so I knew I couldn't go far. Fortunately, all eyes and ears were on that poor blighter in the main street. I just ran as best I could, dumped it behind the hedge at the back of the bakers and hightailed it home on my bike. When I went back last night, miraculously, the thing was still where I'd left it."

"I can't believe it. We've actually got one. Now all we have to do is work out how to use it," Antoine said.

"And where to hide it." Hubert knelt and touched the lid with apparent reverence. "The Boche are going to be on the lookout for it. There's a real risk. We need to decide where to put it before we do anything else."

"Yes, they're going to be determined about this," Luca said.

Hubert ruffled his own hair and frowned. "It's got to be somewhere where we can get at it easily. What about up in the hayloft? Or I could hide it in our barn."

"Up there's the first place they'd search," Luca said.

"Yes, and your place is too far away. What about the old privy behind here?" Antoine gestured with his thumb.

"No, that's too obvious. If they find it, my whole family are in serious trouble. People disappear in the night with no warning," Luca said.

"It wouldn't be just your family, either. It'd be all of us, and God knows what would happen then. We said we wanted a radio, but it's a liability."

"You're not backing out now, are you?" Hubert turned to Antoine and grabbed his arm.

"No, my friend, I'm not, but this whole thing's scary, isn't it?"

"I've got a place here," Luca said. "I'll dig a hole, line it with a *bache*. We've got some old canvas ones lying in the barn. They've been kicking around forever. They used to protect the old press. No one will miss one. Then I'll cover the place over with wood and rubbish. How does that sound? I won't tell you exactly where. It's safer that way."

"We may need to keep moving the thing around, but that would certainly be a good job," Antoine said. "We should do that now and then have a proper look at it when we have more time. The priority must be to hide the damn thing."

"You're right. So, are you going? It's heavy and the digging will be a long job." Luca knelt and stroked the lid.

"I'll stay and help," Hubert said.

Antoine laughed and clapped him on the back. "You like extra work and danger, my friend?"

"No! Remember you're the man of the house. Your mother needs you," Luca said.

"I never forget that." Hubert turned to leave.

After he had gone, Antoine said, "Let me help. I understand the danger, but it will take you ages on your own."

"That's the place over there, with no tiles on the floor. Pull that pile of canvas aside. Underneath will be perfect. We can replace all the stuff after, and no one will be the wiser. The earth will be hard, though." Luca pointed across to the other side. The old red tiles, cracked and worn, ended about three metres from the wall, leaving a strip of hard-packed earth.

So, the decision was made and, with some struggling in the gloom, Luca and Antoine carried the box across the barn.

Antoine stood at the door and kept watch across the yard. The first strokes of the pick seemed to resound. He turned and whispered, "Hell, Luca. That's enough noise to wake the dead, never mind this cousin of yours."

Luca paused in his labours and took a small hand fork and trowel instead, and chipped away more quietly. They took turns to watch and dig.

"This is hot work," Luca said as he pulled his shirt up and over his head. "Better not get this too filthy anyway."

It seemed a long time until the deed was done, the hole lined with the canvas and the box safely stowed. Their bodies were slick with sweat, even in the cool of the night.

"It's nearly two o'clock," Antoine said. "At least the thing's hidden and I'm easier."

Luca nodded his agreement.

Bidding farewell to each other, they shook hands in silence, easing out of the barn and creeping away in their respective directions. Luca walked around the edge of the courtyard and then towards the door to the house.

Rainier couldn't sleep. He'd tossed about, stuck his leg out from under the covers, turned again. The bed was hot. He was thirsty. It must be about two o'clock. All the tricks of counting, repeating a mundane task in his head, mentally filing things away, weren't working.

What's that? A sound downstairs. Someone else who can't sleep? It's stealthy. Perhaps Flora didn't want to wake us as she crept down for a drink of water. What if it's Luca? Is he up to something? Flora thinks so.

That was the deciding factor. Without waking Delphi, he slid to the edge of the big bed. He turned to gaze at her body, slightly curled towards him, her hair mussed on the pillow. She grabbed at his heart still. He groped about for his dressing gown and pulled it on as he stole his way across the room. He lifted the latch. It was impossible to do so quietly. Clack! The metal knocked against the keeper. He paused. Turning, he looked back. Delphi rolled over but didn't awaken. He moved forward and pulled the door behind him. He didn't close it tight, fearing the clatter of the fastening again. He tiptoed to the stairs.

Opening the kitchen door slowly, he saw Luca was at the sink, taking great gulps of water from a glass. The lad turned and some spilled onto his shirt front.

"Uncle, you startled me." He turned away from Rainier and refilled his glass.

"The hour's late to be out, my boy. Is everything alright?"

"Out? I was just having a drink."

"Oh, come on, Luca. Stop pretending. What's going on? You've been up to something, judging by the state of you. You don't get that hot and thirsty sitting around in here."

"Better you don't know," Luca said and turned to face Rainier.

"Better that I do. Maybe I can help."

Luca took another gulp and set his glass down. He said nothing for several moments. From the fleeting expressions, avoidance of eye contact and slight body movements, Rainier was made aware of Luca's internal conflict.

Rainier decided to be open and throw his trust on his nephew. "I hate this current situation, too," he said.

"I'm grateful for you being here. You're a big help with the vines at the moment." Luca said.

Is he deliberately misunderstanding what I said? "I don't mean the vineyard, lad. I mean this political situation. Come on, meet me halfway here. What I'm saying is dangerous, but I'm putting my trust in you because I understand what you think and your views. At the start, I admit I was a Pétainiste. Along with many, I thought he was doing his best to keep us safe. I didn't see him as weak as he is. He was such a hero in my war."

Luca pulled out a chair from under the dining table and collapsed in a single fluid movement. He sat with his head in his hands but still he said nothing. Then he looked up and sighed, and it all came tumbling out. "Yes, that was me in town the other day. I took the box. It's a radio. We've hidden it. No idea how to work the thing or what to use it for." He shrugged.

"Are you working alone?"

"No." He volunteered no names and Rainier did not ask. Then he spoke with passion. "They can't be allowed to do this with no resistance from anyone. What they've done elsewhere, in Poland, Czechoslovakia, this can't go unchecked. And they call this the Free Zone. We're not free, and this puppet government are not protecting all our citizens. What will be next?" He stopped talking abruptly and looked shocked at what he had said.

Rainier let him get all his worries out of his system.

"I didn't mean that, Uncle, I didn't mean it. I'm tired, that's all. I didn't mean it."

"It's alright. I agree. I really do." Rainier came and put his hand on Luca's shoulder. "We've been brought to this state of not even trusting family or people who have always been our friends. I thought Pétain's government was going to protect at least half of France, but what I witnessed in Thorelière shocked me more than I can say. I lived through one war. That was the one to end them all. I'm unbelievably sorry to pick up what's happening." He paused. "Come, time for bed. Perhaps you will permit me to see what you have found, but not now."

They stood and moved towards the door just as it opened.

Luca gasped as he saw Flora in her nightclothes, wrapping her arms around her body as she stood in the doorway.

"Flora," Rainier said. "We're just off back to bed."

"Doesn't look like Luca's *back off* to bed. Not that it's any of my business." She flounced towards the sink and after filling a glass with water, she turned and stared at him.

Breathless, of all things, I'm breathless, mon Dieu, Luca thought as he looked at her. *She's so bold and brave. I've known her forever, but I've never seen her like this. She's on fire. So am I.*

As he crossed the room to the door, a smile played around his mouth. His thoughts pursued him along the hall and up the stairs, which he took two at a time as his mind raced.

Those green eyes are beautiful when they flash like that. She's wild and ... always annoyed me before. How come I didn't see past my worry about the property and sharing it? Too many risks, allowing her to think I've noticed her. Far too much to do now, especially with all that's happening. I've got to do what I can to prevent these bloody invaders. Nothing must distract me, nothing at all. Her body's amazing, though. Calm down, boy. Don't even think of going there.

Luca reached his room and quietly, ever so carefully, he closed his door behind him.

"So, what was all that about? He's late in again." Flora had seen the condescending smirk as he'd turned for the door. "Luca's so lazy, Rainier. Honestly, how can you put up with him? Or were you just having words? There was a definite atmosphere when I came in. Both of you went very quiet."

"We were sharing some views on things, that's all."

"Honestly, you're so patient with him. He's always off somewhere and not working. This is his vineyard, after all. I'm really not sure we should trust him," Flora said.

"He's still finding his feet in these difficult times. Give him a while. We must be patient and let him get used to us being here as well."

Flora sighed. "Two years is long enough." She shrugged and moved to the sink to refill her glass of water. "He really should be alright with it by now." Then she added in a mutter, "Something's not right."

"What? I didn't catch that," Rainier said.

"Nothing."

CHAPTER 20

As the sun dipped towards the horizon, flaring each tiny cloud with a rosy tip, Antoine sauntered into the courtyard as Flora was collecting the washing.

"Let me help you," he said, taking the basket from her before she could argue. "I'm Antoine. Luca and I are good friends, and you must be Luca's cousin."

"Step-cousin. We're not blood related. Rainier is my stepfather and Luca's uncle. Have we met before? We've visited here many times over the last few years and lived here for ages, but I'm sorry, I don't remember you."

"Oh, I only came to this region a few years ago. I haven't visited for ages. I would certainly have remembered you, so I don't think we've met." His gaze scanned down her body and back up to her face. A dimple appeared in his left cheek as he grinned at her.

"Do you know, I think I can manage this." Flora reclaimed the basket from him. A little giggle escaped, belying the scowl on her face. "You, I see, are a great flirt. Luca's over there in the barn."

"And you," he said, undeterred, "are a minx." He wandered off, leaving her to watch his retreat.

Mmm, she thought, her head on one side.

"*Bonsoir, mon ami.* Uncle Rainier is aware of it," Luca said, nodding towards the old cloths and junk near the wall inside the barn. He stretched his back after working on the logs he had been splitting and leaned the *merlin* axe against the pile. Coming forward, he shook Antoine's outstretched hand.

"*Merde.* How did he find out? We better get rid of it quickly," Antoine said. "But it's such a prize. What about taking it somewhere else and burying it? Oh, my God, what shall we do?"

"Don't get in a panic, my friend." Luca put his hand on Antoine's arm. "I'm sure he can be trusted, and he could be useful to us."

"How are you so sure of that? This is very risky."

"If he was going to betray us, he could have done it today. He hasn't. He's been in the fields all day and he's in the house now."

Footsteps sounded outside. Antoine spun round towards the barn door.

"Calm down," Luca said. "That'll be Rainier coming, that's all."

"Hello, you two." Rainier came across to shake hands with Antoine. "Flora said you were here. I gather you've got quite a hot find."

Antoine glanced at Luca but said nothing.

"Don't worry, boy, I shan't give away a thing. You have my complete admiration for what you are doing."

Antoine looked again at Luca.

"Relax, you're safe here," Rainier said. "Maybe later we can have a look at this thing together and work out what's best to do with it. It may or may not work. We shall need to see. In the meantime, come across to the house and take a glass with us before we go our separate ways to eat. Then when it's dark, we can have a look."

They sat around the table and clinked glasses. Rainier went across to the radio that sat beside the dresser. Switching it on and waiting while it warmed, he said, "Let's see if there's some music to lighten our spirits. It's such a gloomy atmosphere."

He turned the tuning dial and odd snatches of words and whining sounds emitted from the great box as he searched. Then, they heard someone speaking French but sounding oddly like an English person. Both Delphi and Flora's heads perked up.

"It's a long time since I heard those tones." Delphi looked at her daughter in surprise. "French has become my native language now. That's a BBC voice announcing the hour."

The electronic whining resumed as Rainier continued to turn the dial.

"No, let's listen for a minute," Delphi said.

"This is against the new laws." Rainier turned to them.

"No one here will tell, will they?"

Flora looked across at the two young men, who both shrugged and shook their heads.

Having found the station again, they were just in time to hear the end: '*au-revoir de Radio Londres*'. Silence.

"We've missed it." Flora sounded disappointed.

"Maybe we could find it again tomorrow," Delphi said.

"There's a risk." Antoine shifted in his chair. "There was a notice on the board at the *mairie*. I paid it no heed, but it was something about listening to foreign radio being 'verboten'."

Luca stood to attention, put a finger under his nose in parody, clicked his heels and laughed as he took his seat again.

"Be careful, Luca," Antoine said, and he looked around at the others.

"No one will betray you here, Luca, but, yes, be very careful," Delphi said. "Many of the workers at the vineyard would cover their backs to save themselves, should it be necessary. Not everyone can be trusted just because we have known them for a long time."

"She's right, lad. We simply can't be certain who we can trust now," Rainier said.

Flora took all this in without saying anything. She really was unsure if Luca had been jesting. Perhaps he was lulling them into a false sense of security. "We shouldn't listen in again," she said.

"I'm sure we all agree with each other here, *ma petite*," Rainier reassured her.

Flora looked at him long and hard, trying to communicate her agitation and unease, thinking he was being gullible.

That night, Rainier and Luca laid the box containing the radio transmitter on the ground between them. Each watching the other, they remained motionless for some time, overwhelmed by the enormity of the find.

"You understand the price to be paid if this is discovered? It won't just be you," Rainier said.

"Are you willing to pay that, or do you want me to remove it elsewhere? You must consider Delphi and Flora, I know that." Luca stirred the earth with the toe of his boot and looked down at it. "That's why I've been loath to say anything before."

"I'll have to speak with Delphi, but I'm not going to tell Flora. She must be protected at all costs, and the less she's told the better."

"Does Delphi need to be in on it?"

"Yes, I believe so. I can't hide this from her and she'd guess something was up anyway. If she's really against it, I'll have to respect that, and you'll have to leave me out of it. She'll understand I must get involved, though. What's happening is despicable. I'm aware of that now." He hunkered down by the box. "Come on, then, let's have a look."

Luca cracked the lid and then glanced up at Rainier, who nodded at him. Opening it fully, he surveyed the contents.

"It all looks in good condition," Luca said as he fingered the headphones, wires and dials.

"I have no idea what the Germans have in the way of vigilance round here, but they're going to be looking for this. I'm not aware of surveillance vehicles, for example. Once we switch it on, we won't have long to try and get it working, though, just in case."

"There are no frequencies or codes or anything." Luca sighed and rubbed his head.

"Wait a minute. Let's have a proper look before we despair."

Luca held the candle nearer while Rainier cautiously lifted the winding handle and worked out where to place it to generate power.

"Let's hope the mainspring inside isn't damaged." Replacing the little handle, he looked down between the radio and the box on each side. He could see nothing, so he patted the lining fabric in the lid. "That's a bit odd, to have a lining, don't you think?" He picked at it with his fingernails and there it was. A little pocket revealed itself and with a bit of poking and tugging, he extricated a piece of silk. "Don't get the candle near it," Rainier said to Luca. "We would be right in the *merde* then."

"What is it?"

"I'm guessing it'll be a list of codes."

"Why is it on that fine fabric?" Luca leaned in to look more closely.

"It's silk. It's fine, as you say, so easier to hide and it doesn't make the noise of paper," Rainier explained.

"It'll be more durable in bad weather too, I suppose."

"Mmm." Rainier was concentrating on the material, trying to make sense of the English lettering. "Shall we give it a go?"

"To be honest, I'm shit scared, so I don't know, but there's no point in keeping it here if we're not going to use it," Luca said.

"Just go outside and have a listen. Make sure you can't hear anything mechanical that might be a vehicle coming." Rainier picked up the small handle again and began winding to create some power.

"All's quiet out there," Luca said as he returned.

Rainier put on the headphones and turned the tuner dial to search for some frequency that might work.

"I've chosen one of those four-letter codes. Anything near suitable would do. I doubt very much if this will work. Firstly, someone has to be listening in, and then we must land on a frequency that works. We can't be too long about it either."

The electrical whining seemed endless.

Rainier continued to turn the dial slowly. "My coding is rusty. It's been years since I did anything like this, and my training was only brief anyway."

Luca went back to the door to listen outside. "Rainier, *Christ, m'aider.*" He came rushing back and thumped Rainier harder than he meant. "There's a car or a motorbike. In the distance, still. Only the Germans have enough fuel for that at this time of night, surely."

CHAPTER 21

Luca and Rainier sat together in the kitchen, trying to fool themselves they were relaxed. There was a thump from outside. Luca jumped up, knocking the table and sending a quiver through the cloudy pastis in the glass before him. Rainier put out his hand. "*Calme-toi*. Take a deep breath."

Luca approached the door and opened it a crack. The German soldier stood impassive but looked determined.

"It's late," he said in accented French. "You are still up."

"My uncle and I are having a drink. Will you join us?" Luca opened the door wider.

"*Nein*. The missing radio transmitter, we are looking for it. Doubtless you know it was stolen the other day," the soldier added.

"Yes, we were talking about it, but we are a quiet house out here," Rainier said from his seat at the table.

Just then, the door to the hallway opened and Delphi poked her head around.

"Ah, my wife," Rainier said. "This gentleman is making enquiries about that stolen transmitter. Remember we spoke of it?"

She wrapped her dressing gown tighter around her as she came into the room. "Will you take a coffee, sir?"

"No, but I will look around. What's that building?"

"It's the barn where we keep old equipment and the cart. There's a stable for just one horse. The presses, sinks and suchlike for the wine-making are in the newer building beyond," Luca said.

"Humph! I will get my colleagues. You will stay here. I don't understand why you are up so late. Do you not have work tomorrow?" Not waiting for an answer, he turned on his heel and marched across the courtyard, calling to his companions.

"Oh, my goodness, what's going on?" Delphi closed the door and came to Rainier, who had stood to wrap her in his arms.

Then Flora arrived, looking sleepy. "Who was that?"

"Flora, go back upstairs to your room. Some Germans are here to look around the place," Rainier said.

"But…"

"Please, do as I say."

Delphi put her arm around her daughter and led her away.

Luca followed the soldiers across to the barn, despite being told to remain inside. He stood in the doorway, watching as they pulled things to one side and lifted others. His heart was thumping. His knees wobbled. He was short of breath. What had drawn them to their lonely vineyard? Only he and Antoine knew of the hiding place, although Hubert was aware it was here somewhere. Had Thibault guessed something?

A soldier moved to where the old tarpaulin covered the place he had used to hide the radio transmitter. He tugged the oilcloth and canvas to one side, shoving and pulling the other bits off.

It was half an hour before the soldiers returned to the house. Rainier was sitting motionless as Luca entered ahead of them.

The officer came in too. "Why are you up so late?"

"We were taking a glass before going up to bed. I told your man, here. Sharing information about tomorrow's work, you know how it is. Men's talk of soil and crops. My wife retired some time ago." He yawned to press the point.

"If you pick up anything, you will report it immediately."

"Yes, of course. Our Protectors are to be made welcome and helped in their difficult tasks," Rainier said and moved to shake hands with the officer as he prepared to leave. Luca copied his uncle.

As the sound of the motors receded, Flora and her mother returned. The family congregated around the table while Delphi filled the kettle.

Rainier poured a Cointreau for each of them.

"My hands are shaking," Luca said.

"But they didn't find anything? We wouldn't be here now if they had."

"No, but I was so scared when they pulled aside the old tarpaulin and moved stuff around. Fortunately, the light in there is not good." Luca looked meaningfully at Rainier but said no more in front of Delphi.

"Why were they so polite?" Delphi spooned coffee, which was still available despite the occupation of the north.

"It's not in their interest to upset regular folk. Things could turn against them easily, even now."

"Are we safe?" Flora asked.

"Yes, that was a routine show of power. If they really suspected anything, it would have been much more intensive."

"I don't think they have the men for more," Luca said.

"What were they looking for?" Flora shivered and her mother put her arm around her shoulders.

"Nothing, my child," Rainier said and glanced up at Delphi. "They're visiting everyone. The light was on and they came to show us who's in charge. As I said, a demonstration of power."

The Cointreau disappeared; coffee followed. "That's it for tonight," Rainier said. "Let's go to bed."

CHAPTER 22

Flora yawned as she threaded the reins through her fingers and the horse ambled along. The sky was grey, which suited her mood. The last time she had been this way, it had been with Rainier on a sunny day that had held much promise, but it had ended with horror. She still had flashbacks to when the boy had lain on the ground with blood oozing from his body.

She was bored rigid at the thought of shopping yet again. She ended up getting the same things each week, depending on what was in season and readily available. She'd get home and prepare the same vegetables, bake the same tarts, make the same dishes as always. Then there was the washing and ironing. It was thinking time, but she needed the external stimulation of planning, composing discussions and paperwork, meeting people, and taking accurate minutes. All this she had got from working in the solicitors' office when they lived in what was now an Occupied Zone.

Having left the horse and cart, she wandered between the stalls, looking at the vibrant colours, sometimes sampling cubes of cheese or dried sausages that were left on plates for passing shoppers. The sounds, colours and smells were all around her. She took in the cries of the traders and smiled as she strolled along, avoiding an elderly housewife here or a mother with umpteen children there.

She made her purchases and headed for the café to have a coffee before returning home again. As she passed the *mairie*, she idly regarded the notices pinned beneath the glass on the board outside. Her attention landed on the announcement in the middle: *Secretaire. I need someone as soon as possible. Previous experience essential.* There was some more basic information, but the message also said to call in for further details.

Flora felt her heart race. Surely this was meant for her. There were few people who had her 'previous experience' with this kind of work.

Perhaps I should go home and consult Mama and Rainier, she thought. *No, I'm an adult. I can make my own decisions. This will be gone if I delay. They may take on someone else far less qualified, and we'd all lose then.*

Taking a deep breath, Flora climbed the ancient steps. She hesitated for two seconds and looked up at the great oak door before turning the handle and entering the stone-flagged hall. Her footsteps echoed as she moved towards a massive carved desk set to one side. She stood before it and waited. No one was there. She looked about her. The columns of the old building soared above her. She craned her neck back to look up at the vaulted ceiling. Not intimidated, she marched forward along the hallway to a door marked *M. le Maire* and rapped smartly on the wooden panel.

A disembodied voice said, "*Un moment.*"

Flora looked down at her dusty shoes and rubbed the toe of each on the calf of her opposite leg. She smoothed her hands down her skirt and prepared her facial expression.

The door opened and she smiled. "*M'sieur. Bonjour.*" She stuck out her hand and the mayor shook it. "I saw the notice outside. I understand that you need a secretary. I have good qualifications and experience."

"Ah, yes, of course," he said, seeming ill at ease.

"I hope you don't mind me calling unannounced, but my last position terminated because the man I worked for retired," she fibbed, "and I really want a job such as this."

"Right, I see," he repeated. "Well, *mademoiselle*, er … please come in."

She followed him through an office and into another beyond. He moved behind his desk and she looked up into his eyes, liking what she saw.

He put out his hand to shake hers again. "I am the mayor. My name is M André Duclos." He was tall but not particularly good-looking in the traditional sense. However, those blue eyes had a light within that was most appealing.

"Er … please, do sit down." He indicated a chair in front of his desk, and he took his place behind. "I haven't been in this post all that long. Our Protectors deemed it a good idea that my predecessor retired. He had disturbingly socialist views." He coughed and began to shuffle some papers. "The previous secretary decided her family needed her attention recently, so I've been managing without anyone for the last two or three weeks. Most inconvenient."

His formality of speech and obvious uncertainty made Flora smile.

"What is your previous experience, Miss … er?"

"Oh, sorry. My name is Miss Flora Harman. I worked for a solicitor previously. I was there for some time and rose from the position of office junior to become his personal assistant. I have letters of reference." She opened her bag and began to dig inside.

He held out his hand to receive her documentation. "So, you are living at the home of Luca Harman. He is your husband?"

"No, no," she said in a hurry. "He's my cousin. My mother and father are there with me too."

They spoke about the work involved and he asked her some other questions.

"Well, Miss Harman, I have one other to interview. That's this afternoon. By chance, your timing seems impeccable."

She produced her most dazzling smile. "Mmm, yes," she said.

Standing, they shook hands again and he held the door open for her. "I shall be in touch."

"*Au revoir, m'sieur, et merci pour votre temps.*"

Outside, the sun had come out and the grey clouds were disappearing.

"Hello, Flora."

Flora turned at the sound of her name. "Hello, Antoine. My, you're looking smart," she added as she took in his clothing and neatly combed hair. He leaned in and kissed her on each cheek, and then kissed her left side again.

"I don't always wear my work clothes," he said. "As it happens, I've been to the dentist, so now I need a treat for being a brave boy." As he grinned at her, his perfect white teeth almost shone. His eyes were merry, and that dimple appeared at the corner of his mouth.

"Antoine, you're an incorrigible rogue."

"You'll come with me for a coffee, won't you?"

"A quick one. I could do with one too."

"Oh?"

"I was on my way to the café when I saw the information board." She nodded in its direction. "I've just been in to speak with the mayor. He has a secretarial job going, so I thought I'd take a chance."

"My goodness," Antoine said. "So, you'd be working in his office."

"I presume I'd be next door most of the time. Typing and whatever."

"But you'd be in his confidence."

"I suppose so. Why are you asking?"

"Oh, just interested. Let's get that coffee," he said and took her elbow to guide her across the square.

CHAPTER 23

Flora was restless the next morning. When she'd broken the news of her interview on the previous day, her mother had been surprised and supportive. Rainier had asked what her duties would be and what hours she would work, as well as several other questions. She'd pondered over his reaction and was worried that he didn't approve. Not that he'd ever minded her working. He was very modern in that way, but she wasn't sure he would like her being employed by someone appointed by the Nazis, albeit indirectly.

"M Duclos didn't telephone yesterday, so perhaps I'm not going to get this job," she said to her mother at the breakfast table.

"Never mind. Now that you've made a move, something else will turn up soon, I'm sure," Delphi said.

They were doing the dishes when the telephone sounded. Flora flung down her cloth and hurried through to the hallway. Her hand was shaking as she picked up the receiver.

"*Oui? Oui, c'est moi.* Thank you, *m'sieur.* Thank you very much. Yes, I will, I'll do that this afternoon. Oh, yes, I understand. As I said yesterday, I am used to that side of things. Thank you again. Yes, absolutely. Goodbye."

Delphi had followed her. "I'm dancing about with anticipation here," she said. "What did he say?"

"The job is mine. M Duclos needs to see my papers again, and I need to go in and sign some others. He reminded me of the confidential nature of the work. Obviously at the solicitors' office I had to be aware of all that, so I said I understood and was able to reassure him."

Delphi came forward and hugged her. "Well done, my darling. Sometimes things are just meant to be. When will you start?"

"Mmm, not certain, but I assume next Monday. Since he's had no one for a little while, I imagine he'll want me as soon as possible. I must say, I'm not sure about it now. I want to work, but in this position…?"

"Why do you say that?" Delphi's face creased in a frown.

"M Duclos is new. He said the previous *maire* had to leave. I suspect this one will be more sympathetic to the Nazis. Rainier's never been a sympathiser, of course, but he seems to think that Pétain is doing the right thing by cosying up to them. Now I'm not so sure. It's all a muddle."

"He said that the *maréchal* is sacrificing a few to save many French people from Nazi occupation. We don't have many food shortages, not as many as in the Occupied Zone, anyway. Parts of the country, especially Paris, were going downhill and becoming quite licentious, too. So, Pétain's brought those wild elements under control. After all, De Gaulle has simply left us. At least *Maréchal* Pétain has remained. But now, Rainier's not such a Pétain supporter."

Flora frowned. "He's not strong enough. He's got Pierre Laval as his vice president. Laval's father worked in a village as a café proprietor, butcher and postman. He was always a self-server. I certainly don't trust *him*. What does Rainier think about this job for me? Is he alright with it, do you think?"

"Yes, of course. Like I say, he's not quite so inclined towards this new government now, with what's happened recently. We're all a bit more circumspect, but see how it goes. If you don't like it or things turn difficult, you can always leave." Delphi shrugged. "Not a problem, I think."

Flora hugged her mother. "I do love you," she said. "You're always so pragmatic and sensible."

Delphi laughed. "Maybe a little more so with age."

That evening, after they had finished their meal, Rainier poured them all a drink, pastis for the men and wine for Flora and her mother. Even Luca was with them for once. Then Rainier moved across to the radio and switched it on. While waiting for it to warm up, he said, "I can't bear listening to *Radiodiffusion Nationale* this evening. I've had enough propaganda from the Vichy government, and *Radio Paris* is even worse with its Nazi messages. I might try and find *Radio Londres* again."

"Is it safe? Can it be tracked or something?" Delphi looked worried.

"It can't be traced, and so long as no one in this room spills the beans, we're fine."

Flora glanced at Luca. Perhaps he sensed her eyes upon him. When he looked up, his eyes met hers but he did not flinch.

The next song was *'Pourquoi pas'* and ridiculed those who were following the Vichy government.

"It's stuffed full of sketches, songs and comic advertising. Little wonder the German's don't want us to listen," Luca said.

The voices sounded tinny and far away. "*Et voici, quelques messages personnel.*" The announcer Pierre Dac's voice became more serious. "My cousin has a big basket. Jean has a long moustache. The old dog will be going to see my aunt." The messages continued.

"What's all that about? It doesn't make any sense," Delphi said. "Personal messages they might be, but they sound ridiculous."

"Just so," said Luca. "I'm sure they're codes of some kind. After all, this is the Free French in London broadcasting. Their sole aim is to encourage resistance right here in the unoccupied areas." He laughed and clapped his hands. "It's priceless. I bet the Boche are listening in and furious. They'll guess they're coded messages, but there's little they can do."

The voice changed again and before the broadcast finished, some regular music came on. It was lively and uplifting.

"Fancy a stroll around the yard and a smoke?" Rainier shook two cigarettes from his packet of *Gauloises*. He smoked rarely after his experiences in the trenches.

"Why not?" Luca said. The men went outside, lit up, and savoured the scent of the cigarettes on the balmy air.

As they left, Delphi crossed the room, moved the radio dial away from its current position and turned off the set. "Can't be too careful," she said to Flora, who nodded and collected the glasses.

Outside, Luca said, "Do you think our radio transmission got anywhere, last night?"

"Honestly? I doubt it. We have no idea what we're doing. There are too many unknowns. Frequency, timing, my Morse code skills." Rainier shrugged. "The message itself. Even if someone picked it up, I'm sure they'd suspect it wasn't a regular messenger. I gathered during the last show that the women who decipher and unscramble these things can recognise the touch of the sender on his key. I think it's unlikely that we'll have success."

"Should we try again?"

"We might, once or twice, but not too often. We don't know what capability the Germans have of tracing the call. I heard today they've brought in a van with a direction finder. I'm not sure if that's true, but it's risky."

"Perhaps we'd better move the set again soon." Luca took a deep drag on his cigarette. "Even if we bury it under a hedge somewhere, it might be safer. I'll have a word with Antoine."

"Be on your guard at all times, lad. You never know who's listening. Letting names slip in a café or among the workers, well… So, who else have you got in your little cell?"

Luca looked at him.

"Come on, you've trusted me this far."

The younger man nodded. "Well, there's Hubert. He lives with his mother. Something happened to his father at the last show. Not sure exactly what. Do you remember him? He was at school with me and Antoine, but in the year below us. Red hair, freckles. Then there's Thibault. He's younger, and to be honest I'm not confident of him at all. He's a wildcard, and he might easily brag to the wrong people or shout his mouth off. He's an arrogant little so-and-so. He likes to follow me around, if he can."

"You don't want to anger him, though, if you're casting him adrift. He could be hurt and turn nasty."

"That's exactly what I said to Antoine. I think it'll be a case of slowly leaving him out or giving him false information."

"Is he aware you have this transmitter?"

"No, unless he suspects something, but he wasn't with us when we retrieved it or when we hid it."

"That's alright, then. I would keep it that way," Rainier said.

When they returned to the kitchen, Delphi had the coffee pot on the stove and the little cups were in a group on the table. Flora was just putting the sugarbowl down as Rainier closed the door behind the two of them.

"So, you've got yourself a job," Luca said to Flora.

"Yes, working in the offices of M Duclos, the new mayor."

Luca nodded but said nothing.

Flora needed to fill the silence and justify her move. "I shall be doing general office duties but, of course, it will be a responsible position, typing *M le Maire's* letters and ensuring things are filed accurately. He will, no doubt, have some quite high-powered correspondence."

"Antoine told me he saw you yesterday."

"Yes, we went for a coffee together just after I had seen M Duclos. We had a lot of fun at the café. He's very amusing."

"He's not to be trusted." Luca frowned.

"What do you mean?" Flora looked at him. She held her chin high and a wary look flitted across her face. Everyone was under suspicion now.

"He's a flirt. He doesn't take people, women, seriously at all."

"Oh, I see. Don't talk such rubbish," Flora said. "He's as trustworthy as anyone else around here." She nodded at him with meaning.

Delphi and Rainier left the table and put their cups in the sink.

"We're off to bed," Delphi said. "Goodnight, my darling." She gave Flora a kiss on the top of her head.

There was silence between Luca and Flora, but neither of them moved.

"At least he smiles and is fun to be around," Flora said after the door had closed behind her parents.

"Meaning...?"

"Meaning you're always so horrid to me. You clearly resent me being here and you're always grumbling about something or other. Antoine makes me laugh. He likes my company. He even complimented my eyes."

"Hmm." Luca stood and put his cup in the sink with the others. "I'm off to bed."

But as he closed the door behind him, he realised he was hurt by her remarks. He was uncomfortable and hot with guilt. He had been mean as a boy, and when the family had come to live with him, he had resented Flora deeply, though not now. How could he tell her he was sorry? How could he say that he admired her spirit and her loyalty? She could have left all this and returned to England back in '39, but she'd chosen to stay.

I can't afford to be sidetracked by anyone, he thought. He had to fight for his country in any way he could.

CHAPTER 24

It was late summer and the sky was darkening as Flora cycled along the lanes towards Thorelière.

She arrived early for her first day of work. Having undone her coat, she placed her beret on the wooden top of a cabinet and sat with her hands tucked under her at what she presumed to be her desk in the anteroom. She craned her neck to look up at the ornate ceiling. A shiver ran down her spine and she hunched her shoulders. Her tummy jittered. It wasn't the work that jangled her nerves. She was confident of her ability, but this new mayor was an unknown, and the complications of allegiance were uppermost in her mind. The outside entrance banged and then footsteps echoed around the capacious hallway beyond her room. As her own door opened, she jumped up, irrationally guilty for sitting.

"Ah, good morning, Miss Harman. A bit grey and dismal today. I'm pleased you're here, though. A ray of sunshine for me. Things have been hectic here for the last week or two. Find a notepad and pen and come through in five minutes." His tall wiry frame disappeared in a flurry of overcoat tails through the connecting room to one side. Her eyes followed him as he tossed his hat. It landed precisely on the top of the coat stand before he kicked the door shut with his heel.

Flora sat for a moment, recovering from the whirlwind that had been M Duclos. Well, clearly she was in the correct place. As she regained her senses, she looked down at the desk drawers and opened the top one to discover a tray of pens and pencils, an eraser and a pencil sharpener. The next drawer down held paperclips and elastic bands and various other office paraphernalia, so she turned to the drawers on the other side and managed to track down a notepad. Her predecessor had been meticulous in her arrangements. Flora imagined an older lady in a brown wool skirt and sensible shoes tucked under this same desk. She roused herself from her reverie and knocked on the mayor's door.

"Come." His voice sounded with deep resonance. An attractive sound, Flora realised. She gulped and, pasting on a smile, went in.

M Duclos stood at the window, peering up into the sky, and turned as she entered. "Please, sit, Miss Harman." He indicated the upright wooden chair on the other side of his desk, gave her a brief smile which didn't quite reach his blue eyes and came to take his own seat.

For the next twenty minutes, Flora took notes and made lists of all the things he wanted her to start on. Occasionally he pulled a folder from the pile in front of him and referred to it before nodding and proceeding with instructions.

"As you can tell, the last incumbent of your position was neat but not very imaginative. As for my predecessor, he definitely worked well outside his comfort zone in these changed times." He stood and wandered back to the window, looking out. As he spoke in this vein for several minutes, Flora listened, but her eyes roamed across his desk. The usual blotter, pen and ink, and large black telephone sat innocently. There were several buff card folders, and each had a cream label outlined with a brown line. Then there was a photograph in a silver ornate frame. A lady with blonde wavy hair held a young child. The child wore short ankle socks and buttoned shoes. A little knitted beret sat on her head at a jaunty angle, from which her curls escaped. She wore the widest and most infectious grin that Flora had ever seen. It brought a smile to her own face.

M Duclos turned and glanced at the image upon which Flora's eyes still rested, and then looked at Flora. He pushed his sandy hair from his forehead. It seemed to have a habit of falling forward. His voice changed, became soft and wistful. "My wife and child," he said, but he did not elaborate. "Right!"

Flora jumped.

"That'll be all. Any questions, Miss Harman?"

"No, sir, I'll make a start straight away." She took the folders he gave her and turned, trying not to scuttle as she left the room, but his rumbustious manner was not encouraging.

I'll see how things go. I don't have to stay, but it's early days. Give it time. Perhaps he's as nervous as me, she thought as she sat at her own desk.

The second task was almost complete when the connecting door opened and M Duclos came hurrying out with his coat flapping, his hat firmly planted. "I have to visit the *gendarmerie*. I'll be about an hour," he said without pausing.

"Right, sir."

"You don't have to call me 'sir' all the time. That's how I had to address my father. M Duclos will do for now."

"Thank you," she managed, and then the space was quiet and empty.

As she pedalled home that evening, Flora's thoughts were in a whirl about her busy day typing letters, sorting files and making notes of things that needed following up. There were several questions on her pad, things to clarify with M Duclos. She found she was looking forward to her return the next day, as the work seemed interesting. Then her mind turned to her boss. What had she made of him? The jury was out on that one. She would have to wait and see.

"So, how did it go?" Delphi asked when Flora returned that evening.

"It was fine. The work was varied. M Duclos seems pleasant enough, but he was brusque and always in a hurry."

"What sort of age is he? Does he have a family?"

Flora pondered for a moment. "He must be fortyish. There's a photograph on his desk of a lady holding a beautiful little girl. He caught me looking at it and then was rather short when he mentioned them." She shrugged. "Who knows?"

When Rainier returned, Luca was with him. "What sort of things did the mayor ask you to do?" Luca asked.

Flora answered their questions with a summary of her day, Luca glancing at Rainier from time to time as she spoke.

"So, he left you alone in his office?" he queried.

Flora looked at him. Unease fluttered inside as his dark eyes scrutinised her. Why was he interested in that? She wasn't daft. His shoulders tensed. He wanted to hear more, she realised, but why? Maybe he was being critical that M Duclos had left her alone in the office when there must be confidential documents around. She would be most careful what she told him.

Flora crossed to the stove to heat a pan of water for coffee. "I wish Edith was here. She would have an opinion, for sure. Writing isn't the same at all, and letters from her seem to have stopped altogether. I do hope she's alright."

"Trying to survive and very busy, I expect," Delphi said. "As are we all."

Towards the end of the week, Flora headed to the café across the square. It was busy with wives and their baskets and men in the blue trousers favoured by all French country workers. A *croque-monsieur* would do for her lunch. There would be no ham, but there might be an egg to go on top. Having concentrated hard on her tasks, breakfast seemed a distant memory. Thoughts of the tangy cheese on toasted bread were making her mouth water. Yellow yolk oozing over the stringy Emmental, the egg white slightly crispy underneath. Oh yes, perfect.

"Hello, again. Your mind seems far away." Antoine grinned at her with impish enthusiasm.

"Oh, Antoine, hello. I was thinking about my lunch. I'm famished."

"Mind if I join you? I've been seeing the seed merchant. Business is done now, so I'm grabbing a quick bite before heading back to the farm." Once they'd seated themselves and placed their orders, Antoine asked, "How's your job?"

"The work is fine. I'm getting used to my new boss, M Duclos."

"Just one minute." Antoine left the table and spoke to the bartender before returning. "What does it involve?" he asked as he returned.

Flora gave him a *résumé*. "Why is everyone so interested in what I do?"

He leaned towards her to speak. "Because he's a new mayor and probably aligned with the Germans. It makes for a powerful position. We're interested in how he's thinking and what he's doing. You could be useful to us, working there."

"Antoine, forget it. Everything I do is confidential, and anything I see would be the same. I must have loyalty to my boss. I had to reassure M Duclos of that before I got the job. Who is 'we', anyway?"

"Oh, just me and a few friends."

"You're reckless. You need to watch what you say and to whom. What about Luca? He's your friend. Where does he stand?"

"I couldn't possibly say." Antoine grinned at her and winked. "What are you doing this weekend? We could go and have dinner. We'd have lots of laughs, you and me."

Flora looked at him. It was tempting. He was amusing, and it had been a long time since she'd had diverting conversation. Then he reached over and took her hand as it played with the stem of the water glass in front of her.

The food and a whole bottle of wine arrived.

"I only ordered a glass," Flora said to the waiter.

"*Mais, non, mademoiselle. M'sieur,* he changed his mind," he said, indicating Antoine as he placed the bottle on the table.

"Live a little, Flora." Antoine winked at her. "So, what do you say to dinner?"

"Sorry, Antoine. I really can't. I have too many things to see to."

"I'll wear you down, you wait." He grinned again, not put off at all.

CHAPTER 25

"I'm so pleased with your work, Miss Harman. Now you've been here for several weeks, are you happy with this position?"

"Yes, thank you, M Duclos. I hope I'm doing everything correctly."

"Oh, certainly. I can trust you with almost anything. And how is it going, you living at your cousin's place?"

"We jog along together, I suppose. My stepfather has a vineyard too, so he can cope with all of that. Luca, my cousin, is on his own since his father died, so he welcomes the help."

"I met Luca a few times some years ago, when my wife was alive. He's younger than me, of course. He can be reckless. Tell him to stay on the right side of things. It wouldn't go well for him if he was foolish."

"Oh, M Duclos, Luca has grown into a sensible man." Flora mentally berated herself for the lies she was spouting, but family feud or not she didn't know this man well enough to trust him. Determined to change the subject, she asked, "Is your wife no longer with us, M Duclos? Forgive me for asking."

M le Maire didn't answer for several seconds, and Flora began to think she had overstepped the mark. He sighed and said, "My wife was killed, along with our beautiful daughter. They were in a car accident. Nobody can be sure of what happened. Maybe she was distracted by something. Perhaps she was tired. No one else was involved. The car hurtled down a ravine about thirty kilometres from here. They were returning from her mother's."

"I'm so sorry."

"No, that's alright. Better that you get it from me now. They died nearly three years ago. Our little Chloé would be almost five now." They both sat in silence until M Duclos said, "Well, life goes on for me, although I have few friends these days. It's amazing how they disappear when tragedy strikes. They hang around for a while, and then slowly they find it too awkward and…" He shrugged. "My work keeps me busy. I'm doing some good for the citizens of Thorelière, of that I'm sure. These Protectors will not harm us if we help them as best we may."

"I hope you gain inner peace, *m'sieur*." Flora stood to get on with her work.

"Thank you, my dear," he said.

Back in her own room, Flora sat at her desk for several minutes and stared into space. *What a sad man. His life seems empty, despite what he says, and I'm sure he's putting on a brave face and trying to believe his own words. I wonder what he'll do for Christmas. How miserable to be on his own. He wants to keep the Germans happy, but I haven't seen signs of actual collaboration.*

As she cycled home that evening, the wind blew in Flora's face and made her nose run. She wobbled as she held the handlebars with one hand and searched for her handkerchief with the other. Finding it, she had to stop to blow. The silence was palpable. Then a whisper of a breeze stirred the foliage. Something tiny scuttled in the undergrowth. An owl made the distinctive *hoo-hoo* sound of a tawny male some distance away. There was no answering *kewick* of a female. Poor owl. Lonely, like M Duclos. The stars above speckled the sky. Flora and her concerns suddenly seemed miniscule.

The reverberation of motors broke the peace. This wasn't a tractor, though. It sounded like a motorbike. No, more than that — a small cavalcade. No one had the fuel to move around like that at night. No one except the Germans, of course. Then there were voices, indistinct but male and not gentle. Flora remounted her bike and pedalled home with as much speed as she could muster.

She freewheeled around the corner into the courtyard and up to the barn door. Pulling it open, she hurried to put her bicycle away.

There was a sudden scrabbling as she entered, and a torch was switched off.

"Who's that?" It was Antoine's voice.

"*Fils de pute*," added another voice, which Flora recognised as belonging to Luca.

"I'm not anyone's son," Flora said, indignant at his swearing. "What on earth are you up to, anyway, lurking about in the dark? Put the light on." She reached out and fumbled next to the door. Finding the switch, she clicked it on.

The two young men stood up with a single bound, shielding something with their bodies. In the gloom of the dusty lightbulb, it was difficult to see. Leaning her bike against the wall, Flora approached them. She laughed at their expressions.

"Come on. Is it dirty magazines? Most women today are not that easily shocked. Perhaps it's stolen goods, or something tasty from the black market?" She assumed a wheedling expression for Antoine's benefit and tilted her head sideways to try and see. "What on earth is that?" Her voice became sharper. The box with its dials and wires had a set of headphones trailing out onto the dirt floor. "*Merde*, boys. Is that what I think it is? You better hurry up and hide it well. I'm sure there was some sort of convoy around as I was pedalling home. That's what it sounded like. Only Germans have enough *gazole* for vehicles. There are none stationed round here, but who else could it be?"

Antoine and Luca packed the whole thing away and lowered it into a hole that she hadn't noticed before. She crept back to the door and listened.

"I'm sure it's vehicles. Oh, do hurry."

The two men pulled the canvas sheet across the hiding place and dumped some other old bits on the top. Scuffing their feet across the earth ensured no footprints were left to give them away.

Flora pushed her bike further in. Turning off the light, the three closed the door and hurried across the courtyard to the house. They snuck in through the smallest crack to prevent light pouring out and sat at the table.

Delphi looked at them with surprise and puzzlement. Ever a quick thinker, she collected cups and half-filled each one with coffee from the pan on the cooker. The ancient black *Godin* with its wood-burner kept the range hot all the time.

Luca pushed his hair off his forehead. Antoine leaned back in his chair and crossed his foot over his knee, trying to look casual. Flora took off her hat and coat and threw them over the back of the fourth chair. To any observer, they would look as if they had been sitting for a while.

An almighty racket sounded in the courtyard. Motors thudded, gravel crunched and voices shouted.

Rainier came from the back of the house into the kitchen. "What on earth is going on? I was doing some figure work." He saw Antoine, nodded at him and shook his hand.

There was a thump on the door. Luca stood to open it. A soldier in grey uniform and a member of the *gendarmerie* straightened up, touching their cap and kepi respectively. The officer's copper-brown shoulder insignia heralded him as a motorbike *Oberleutnant*. Others hovered in the background.

Please, God preserve us, thought Flora. *At least they've the sensitivity not to give a Nazi salute. Probably been directed not to antagonise the locals.*

"We have gained information that someone is in possession of a radio transmitter."

"Really? How could that be, and what would be the point?" Luca held the door wider.

Flora steadfastly refused to glance across at her mother but instead focused on Luca. He tried to appear both innocent and concerned.

"Surely it would be no use to anyone without codes or frequencies or something like that," he said.

"You will remain here while we search your premises. What is that building there and the other one behind?"

"There's the old barn. It doesn't hold much these days. Some of your people looked in there once before when that radio went missing some time back. You're welcome to have another look, of course. The horse is stabled there. Not much else; my cousin's bicycle and some ancient rubbish from previous times. Have a good poke around, but you'll not find anything there. The other building is for the wine production. Please don't make it dirty. There are vats on the go, not many empty; a couple awaiting the late harvest. We're hoping for the predicted frosts, so we're planning to start that next week."

"Ah, *Eiswein*," the soldier said. "Not as good as our German wines, but passable, I'm sure."

"You should come back later. All the workers are given some grapes for their own use. It's a small bonus, so to speak." Luca smiled at the officer, who turned and strode across the courtyard, beckoning for his comrades to follow.

Flora crossed to the doorway and stood next to Luca. The others peered through the window.

They could hear banging and clattering. One of the soldiers appeared at the door to the barn. "What's this pile of canvas and bits?"

"I don't really know. Some old junk left over from my father's time, as I said before. Have a poke through it if you wish," Luca replied.

Flora took a sharp breath at his side. When the soldier disappeared inside again, she said, "That's a risky strategy."

"It is. I'm gambling on them being tired and fed up. We're evidently not the first visit they've made tonight."

The sound of the latch of the stable being pulled back and the rustling of straw came to them. Then all the men reappeared and headed for the other outbuilding, while two strode towards them.

"We'll search the house. You will remain here."

Thudding and banging emanated from upstairs as the men presumably opened wardrobes and looked under beds before returning ten or fifteen minutes later. By that time, the others were congregating back in the courtyard. The officer approached Luca.

"If you hear of anything, you will inform my companion here," he said, indicating the member of the *gendarmerie*. The Frenchman avoided looking at Luca directly but saluted and turned away.

The small cavalcade left in a whirl of exhaust fumes and noise, and Luca closed the door and leaned against it. Flora glanced up and found his eyes on her. What was he thinking? Was that relief, or was it something else? She wanted to sink against him but resisted and hurried to her mother. They enfolded each other.

Rainier and Antoine moved towards Luca, and the older man said, "Let's have a quick look in the barn and see how close they came. Clearly, they found nothing, or we would not still be here."

Flora watched as they crossed the courtyard. Unable to contain herself any longer, she followed the men.

As she entered the barn, Luca said, "My God, they did come close. They've pulled all except the last *bache* away, and all the other bits are scattered. If they'd moved that last canvas, we'd have been sunk." He put his head in his hands.

"But they didn't." Rainier placed his hand on the younger man's shoulder. Flora's eyes stung with tears which she steadfastly tried to prevent from falling as she watched Luca.

CHAPTER 26

"I've heard nothing from you in quite a while," Thibault said. He had called to see Luca and eventually found him in the vinification room, where he was checking the vats and lines before the next harvest began.

"It's a busy season coming. Look at me in here, at this time of the evening," Luca said.

"I understand you got raided the other night. You weren't alone. Several others said the same thing. Scary, no? Were they looking for this radio that's still supposed to be in the area?"

"Apparently." Luca was concentrating on his work and did not turn around.

"Do you know where it is? We could certainly do with it."

"Don't let your imagination carry you away," Luca said. "What would we do with it? It would be a danger and of no use to us without any knowledge of how to use it. Don't be a fool, Thibault." He immediately regretted his insult and softened his words. "So, what have you been up to? We need a planning meeting soon. Any ideas?"

"I haven't done much. I've been awaiting a call from one of you." Thibault looked down and scuffed his foot around, looking sulky.

"You're right, of course," Luca said, approaching the lad and placing a hand on his shoulder. "Thank goodness you keep us on our toes. We've been too lax. I'll catch up with Antoine and Hubert, and we'll fix a time when all four of us can meet again."

Thibault looked happier and smiled at Luca. "That sounds good, my friend. We need to keep sharing all our information."

"Yes, indeed. Would you like to help me here for a bit?"

Adoration and hero-worship flitted across Thibault's face. "I would, but I have to get home. There are jobs to finish," he said with importance. "My mother depends on me since my father went."

"Of course. I'll be in touch soon." Luca waved his hand as the gawky figure left, before turning back to the task he had to finish.

When he caught up with Antoine and Hubert, he confessed his shortness with Thibault and recounted how he had backtracked and made to include him.

"I nearly upset him badly. We must tread carefully around him. I don't trust his sense of loyalty at all. He would give us away out of youthful boasting, or even spite, quite easily. He craves importance."

"We'll meet up late one evening to keep him on our side, but we won't tell him any real information," Antoine said.

M Duclos called Flora to his room. "I need you to take a letter down for me and get it typed up. It must go to the Hauptmann quickly."

"Yes, M Duclos." Flora opened her notepad and waited while the mayor organised his thoughts. She had time to study him again.

His collar looked slightly frayed and old, although white. His tie was conservatively striped and his jacket brown and plain. His hair was short and neat and, overall, he was unremarkable, until he looked at her. Then his eyes made her blush. They were very, very blue and seemed to stare right into her thoughts. She lowered her eyes to her pad to avoid his piercing gaze. When she glanced up again, he was still looking at her.

"*M'sieur?*"

"Right, yes. Here we go. *Cher Hauptmann Schultz*," he dictated. "I understand that you had no luck with finding the missing radio transmitter. Information came to me last evening that it has been sent west towards the coast, but the person from whom this news originated has also gone, which makes me think it is true. There are groups of resistance operating in the *Vendée* and the *Département de Loire-Atlantique*. I thought you would wish to receive this, so that you might inform your colleagues there. I hope this is of help to you, as I gather you have few personnel in this area for carrying out the searches that you must undertake, and now you will be able to concentrate your great skill and energy on other worthwhile tasks. Yours etc., etc. Thank you, Miss Harman. Will you please get that sent off as soon as possible? He will pass the information to Oberleutnant Weber here."

"Yes, M Duclos. I could carry it to the post office in my lunch hour."

"It's not necessary to go in your own time. Take it as soon as you have typed it. I shall be here."

Managing to keep a straight face in front of M Duclos, Flora sat at her desk and grinned to herself. This would be good news to pass to those at home.

She was typing up the all-important letter when M Duclos's door opened, and he stuck his head around the corner. "Oh, and would you organise some flowers to be sent to my mother, please? It's her birthday. I nearly forgot." The rest of him appeared and he added, "The address will be in the book. My wife used to deal with all those things." He shrugged and disappeared, closing the door behind him.

Flora's glee evaporated. *Such a sad, lonely life he must lead now*, she thought.

Flora pedalled home that evening with her news regarding the letter uppermost in her mind. As she cycled up the lane, the sounds of the harvest greeted her. Voices carried on the still air. Each year, itinerant workers arrived at the right time. Long years of experience had taught them when they would be needed in each region. She guessed they travelled from Bordeaux, Provence or Languedoc-Roussillon having finished the *vendanges* in those areas and prepared to continue the back-breaking picking here. She stopped at the gate and looked across the fields. Heads and shoulders bobbed up and down as the pickers bent and stood, their figures silhouetted in the last rays of the lowering sun. The horse was on the path between the vines. The boxes were piled on the wooden sled behind it, ready to take to the vinification shed where the grapes would be placed on the conveyor belt. The noisy generator would enable the fruit to be carried up and tipped into each vat.

Long, lazy days, cloudless blue skies and more solitary work of pruning, treating and hoeing had come to an end. Luca and Rainier had been anxiously tasting grapes and estimating the ultimate time for picking. Now was the season for community and contagious energy.

Rainier spotted Flora and waved. She waved back, but realised her eyes were raking the scene for sight of Luca's broad shoulders. Among all the dark-haired heads, his was quite easy to spot since he was so tall. He hadn't noticed her. His back was to her and he was directing someone to a new place to pick.

"Humph!" Impatient with herself, Flora remounted her bicycle and pedalled the short distance to the house. *Makes a change to see him working hard, although it seems he has other things to do now too*, she thought grudgingly.

Old François was hobbling across the courtyard with a rake over his shoulder. His bow legs and mild limp were distinctive. Flora greeted him with a smile. He made a pretence of working, but these days he did little. Delphi was in the kitchen preparing supper when she went in. The smell of cold ham from a huge plate in the centre of the table made her mouth water. The clear, pale jelly around the slices would be delicious. It was a rarity to see it these days.

"That looks good. Where did you manage to get it? I thought most of the pigs were purloined for the Germans."

"I was in the right place at the right time. I heard a rumour and cycled over to the Dubois' farm. *Madame* Dubois had taken a delivery of a whole side of pork. She owes me from when I helped her with all that pickling."

The steam rising from a large pan of vegetables gave a warm, damp atmosphere to the room, but Delphi was lighting the wood-burner on the wall, so it would soon be cosy and bright.

Returning from hanging up her outdoor things, Flora hugged her mother briefly and started to set the table. "I had a good day today," she said.

"Oh? What made it so?"

"I don't know. I just felt M Duclos was a bit more open and I had to go to the post office, but he let me go in work time rather than during my lunchbreak. He's nice really."

Delphi smiled at her. "Is he, indeed? What will he do for Christmas?"

Flora shrugged and shook her head. "He seems lonely. It's so sad about his wife and little girl."

The door opened, so the subject was dropped. Rainier and Luca came in to eat.

Once they were all seated and the business of serving and pouring had been done, Flora decided to share her news. She was gleeful again at the thought of what she was about to impart.

"You'll never guess what happened today," she started, then proceeded to tell of the letter to Hauptmann Schultz.

"That's more like it," Luca said. "That's the sort of useful particulars we need more of."

"Now, lad," Rainier said, "Flora works for this man, but she'll not go divulging confidential information which could put her in an awkward position."

Flora looked at her stepfather with gratitude. "I shouldn't have said anything this time," she said. "I had to sign a confidentiality clause in my contract. I should know better. It's just that…" She sighed. "It's just that you were all worried after we had that raid, and now it seems safer. I wanted to tell you."

"Of course, darling," Delphi said and reached out her hand to Flora. "Family comes first, doesn't it? Always."

CHAPTER 27

The secondary grape harvest lasted for the best part of a month. The horse with its sled and the carts of the workers trundled back and forth to the vinification room. The men, including travelling visitors who had come for the season, bent and stretched until their backs were sore. Fortunately, the weather continued in hues of gold, russet and blue, although the early mornings and late evenings had a nip in the air and the week after the raid the frost had struck, as desired. So, it was some time before Luca and the others met one night. The topic of conversation started as it had in many other circles — 'Case Anton' and the German annexation of the whole of France.

"It's a cold wind tonight," Hubert said as he hustled into the room at the back of Luca's barn. The candle flickered with the draught from the door. He shook hands with Antoine and Luca. "No Thibault?" He sat and rubbed his fists in his palms. Then he gladly accepted the pastis that Luca passed to him.

"I'm sure he's on his way. Wild horses wouldn't keep him out," Luca said. "We must be careful with him, though. As I said the other day, he's too young to be trustworthy. Nor can we afford to upset him."

"I agree," Antoine said. "We're going to need to be especially watchful now, with so many more Boche around. There's no pretence anymore."

They discussed recent events. At the beginning of November, while the German army had moved from the south coast across to the Spanish border and inland to Vichy France, the Italians had taken Corsica and occupied the French Riviera.

The Germans had planned to annex the French fleet, but it had transpired that naval commanders had managed to delay the taking of this by demanding negotiations and through subterfuge. This had given the French commanders long enough to scuttle all fifty-eight ships, including three battleships and twenty submarines.

"The Nazis bragged that it denied Charles de Gaulle, but they must have been disappointed," Luca said.

By the end of November, the actuality of a Free Zone had evaporated, although the pretence remained. The original Armistice in 1940 had served the Germans in stopping France allowing access to Allied troops into her colonies, but that had disappeared with some landings in those regions of North Africa. Laval, ever the self-seeker, had given his permission for Italians and Germans to take the moves they had. Pétain's government had made a few broadcasts of objection but little else. Germany had countered the objections by saying that France had negated the 1940 Armistice by permitting allies into North African colonies. If the Germans hadn't been able to stop that, then, in truth, it had been nothing to do with the French. So the Free Zone continued, but in name only.

A knock sounded three times and then after a few seconds once more.

"That'll be Thibault now." Luca stood and greeted the newcomer.

Having all shaken hands with each other, they sat down on bales of hay. Luca glanced around the little group. Their faces looked determined. A candle in a jar flickered on the low box in the centre, casting shadows upwards. There was a surrealism about it all. A couple of years ago, Luca wouldn't have believed they would be in this place with plans of sabotage in their minds.

"Right, listen to this," he said, and he shared the snippet of news Flora had given him about the whereabouts of the radio. He managed not to look at Antoine as he spoke.

"That's so annoying. If we'd had it, we could have used it," Thibault said.

"Hardly," Antoine said. Then he felt Luca's foot against his own and modified his tone. "The trouble is, my friend, we have no codes and we've no information on frequencies."

"What do you mean, *we* have no codes? You make it sound like we've got the radio but have no way to use it." Thibault was quick to spot Antoine's slip.

"Well, we don't, do we?" Luca jumped in to ease the discussion.

"Mmm." Thibault frowned down at his feet and Antoine glanced at Luca, shrugging and raising his eyebrows almost imperceptibly.

"We need to plan a campaign," Hubert said.

"There's simply nothing happening round here," added Thibault. He paused. "I have an idea. What if we slipped in and out of the Occupied Zone? The border's not that far away. Surely we'd be able to do something there."

Antoine was about to dismiss the idea because Thibault had come up with it, but then he hesitated. He looked at Luca and raised his eyebrows in an unspoken question. Hubert sat without a word and hunched his shoulders, frowning.

"I suppose that might be possible. How would we get across? The river's wide and becoming more so, especially at this time of the year. I wonder if there's any way we could use the château. It spans the river. Perfect, if we got in and crossed the gallery. The borderline runs right through the middle."

"Didn't the concierge's son go to our school for a couple of semesters? What was his name? He seemed a good bloke at the time. Do you remember when he shut that piglet in the paper cupboard?" Antoine chuckled.

"Oh, yes, that was so funny. I'd forgotten about that," Luca said.

"We laughed until we ached. It was perfect. We had that awful old hag for a teacher. Her backside was huge and used to wobble as she wrote on the chalkboard," Antoine added.

"What? What happened?" Thibault was too young to have been there, and Hubert had been in the year below, so he wasn't in on the joke either.

"You should have seen it," Antoine said.

"Why? Tell me." A whine crept into Thibault's voice.

"He shut a piglet in the cupboard, but he'd greased it thoroughly, so when it squawked and the teacher opened the door to see what it was, it ran out…" Luca began.

"And she couldn't catch it," Antoine finished for him.

"The animal kept slipping through her fingers. It was so funny."

"When she found out who'd done it, she was so angry."

"Yes, he left soon after that. His parents couldn't stand the embarrassment. Anyway, his dad got the job of concierge at the château and he's still there," Luca concluded.

"What would we do if we got over?" Hubert frowned.

"Well, what about cutting telephone wires? That might be easy enough, I should imagine. That would be disruptive too, surely," Luca said.

"Yes, yes, let's do that. That's a splendid idea. When should we go?" Thibault almost bounced in his seat.

"Slow down, lad," Luca said. "There are several practicalities first."

"Yes, we'd need to contact Pierre. That was his name. Sussing him out would be critical, and we must be careful how we do that. He may not be safe or may not even be there still. We were lucky that we didn't have to sign up because we work on the land, but he may well have done. Perhaps we could get hold of his father and find out if he's sympathetic to us or the Germans." Antoine stroked his chin as he thought aloud.

"We'd need to do a recce. Antoine, what if you and I head over that way one afternoon and see what we can find out? Then if we report back and things are good, we can make a proper plan," Luca said.

"Yes, let's do that as soon as possible. I want to come too." Thibault leaned forward.

"We can't have too many going. That alone would look odd," Luca said. "Anyway, your mother needs you. You told me that the other week."

"Yes, she does. She relies on me now."

"Exactly. You had the idea, though, so great job, Thibault." The lad smiled, pleasure shining in his eyes at the compliment.

Flora helped her mother prepare the supper.

The men were yet to appear, although night drew in early. The days were short as Christmas neared and the mornings dark for longer.

"It must have been easier in the olden times when people almost hibernated. I read that they used to do that. M Duclos and I were talking about it at work. He seems very lonely, Mama."

"Has he no friends?"

"It doesn't seem so. He never mentions anybody and never seems to go to anyone's home for a meal or anything. I asked him what he did last Saturday and Sunday, and he said he sat and read and did some household chores. Can you imagine?"

"Do you want to ask him to supper one evening, or perhaps for dinner at the weekend?"

"I'm not sure Luca would be at all happy, and Rainier might not be pleased either."

"I'll speak to Rainier and see what he says," Delphi volunteered. "It's always useful when the mayor is a friend."

"He doesn't like to do the Germans' bidding, I'm sure. After all, he informed them the radio transmitter was no longer in the area, and I'm not convinced he really did have information regarding that, as he wrote in his letter."

"Leave it with me. Before we say anything to Luca, I'll speak with Rainier."

Flora sat on the stairs later that evening, listening to her mother and Rainier. There was no sign of Luca.

"Mmm, I see," she heard her stepfather say.

"It wouldn't do any harm, and it might even help to have an important person such as the mayor as a friend," Delphi said.

Delphi's voice lowered and Flora had to strain to catch her words. "I think she might be interested in him. She could do worse. By all accounts he's personable and seems kind to her."

"Now, Delphi, don't be getting ideas."

"Why not? It's about time."

"Let's stick to the point. Do we want him here or not? We'll need to watch what we say. There can be no question of the slightest show of criticism of the Nazis."

Flora had gone to bed early, but sleep eluded her. In the end, she put on her dressing gown and stepped silently down the stairs to make a cup of warm milk with some sugar in it. Perhaps that would help her to relax. Her mind was all a dither about the conversation she had overheard Delphi and Rainier having, and now she wondered what Luca was up to, as well.

She was still undecided about whether he was lazy and up to no good or against the Germans and prepared to do something about it. If this was the case, he would be putting himself and them in danger. The radio she had glimpsed was evidence of that. Maybe, though, he was simply flirting with ideas and taking nothing seriously.

She entered her bedroom again. Carefully carrying her cup, she closed the door, not wishing to disturb her parents. Then she became aware of stealthy sounds.

Luca must be returning from wherever he had been this time. Her parents' door opened then closed, and footsteps padded past her bedroom. She waited. Placing her cup down, she decided a little more covert listening would not go amiss.

At the top of the stairs, she stood still and listened with ears straining. The sound of some clinking glass or china and then the murmur of male voices came to her. This was no good. She would need to be closer. She hurried back for her cup. If she was caught, she could say she had been about to return it. She crept down.

"So how did it go?" Rainier's deep voice was sonorous.

"We found Pierre's father and made up some stuff about visiting his son. I'm not sure, but he probably thought that a bit odd after all this time. Anyway, Pierre's not there. He's a prisoner of war over on the Belgian border somewhere."

"That's a blow."

"Yes, in a way, but after a lot of skirting around M. Martin gradually started to open up. I think he'll be our man. He seems sensible and categorically denounced the Nazis. He knows of some of the Germans occupying the village of Chenonceaux and seems to have some idea of the routines around the château regarding them."

"Did you get to share anything more obvious with him?"

"Not really. It's all so risky. We must be certain of him. We said we'd pay another visit next week."

"Well, it's a step forward. If we can gain access that way, I'm sure we can do some damage. Sounds like a good evening's work, lad."

"I'm truly whacked."

"I'm not surprised. Leading this double life, up early and to bed late. Get some sleep now," Rainier said.

Flora turned and scooted back upstairs. She managed to seek the sanctuary of her room before heavy footsteps approached from below.

CHAPTER 28

The next morning, Luca discovered the plan to invite M Duclos to dinner at the weekend. His reaction was not what Flora had expected. They stood opposite each other, she with her arms folded and he with his hands on his hips and his head to one side. There was a calculating expression in his eyes.

"Mmm, I see," Luca said. "That could be useful."

"Useful? What do you mean by useful?" Flora was tired and not a little resentful of Luca. He was up to something, and she couldn't work out what.

He shrugged. "It can't hurt, having the mayor as a friend. That might help us to understand what he and the Germans are up to now."

"I'm not spying, I'm offering friendship," Flora said.

"Right. Friendship, is it?"

"Meaning … nothing else." Flora crossed to the sink, put her plate and cup in the bowl and left the room with a glance that would have made Medusa proud. As she headed for her bedroom, her fingernails dug into her palms and she gave a silent howl of frustrated anger. He didn't seem to be a closet collaborator, but he was still grumpy and mean and sneaky.

Luca had travelled a reasonable distance yesterday, and all the hedging about the older man at the château had made him tense.

Now what've I done? he thought. *This bloody war. Nothing is straight. Everything is warped. I've come to understand that my petty adolescent jealousies were unfounded. Would I have had a relationship with Flora? I might well have done. After all, she's very attractive, and*

175

despite her flouncing around she has courage and strength. His groin grew tight. *Humph! But she's becoming interested in this Duclos, and I need to go along with it in case he is useful. Loyalty to an ideal is so difficult at times.*

He left the kitchen and went outside to see how the ice-wine grapes were doing. There weren't many this year. It was always tricky to get them picked after a frost when the concentration of sugars and acidity were greater, but before they rotted on the vine. Then they had to be pressed before thawing, which was an all-night job. Normally, he wouldn't produce this and nor would any neighbours, but Luca knew, from visits to Alsace and Germany before the war, that it was a speciality and much prized. It was an experiment he had been keen to try, but only a small sample for family consumption. He needed something normal, away from all the intrigue and stress and thoughts of his step-cousin. He strode across to the vinification room.

When Flora arrived at work, M Duclos was there before her. The door to his room was open, and he called through a 'good morning'. She withdrew the letter from her pocket and looked at the envelope for several seconds, before taking a deep breath and knocking.

"Come in. No need to be so formal," M Duclos said, looking up and smiling. Crinkles appeared at the corners of his eyes, and there was a dimple in his left cheek. Blue eyes pierced her thoughts.

"My mother and stepfather are inviting you for dinner. I hope that's not too forward." Her neck became warm and she fumbled with the letter before handing it over. She shrugged. "You don't often seem to go out... They wondered if you'd like some company, but if it's not convenient..."

"That's so kind." He nodded and opened the envelope. Perusing the note, he looked at her and said, "Please tell your mother I'd love to come. That would be splendid. It is a bit of a lonely job, this." He made no mention of his personal circumstances. "Here are some letters for you to type this morning." He handed her a folder, indicating an end to pleasantries and the continuation of work.

The weekend dinner came around quickly. A knock on the door heralded the arrival of M Duclos but when Flora opened it, all she saw was his back as he bent to remove the cycle clips from his ankles. He raised his head. "Didn't want to get my good trousers caught in the chain."

She stood back and pulled the door wide.

He kissed her on each cheek as a greeting, rather than a conventional handshake. "We are familiar enough with each other now, *n'est-ce pas?*" he said in his formal manner.

Overwhelmed with confusion, Flora ran her fingers through her hair and smoothed her skirt, giving herself time to face the family.

As the mayor entered the room, Rainier and Delphi stepped forward to shake his hand. "So pleased you could come," Delphi said.

"Please, let Flora have your coat and do take a seat. What may I get you to drink? A little apero always helps." Rainier indicated a tray of bottles and decanters. "I might have a small whisky. I have a shot or two left from before the war. You are most welcome to join me, or I have here an exceptionally good pastis from *Distillerie Combier.*"

"Ah yes, *Combier* in Saumur. It's not often I taste that one. It's particularly smooth, but I cannot deny a whisky would be an exceptional treat. *Merci*, M Harman."

"It's Rainier, and my wife is Delphi. First names today, I think, as this is a social occasion."

"Yes, indeed. I am André. I'm very pleased to be here. Thank you, Rainier." He raised his glass to the family.

"My dears, what will you have?" Rainier turned to Delphi and Flora.

Typical Luca, Flora thought while drinks were organised. *He's done his disappearing act again. He's so rude.*

When everyone had a drink, they all clinked glasses. Raising them, they chorused "*Salut!*"

Luca arrived at that moment from somewhere deep in the house. Flora glanced at him and was sure the tension must be showing in her eyes. She was aware her shoulders were taut, too, and tried to relax. He gave a broad smile to the guest and with an outstretched hand, came across the room. "I'm so sorry, I didn't hear you arrive," he said.

Whether this was true or not, Flora couldn't be sure, but as she looked at him, she had to admit that he looked particularly handsome out of the blue overalls and thick cotton work jacket. His dark hair shone cleanly and curled onto his collar. It was unfashionably long, but it suited his square Harman jaw and straight nose. His eyes were merry for a change, and a smile lit his face, transforming his whole demeanour. His body had long since attracted her, despite her resolve. Luca was taller than M Duclos, and his shoulders were broader. She recalled seeing him in the courtyard under the pump that day she had peered from the window. She became aware of her heart beating and her neck warming. Still, physical attraction was nothing compared to respect.

The meal was delicious. Delphi was a cook with high standards and professional experience. The lamb was tender, pink and succulent, the vegetables done perfectly. The salad course, even at this time of year, was clean and crisp and the cheeses, made locally, were creamy.

"You did well to find such a good cut of meat," André said.

"One of our farmer friends has been bringing on a lamb, and it reached hogget stage at just the right time. We were fortunate indeed. Not too small and not too old and tough," Delphi said. "No dessert, though, I'm afraid. Some things are in short supply."

"I've eaten too much already. I can't remember when I last ate so well. It doesn't seem worth spending time on preparation for only me at home. I tend to peck at things."

"Do you have family locally?" Delphi collected plates as she asked.

"My parents died a few years ago. They were both quite young. My father-in-law is still with us, but he's on his own now. He suffered badly with my wife's passing. *Ma belle-mère* lives apart and moved to the Swiss border. We don't meet often. Less and less, in fact. It took my father-in-law a long time to accept it all. It distresses him to be with me on my own and to remember what my wife and I had together. There are moments when I'm bitter about everything, but life continues, so I work hard and get by. Things get easier with time."

Flora's throat developed a lump. She swallowed. *Poor man. I'm glad we invited him today.* "Will you take coffee, *m'sieur*?"

"Thank you, Flora. That would be lovely." When he smiled, her heart jumped again. She was in such a tizzy.

"Let's go through to the *salon*," Delphi said. "We'll be more comfortable, and the fire is lit so it's cosy. Will you make the coffee, Flora?"

"Yes, it won't take long. The water's hot already."

Once they were seated, and the cups and sugar cubes were distributed, Luca asked, "Do you have many dealings with our Protectors, *m'sieur*?"

Rainier looked at him and coughed. Flora guessed he was hoping to catch Luca's attention and warn him of dangerous territory. Her gaze darted between them, but Luca refused to be intimidated and would not look at the older man.

"Inevitably there is correspondence, but they leave me to get on. I'm unsure of the future, though, especially with these recent changes. It's difficult to predict. We'll all be fine so long as we obey their rules and don't rock the boat," he said with a nod.

Rainier said, "André can't tell us much about his work, Luca. We shouldn't ask. It's confidential." He turned to their visitor. "We don't want to place you in an awkward position, *m'sieur*."

Time passed in pleasant conversation, as all strove to keep away from anything sensitive. It grew late.

"I must be going," André said. "Thank you so much for your invitation. It has been wonderful to have company and such good food."

As he went to leave, Rainier held his coat for him and Delphi gave him his hat. "You must come again," she said.

"Why not come and share our Christmas meal on the 24th? You would be most welcome," Rainier said, looking at Luca for confirmation.

"Yes, indeed," Luca offered obligingly.

Flora looked at her step-cousin. She was sure surprise showed on his face and then excitement sparkled in his eyes. She busied herself collecting coffee cups. *What's he up to now? Is he going to fish for more information, or is he just cosying up to André? That would be a dangerous game. I must speak with Rainier about him.*

"I'll see you in the morning, Flora," André said. "Thank you for your hospitality, too."

He came across and kissed her on each cheek. Flames engulfed them and she smiled at him, avoiding Luca's eyes but uncomfortably aware of him watching her.

CHAPTER 29

It was late in the afternoon by the time Luca and Antoine arrived at the Château de Chenonceau. They rested their bikes behind a tall hedge and skirted the property, keeping out of sight of the château's windows as they searched for the concierge, the father of their old school friend. They found him in his tractor, picking up ash logs with the fork fixed to the front. It was dank and drizzly, so he was well wrapped up. He already had a trailer loaded with cut wood to be moved from the tract of forest to the back of the château, where the logs would be stored in an outhouse and taken when needed for the ancient and enormous fireplaces.

Since the flood earlier that year, the beautiful gardens had become sorrowful. The river had ravaged them. The gardeners had been called to the war, leaving the concierge on his own. All he could do was keep the house warm enough and perform some minor maintenance. Despite all the money from their chocolate enterprises, the incumbent Menier family had an uphill battle on their hands. Though *Madame* Simone Menier used private rooms, smaller and cosier, the old building had to be kept warm and aired if it was to survive, even the long gallery. It was this part of the château that Luca and Antoine needed to access. The gallery had been built above the bridge of Diane de Poitiers, who had been the king's mistress in the sixteenth century. It spanned the River Cher, and so was the gateway from Occupied France into the Free Zone.

Luca waved and caught the attention of the concierge behind the tractor wheel. The noisy engine died as he turned the key.

He touched his cap. "Boys."

"*M'sieur*," they chorused and reached up to shake his hand.

"Have you any news of your Pierre? I hope he's alright, *m'sieur*," Luca said.

"No news," the fellow said. "But I suppose that's good. My wife and I might have heard if it was bad."

"Yes, indeed."

"So, what brings you this way? Twice in as many weeks? You have something on your minds. I can guess what."

Neither Luca nor Antoine ventured to say anything. This was risky business.

"Oh, come along now. Don't be shy."

Was the old man teasing or testing them? They could easily show their hand and regret it.

"This place is unique, *n'est-ce pas?*" He grinned at them, exposing gaps in his yellow tobacco-stained teeth. "We all sense the possibilities. In fact, I've used it myself. I was offered a side of pork. Am I going to turn that down? Of course not. Pfft! I had to fetch it, though. It's not that hard. *Madame* Menier unlocks the door at times … when we need it so." He guffawed, showing a wide mouth and many crinkles around his eyes. His nicotine-stained moustache had gathered moisture from his labours, and he took a grubby rag from his pocket and wiped it. "So, my boys, does that help you?"

"Yes, indeed, sir," Luca said. "We are speaking the same language here."

"All of us have to be so careful these days," Antoine added.

"So, what is it you wish to do?" The old man sniffed loudly.

"We'd like to go across to the Occupied Zone and return the same night," Luca said.

The man nodded. "When?"

Luca looked at Antoine, who shrugged.

"Next week, maybe. There's an old moon on Thursday, I worked out, so it will be darker," Luca said.

No other information was divulged. All three understood that to know as little as possible was wise.

On their return journey, Antoine asked, "Do we ask Thibault to come along?"

"I think we have to this time. He's beginning to get restless at not being included. At least if he comes and takes a full part in this outing, he'll have incriminated himself too, so it'll be harder for him to inform on us."

"Let's not tell him until the last minute, then. He won't have the opportunity to let anyone else in on it."

"We could ask him to join us but not share with him where or why until it's time to leave," Luca said.

"Exactly. That's the best plan."

"Will you tell Hubert? You're more likely to see him before me. Let's meet at my place. Say at 22.00 hours?"

"Shall we make it 23.00? There'll be less people around. Whatever time we choose is after curfew, so that makes no difference. *M'sieur* back there better make sure he keeps that door open until we're ready to return. We've no idea where to go or what to do when we get over there." Antoine looked worried.

"It's become real suddenly." Luca voiced their fears. "We're familiar with the area, though. Before the occupation, it was a regular journey for us when we went selling our wine."

"True. We better come up with a firm plan of exactly where we're going and what we'll do." They continued to discuss their ideas in lowered voices.

By the time Luca reached the haven of his own kitchen it was late, and the family were upstairs preparing for bed. There was a smell from the meal consumed earlier that set his stomach rumbling. He scouted around to find something to eat. On the range, a pan full of garlicky liquor had grown cold. When he looked into the pantry, a plate of snails lay prepared on a marble slab. Ah, he hadn't had those since his mother had died. Flora and Delphi had been out looking in all the damp places under hedgerows and bushes a couple of days ago and had returned with a bucket of the huge white-shelled variety. These would be the first course of their Christmas dinner. Beside the snails was a bowl containing the remains of the garlic-flavoured butter that had been used to season them.

Cutting himself a hunk of bread, Luca slathered it with the butter and returned to the kitchen. Taking a big bite, he flopped onto a chair. He was exhausted. His back and shoulders ached with tension.

Just then, the door opened and Flora stood there, looking at him. Her hair was tousled and her dressing gown was loose, exposing the lace of her nightdress.

"Do you want some?" Luca waved his crust at her.

"Mmm, why not? Where've you been off to so late?"

"Better you don't know." He recognised her cynical look. "No, really, it's safer that way."

She stretched across him to reach the butter and their arms touched.

"Oh Flora," he said and looked at her, his consuming weariness causing his broad shoulders to slump. "What a state we're in. I wish we could go back to how we used to be before all these political complications."

He was aware that her eyes rested on him. When he glanced up, he saw that her cynicism had been replaced with concern. Luca wanted so much to rest his head on her shoulder and let her take some weight from him. He leaned towards her but stopped himself and stood, knocking his chair back.

CHAPTER 30

On the 24th of December, Flora and her mother were up at dawn. They had a busy day ahead. They would be providing *apéritifs* for the workers before their own dinner commenced at about nine o'clock that night. The family would all be there for that, and André Duclos had been cordially invited too.

"Luca has been surprisingly complacent about inviting him," Flora said to Delphi as she flattened out pastry for the mini *tartelettes* that would later be filled with tiny shavings of olives in the savoury egg mix.

Due to food shortages, there would be no ham or rolled salmon this year. Still, the two women could be inventive, and they would prepare some tasty appetisers for the men and their families. Mother and daughter had yet to cook a huge batch of beans. Once they were finely chopped and had a warm mayonnaise and garlic dressing, they would be filling and delicious. Whilst not a traditional dish for the *apéritifs*, the estate workers would appreciate the reasons. Once they'd had a few glasses of wine, they would be happy enough.

As Delphi disappeared down to the cellar, she called back over her shoulder, "Luca appreciates we need to make an effort. It's a good idea to have André sympathetic to us as a family. And you like him, I think."

"Mama!" Flora said to the back of Delphi's head as she vanished down the steps.

Earlier in the year Delphi had used tomatoes, which had been plentiful, to make a sauce and had bottled it. "What about spreading this on some pastry and fashioning tiny *roulades*?" she said, having retrieved a jar and holding it up. "What do you think?"

"Good idea." Flora nodded.

They busied themselves in companionable silence for several minutes until Luca and Rainier came in from the courtyard.

"The tables are up in the sheds and the barrel is ready. What else do you need us to do?" Rainier came behind Delphi and folded his arms around her waist.

"The white cloths are up on the landing."

He reached past for a few olives as she chopped them. "Hands off," she said. "There are few enough as it is."

He nuzzled her neck, but she shook him off with a laugh. "That's unfair, M Harman. I have floury hands."

"I know it well." He chuckled and gave her neck a kiss.

Luca looked at Flora and she gave him a merry smile, entering the light-heartedness of the morning. He reached past her and lifted the spoon from the mayonnaise mixture. About to put it in his mouth, she made a grab for it. "Oh no you don't," she said, but he dodged away.

She stood with her hands on her hips and her head on one side, grinning at him. The lambent light from the open doors of the wood-burner stole the shadows from his face. Was it the warmth from that that she felt? He suddenly turned serious, and so did she as they regarded each other. They both seemed to recognise a tension of a different kind.

Flora cleared her throat and held out her hand. Luca stood still, watched her for several seconds and then handed over the spoon. He left the room and she heard his feet on the stairs.

When Luca reappeared, he had an armful of crisp, white linen for the tables outside. He avoided Flora's gaze and left. Rainier followed him out. Flora returned her attention to the cooking tasks. There was the guinea fowl to pluck and prepare, so she headed to the pantry to retrieve it. There it lay, among the other ingredients for the special meal. Vegetables and local cheeses were still plentiful. Somehow, Delphi had made apple tarts in spite of the rationing. There was five hundred grams of sugar, two hundred grams of butter and two hundred grams of margarine per week for each of the adults. Carefully managing their supplies, Delphi had had a baking spree over the last few days. The results sat on the shelves. There was even a *bûche de Noël* made with puréed chestnuts and a small amount of chocolate, skilfully ruched to look like bark. Where Delphi had found the chocolate, Flora had no idea, but it was a lovely surprise.

Rationing in the Occupied Zone seemed significantly worse. Flora had heard stories of long queues forming on certain days each week. There were also tales of unrest in the bigger cities and towns. Apparently, herring had washed up on the Normandy beaches from where they had become overpopulated in the sea between France and Great Britain. The fish had been gathered and shipped to Paris to help the hungry people there. Thankfully, here, they were protected from such desperate measures, another notch in Pétain's argument for his so-called Free Zone. Flora shook her head and grimaced.

It was soon time to feed and entertain the estate workers and their families. Having peeked at the guinea fowl and given it a baste in the oven, Flora bundled on a coat and headed out to join her parents and Luca in serving their guests. She nodded to several people that she now knew better and took up a couple of plates to start handing round the little tarts and pastry pinwheels they had made earlier. She went across to where Delphi stood next to a rotund man with a fresh complexion and a tall, slim lady. They all shook hands and made small talk for a few minutes.

"Are you alright? You look anxious," Delphi said.

"I'm fine." Flora paused before admitting, "I'm unsure how this evening will go. Will Luca be polite to André, do you suppose?"

"I'm sure it will be alright, but I'll have a quiet word with Rainier, and then he can speak to Luca. After all, we can't afford to upset the mayor, can we?"

"Exactly."

"And we want all to be smooth between us and him for your sake too."

"Mama! I work for him, that's all."

"Yes, darling, but you like him too, don't you?"

"Mmm ... I'm sorry for him." Flora knew she sounded uncertain.

As time passed, the small crowd became noisy. Since Rainier had told them to help themselves from the barrel, they were content. There was plenty of grape or apple juice for the children.

Rainier, Delphi, Luca and Flora said their goodnights and left for their own dinner. The smells that hit them upon opening the door were remarkable.

"We better get to it, Flora." Delphi took off her jacket and reached for her apron.

"What time is André Duclos arriving?" Luca turned to Flora.

"Anytime now, I should think."

Sure enough, after ten minutes there was a knock at the door and Luca opened it to the mayor.

"Come on in. *Joyeux Noël* to you." Luca held out his hand to the newcomer, who shook it and smiled as he came into the room.

André shook hands with Rainier and kissed Delphi on both cheeks, giving Flora time to take a deep breath before it was her turn. When he kissed her, she took in the heady, manly scent of citrus, spices and musk. Heat rose up her chest and neck. She turned away with his coat to hide her confusion. Flora glanced across at Luca, and she saw him observing her emotions. Her heart pounded. She hadn't experienced turmoil quite like this before.

Wine was poured and passed, and Flora took a gulp before placing her glass on the table and going to help her mother. Once they were all seated, Delphi brought the great platter of garlicky snails to the table and Rainier sliced the bread.

"Flora and I gathered and prepared them ourselves," Delphi said, following André's enquiry.

"I haven't tasted such good ones in a long while," he said. "At home before the war, my mother used to do them, but that was several years ago now."

Flora saw Luca watching André, but his expression was inscrutable. She passed the breadbasket to the others. Each of them used a slice to mop up the remaining slathers of flavoured butter.

"More wine?" Rainier did not wait for an answer but refilled each glass as the men sat back. André sighed, and the women stood to clear the dishes.

Carving and serving the *pintade* and passing the vegetables was an art performed with a customary flourish by Rainier.

"It's a long time since we've eaten so well and with such leisure," Luca said, looking at André. "Still, we don't have the deprivation that the Occupied Zone seems to be suffering, even at Christmas," he added.

Unease crept over Flora.

"We are indeed fortunate here, Luca, and André is proving to be a dedicated mayor, is he not?" Rainier passed the gravy boat to their guest with a smile.

"Absolutely." Luca inclined his head with grace and Flora breathed out.

"Perhaps, after the holiday, you might all accompany me to dine at *La Grotte de la Reine*. As mayor, I have a pass to get in there. I should like to repay your hospitality."

"My goodness, that is very fine dining, I hear," Flora said.

"We certainly cannot match that," Luca said. "But sadly, it will be difficult to escape my duties here."

"The same goes for us," Rainier said. "Perhaps you would take Flora. It's a long time since she was entertained anywhere, never mind somewhere so wonderful."

Flora was trapped. She glanced at Luca. He glared at her. Was he daring her to refuse? "That would be a treat, André. Thank you so much." She tried to discern Luca's reaction, but he looked down at his hands so she couldn't see his eyes.

Rainier passed the wine again and the meal continued. On the surface, all was relaxed and happy, but each time Flora looked at Luca, his eyes bored into her while he smiled at André with polite restraint.

The *bûche de Noël* was the highlight of the meal.

"I haven't had one of these since my wife died," André said with delight. "My daughter wanted a little toy robin to sit on ours the last time. She said it looked like a real Christmas log. Yours is impressive in these troubled times, *Madame* Harman."

"It's Delphi, remember."

"Yes, of course. Please, may I propose a toast? I should like to thank you, most sincerely, for inviting me here tonight. I raise my glass to each one of you. *Salut!*" He drank to them. "And the wine is delicious." He chuckled.

Rainier smiled and returned the well-meant expressions. Luca nodded, but there was no smile from him.

He's still smarting from my acceptance of André's generous invitation, Flora thought.

The evening broke up after coffee, with whisky and pastis offered and accepted.

"This is the last of our grounds. I've been saving them, but I cannot imagine a better way to use them," Delphi said.

"Perhaps I might find you some," André offered.

"I'm sure it would be safer for us to manage as our neighbours will," Luca said. "We don't want to be accused of anything shady."

"Luca, really!" Rainier frowned as he remonstrated with his nephew.

"I apologise, *m'sieur*. I did not intend any insult." Luca inclined his head.

"And none taken, Luca. None at all. These are sensitive times in which we live."

Eventually André took his leave with thanks. Handshakes and kisses were exchanged, as well as wishes for a peaceful Christmas Day. Flora gave a final wave as he mounted his bicycle and turned the corner, before she closed the door.

"You really shouldn't have been so surly, Luca," she said. "He's only showing his gratitude by taking me out."

"You think?"

She was saved from saying more when there was a knock on the door.

They all looked at each other.

"Perhaps he left something. His gloves, maybe. I saw he took his hat," Flora said.

Luca went to open the door. Flora came up behind him.

"What in the name of…?" Flora gasped. "Edith!"

CHAPTER 31

Flora instinctively knew this was a covert visit, and not just from Edith's nervous look over her shoulder before entering.

"Come in, quickly."

Even in the Free Zone, it was highly irregular for an English girl to be wandering the French countryside in the middle of the night at Christmas.

" Luca!" Edith turned to him. "You've changed since we last met."

"It must be eight or nine years since you came to visit us," Flora said. "What on earth are you doing here?" Flora opened her arms and gave her best friend a hug, then stood back to take in what she saw.

At school, Edith's hair had been golden, like the barley in July, and she'd been as voluptuous as a ripe plum. Now her hair looked badly cut instead of shaped and shiny. Her blue eyes had dark smudges underneath, but nevertheless they shone with excitement. Her clothing looked outmoded and shabby. She'd been clothes-conscious before and had always managed to look fashionable, even in the shapeless school uniform. Now she looked like any other local person, making do and tired.

Good thing, Flora thought. *I hope nobody has seen her.*

"I cannot believe this. It's been so long. I've written, but I didn't hear back." Flora shrugged. "It's trying times here."

"Would you mind closing the shutters?" Edith looked at Luca and then at Rainier. "I'm not supposed to be here, of course. I'm sure I've not been seen." She said this as if trying to reassure herself. "It's why we chose today. Everyone should be indoors, celebrating Christmas."

"How did you get here? What are you doing? Why now? It seems so strange," Flora said.

"Let her catch her breath." Delphi invited Edith to sit. Then she went to the stove to reheat the last of the coffee. "This is the best I can offer, I'm afraid."

"It's a lifesaver." Edith took the cup and wrapped her hands around it. "There's a cold wind tonight."

"What about food? Are you hungry?" Delphi, ever practical, started to bring things from the pantry. Cold meat, the rest of the savoury roulades put by for tomorrow, the bread from the long drawer in the table.

"You're safe here," Rainier said. "All of us here will keep your secrets." He clapped Luca on the shoulder and went to put his arm around Delphi before heading outside to close the shutters.

"There was a radio transmitter message from very close to here. Someone sent word. Slightly garbled spelling, but the people I work for picked it up and pinpointed the location," she said.

"You can tell us everything." Flora looked at Luca with more understanding, remembering the box she had seen in the barn.

"How on earth…?" Luca came to the table and sat. Rainier joined him when he returned.

"I knew you were all here, of course, from your letters, Flora. I remembered visiting all those years ago, too. We need to know who sent that message. It's quite urgent. Several people like me are training in England, but we're not ready to send them all over yet. Give it three more months and several of us will be arriving. It's vital to know who we can trust, and then we can make contact."

"How did you get here, though?" Flora was still very puzzled.

"And what do you mean by *us*?" Luca was frowning.

"With the fall of France, Great Britain started a unit the following month. I can't say too much, but I've been training with them since August last year. We want to set up networks to support any anti-Nazi disruption. We can train people in all sorts of stuff, and even get access to weapons. We're also going to be involved in propaganda, distributing leaflets and the like."

"How did you get into the middle of France? Edith, tell me, please." Flora was pleading by this stage.

"I was dropped off by aeroplane. We have a type called a Westland Lysander. It doesn't carry many people, but since it was only me this time…"

"What? You parachuted in or something?"

"No. I've received the training, but I didn't need to parachute this time." Edith gave a chuckle. "The Lysander only needs a really short runway. Not even four hundred metres. I was landed in a field not far away. I've walked from there. They're coming back for me the night after next, so I must be away and ready. It's a very quick turnaround, as you can imagine. There are so few Germans in this region still. It's not too bad, but of course there are some French *gendarmes* who might be happy to earn a little extra by giving information. I'm putting my trust in you all." She looked around at each of them.

"But how did the pilot know where to land?" It was Luca's turn to demand answers.

"Yes, well, that was a bit tricky this time, but by April of next year we should have even more operatives and friends on the ground to signal. We'll also have a handy bit of kit to help with that. We call her Rebecca, or sometimes Eureka. I can't say more now."

Luca shook his head and frowned.

"We're still finding our way with all this. That's partly why I'm here. I don't have much time. I need to connect with whoever sent that transmission. We need to start building contacts."

"When you say 'we', that's this group you were talking about just now?" Flora asked.

"Yes, I'm in F section. I got in because my French is reasonable. The accent's a bit different because I learned mainly in Switzerland, of course, but it'll be alright. There's RF section who are mainly native French. They'll be doing more dangerous stuff than me."

"Just you being here seems frightfully tricky to me," Delphi said.

"We have so much to do. There'll be many opportunities very soon. Can you help, at all? Even an inkling will do."

The family looked from one to another but said nothing.

"We have to trust each other, or we'll get nowhere. I must find out who has that radio," Edith said, taking a bite of food from the plate Delphi had placed in front of her. Her gaze rested on Luca. "You know, don't you?"

Flora saw him glance at Rainier, who nodded almost imperceptibly.

"Yes, it's us."

"Really? Oh, that's wonderful. That makes life so much easier, I can't begin to tell you. How on earth did you come by it?"

Luca and Rainier, between them, told the story. Flora didn't want to remember that day when they must have acquired the set.

CHAPTER 32

The next day dawned bright and clear. The cerulean sky sang in tune with Flora's heart. It was so good to have her friend close. It was Christmas morning and the world had retracted. She could pretend there was no work and no André, no secrets, no shortages, no complicated relationships, no war. She sang as she collected the eggs for breakfast. She and Edith had talked into the small hours as they'd squashed up in Flora's bed together, eventually sliding into a deep and exhausted sleep. It had been as if they were back at the school, creeping into each other's beds for warmth.

"Good morning, Mrs Henrietta, hello, Beaker. You're in fine plumage today. Where's Dixie chick? Is she sitting on one still?" Flora spoke with the family's turkeys. There was also Chanticleer, Monet, Flossy and Bossy. The oldest was Tyrannosaurus Pecks because of his ferocity.

"You haven't named them all, surely?" Edith said as she approached Flora.

"Only a few. Luca thinks I'm insane. To him they are future food and no more. He doesn't get the joke of their names at all, of course. I did hear him talking to them the other day, though, so he's not as hard as he'd like me to think. He doesn't know I was listening. I was upstairs watching from the window." She laughed.

"So, he has no idea you secretly observe him." Edith nudged Flora's arm.

"No, and don't you dare say. For ages, I've been wondering if he can be trusted." Flora picked up a final egg.

"Now you tell me." Edith looked concerned.

"No, listen. When I found them in the barn that night and discovered what they were up to, his unexplained absences became clearer. It's like I said last night: I do believe he's okay and on the right side. But he can be very surly."

Together they made their way back to the kitchen.

"Mmm," Edith said. "After all our chatter last night, it sounds like you're clearly drawn to him for one reason or another. It's a shame I won't get to meet this André, though."

"That would be risky. Inevitably he works in close connection with the Boche. He was their choice, after all."

"He sounds really nice despite that, and rather in need of cheering up. He could be useful to us, Flora."

Flora hefted the basket into her other hand and looked at her friend. "Useful?"

"There is much to talk about today," Luca said as he regarded Edith with a serious gaze over breakfast.

"Yes, indeed. Is there anyone else I should meet? It's Christmas, but this would be one of the safest times. Most people will be indoors, recovering from the excesses of last night."

"What about Antoine?" Flora looked at Luca and then across to Rainier.

"Antoine?" Edith raised her eyebrows in a question.

"He's a friend of Luca," Delphi said, turning from where she was cooking the eggs. There was a glorious aroma of garlic and warm bread, as well as the sound of sizzling lard in the pan on the stove.

"I do appreciate all that you're doing for me," said Edith. "It's almost like coming home after a long absence."

"We normally have more than bread and coffee at Christmas. One more to cook for is a joy, especially one who is so appreciative," Delphi added.

"So, what about Antoine?" Flora pursued the original question.

"Antoine should be brought in, and possibly Hubert," Luca said.

"And Thibault?" It was Rainier's turn to ask.

"No, definitely not."

"Who's Thibault?" Edith took a plate of food from Delphi.

Luca explained their reservations as breakfast was distributed.

"I would agree about this lad, Thibault. We are talking serious stuff here. We can take no chances at all." Edith took another forkful of the eggs. "And what do you see as your priorities? There's so much we can do together."

"Recently, we've arranged a passage into the Occupied Zone." Luca explained about the Château de Chenonceau and its unique position spanning the River Cher. "We're going at night to cut telephone wires."

Flora looked at him with fresh interest. Her heart beat faster. She'd known nothing of this. This was perilous. Edith being here had been a game until now, something fantastic and intoxicating. Last night, she had been transported back to their romps and pranks. This new information was frightening, and involved people she cared about.

"Now that would be useful, coming across this way too," Edith said.

Flora was puzzled, not really understanding the implications of that. She made a mental note to ask later.

"Can you get Antoine and Hubert here today? Perhaps too many questions would be asked at their homes," Edith said. "It would be helpful to look at the transmitter together. Maybe I can help you with it. I have had quite a bit of training in that department." She turned to Flora. "I was stationed in Scotland after the prelim school. It was gruelling at times, but you'd be surprised what I learned. Then I was at Beaulieu."

"Down in Hampshire?"

"Yes. I wasn't able reply to letters because half the time they didn't find me, and the other half there wasn't time to turn around, never mind write."

"Don't worry about that now. I can see there's a frightful amount to do before you have to leave."

"I'll get Antoine here and Hubert too, if possible," Luca said.

After lunch, they gathered in the barn. Flora watched as Luca uncovered the transmitter from its hiding place.

"That's impressive. It should be safe enough there. The only thing we wondered about at the training sessions was whether the Germans have direction finding kit and how successful they are. It's too soon to say yet, but it's too late if they find you. You should move it around as much as is safely possible," Edith said.

"We talked about that." Rainier nodded as he spoke. "We'll start doing it, Luca."

The younger man looked up from his task. "Mmm."

Edith knelt next to Luca. A sound was discernible in the lane.

"Oh my…" Flora said and rushed to the door as she heard Luca pulling covers back over the box in front of him. *How to explain all of us being in here on Christmas afternoon?* Flora thought, guilty fear filling her heart.

She fumbled with the catch and opened the barn to see Antoine approaching. She grasped the edge of the wood. They had been unable to get to Hubert. He lived a little further away.

"You gave us such a fright. We all imagined the Germans arriving. Come in quickly."

As they entered the gloomy interior, they saw the family group standing around the old wine vat in the corner, trying to appear as if they were debating over it. It didn't fool Flora, and she wondered if it would have deceived any unwanted visitors.

Everyone shook hands and introductions were made. Flora watched Antoine as he took Edith's small hand in his and said, "*Enchanté, mademoiselle.*" He gave her one of his piercing looks.

Mon Dieu, he's such a flirt. He was doing that with me only a few weeks ago but not now, thank goodness. He knows me too well and understands I'm not taken in by him. He does it with all women, I've discovered. She smiled to herself. *He's incorrigible. I must warn Edith about him.*

As they knelt around the box and Luca unpacked all its components, Flora's head was close to his. She became aware of him. She smelled his earthy masculinity, and glancing across she could see the dark shadow around his chin and concentration creasing his forehead. He swept his hair from his eyes and she sat back on her heels, distancing herself. A deep breath calmed her racing heart. He looked at her, but she could tell he was in a distant place, his mind on nothing but the task in hand. Edith's voice broke her thoughts, explaining about frequencies and controls.

"There have been few Germans in this region, but that's changing since Case Anton in the south. They've been allowing the French some autonomy. It's in their own interest, but it might not continue for much longer. They have their spies, as well as increasing troop movements all over France. Be careful. I have a list of codes here. You must do this." She demonstrated how to tap out a message. "If you learn these by heart, it will be quicker and safer. These are the frequencies for you to use." She showed them another piece of paper. "It goes without saying that these must be kept safe and not with the box. Destroy this." She held out the information they had used previously. "This is obsolete, and you're very lucky it was picked up by someone back at home. At the moment, it's a clean machine. From what I understand from you, Luca, they think it's gone to the coast. Let's keep it that way. It'll be very useful indeed, back at the ranch, to know we have you and it here. The more musicians we have, the better."

"Musicians?" All this seemed alien and disturbing to Flora.

"Radio operators. It's slang," Edith said. "The other thing we're considering is developing more messages to send to agents over here via the BBC evening broadcasts. Up until now, they've mainly involved those in Paris."

"We've heard some of that," Flora said. "We call it *Radio Londres*."

"Before I leave tonight, we'll write some random times down as a list, and for now you must stick to those for sending and receiving messages. That way, we can communicate until I return."

Heading back to the warmth of the farmhouse, Flora walked beside Edith and snatched her opportunity. "What do you mean when you say the château might be useful 'coming this way too'?"

"We need a route for airmen who have been shot down. Another way to get them out of France. If we smuggle them into this so-called unoccupied zone, we could get them down to the south to Spain and out that way."

"But they'd need places to stay en route," Flora said.

"Yes, they would."

Back in the kitchen it was a merry group. Release of tension was causing much chattering from the younger generation, and

Rainier and Delphi were happy to serve the drinks and pre-lunch snacks.

"I must tell you my cover name and story so that we're all on the same page if questioned," Edith said. "Sorry to be serious again for a moment, but it's for everyone's safety."

They all looked at her.

"I'm Colette, and I'm your cousin, Flora. Just as Delphi married a Frenchman, so did my mother, your sister, Delphi."

"But…" Delphi started.

"I know. They're both in England. Rose is with Michael. This is Izzy I'm talking about. Her recent history is perfect. She visited Germany a lot before the war, didn't she? That helps. They'll see her as sympathetic to their cause. It's alright. She's not. They can't check that she's in England either. In fact, they will be led to believe she moved to the USA after my father died. That was a traffic accident. He went down a ravine and the car burst into flames. *Très tragique.* I am alone and so that's why I visit you here when I am able. You must call me Colette from now on. Never forget or be careless about this. But enough. *Joyeux Noël.*"

"Here." Rainier offered the bottle again and they were all happy to take a glass and move off the narrow path of danger they all walked.

CHAPTER 33

When Flora entered the office after the holiday break, André was already there, unoccupied and perched against her desk as if awaiting her arrival. She glanced at the clock above the new framed emblem of Philippe Pétain. The motto on the wall had changed, too. Gone was the familiar '*liberté, égalité, fraternité*'. It had been replaced with the stylized throwing axe in French colours and the words '*travail, famille, patrie.*' Flora looked with contempt. *Such arrogance. We've always respected work, family and our homeland. We don't need reminding. France stands for things far deeper and more philosophical.*

Turning to her employer, she said, "I'm not late, am I?" She removed her hat with haste and went to hang it along with her coat on the stand in the corner.

"No, I wanted a word. That's all."

Now she was nervous.

"I had such a good time with your family at Christmas. I would like to return the favour and take you out for dinner as we discussed. I'm sorry your parents are unable to come, but it would give me much pleasure if you would honour me." He spoke with sincerity, but it still sounded somewhat pompous.

"Oh. Oh, I see," Flora said, playing for time.

"*La Grotte de la Reine* is the best restaurant, and they will not have the shortages that are beginning to appear elsewhere. I can assure you it will be *magnifique.*"

"Well, I'm not sure," she said, ferreting around her mind for a suitable excuse.

"I insist, *mademoiselle.*" The mayor bowed his head in old-fashioned deference. "Really, I owe you this small thing, and I should very much enjoy your company. Please, say yes. Evenings are lonely, and it would be a joy to have you with me."

Flora looked into his pleading eyes and took pity. "Yes, M Duclos, indeed I should be pleased to accept."

"Yes, it is best to stay with surnames at work, but I hope you will call me André when we are out together."

She smiled, unsure how to respond.

"Shall we say this Friday?"

"So soon? Will you be able to take a reservation that quickly, *m'sieur*?"

"I shall try this morning. In fact, right now." He hurried from her room to his.

"I shall be going out with M Duclos on Friday," Flora announced at dinner that evening. She glanced fleetingly at Luca, but couldn't read his expression.

"How marvellous, darling," Delphi said. "It's about time you had some fun. Is he taking you to *La Grotte de la Reine*? He mentioned it when he was here."

Flora nodded and smiled.

"That's so exciting. We must plan carefully what you will wear."

Flora looked directly at Luca, daring him to comment.

"That is indeed marvellous," he said. "It's a splendid opportunity. He seems an admirable chap. Of course, he is the mayor, a most important fellow. Well done, Flora." His voice was flat, and didn't reflect the enthusiasm of his words.

Flora was uneasy and looked away. Was he pleased? A trace of his old resentment of her had seemed to inflect his speech.

"What have you to wear? I know — there's your emerald green dress. You haven't had the opportunity to show that off for such an age. Perfect. We must hang it out in the sunshine to air. You don't want him to remember you by the smell of mothballs like some ancient maiden aunt." Delphi was bubbling with excitement.

"It's a bit revealing. The straps are so thin," Flora said.

"You could have my silk scarf around your shoulders. It's the right colour and shade, and if it seems appropriate you can remove it once you are seated. Will there be dancing?"

"Come on, Luca. Let's leave the women to their planning. You enjoy yourself, *ma petite*," Rainier said. He kissed the top of Flora's head before they left the room.

Friday came too quickly. Flora was all a-jitter. First, she had a long bath and washed her hair. Then, with her dressing gown firmly tied over her underwear and petticoat, she knelt in front of the fire to dry it and then brushed it. The motion of the hairbrush was soothing. It gave her time to think. Delphi was somewhere in the house, and the men were outside. Alone, she thought of little else but the evening ahead. Her mind wandered briefly to Edith, and how much she would have liked to share this. Her friend's Resistance work had taken her Flora knew not where, but it must have been important, the way she disappeared like a shadow with the retreating sun at twilight.

André was coming at seven thirty. Should she be ready or make a pretence of being late? No, that wasn't her style. She would be ready. *I'm going to make sure I don't drink too much. I wonder who else will be there. Will the room be full of uniforms? I hope the dress is not too over the top. What if all the other people are in winter skirts and pullovers? Don't be silly, Flora. It's like a night club. Should I bother with Mama's scarf? Yes, it gives you an extra option.* She heaved a sigh and put the brush down. *This won't do. Make-up next.*

Delphi knocked and came into her room as Flora applied her lipstick. "That's getting low," her mother said.

"Mmm. *Madame* at the *pharmacie* suggested I buy another as soon as possible. She suggested there would be a shortage of make-up. I'm not sure if she was just being a pessimist or trying to make an extra sale."

"Here, let me help you with your frock. He'll be here and you won't be ready." Delphi took the emerald dress from its hanger. "This really is the most gorgeous colour. It suits you perfectly." She sniffed it. "It's fine. No trace of mothballs," she added.

Flora stepped into the dress and slipped the thin straps over her shoulders. Her mother fastened all the tiny buttons at the back.

"Turn around and let me see," Delphi said. "Oh, my darling girl. You remind me of myself on the ship coming from Australia. Do you remember the balloon ball? I danced with Rainier that night and knew that I loved him." She smiled. "Mind you, it was a while before we met again, wasn't it?"

"But it all ended happily." Flora gave her mother a hug. "Love you both," she said and saw tears in Delphi's eyes.

"I'm so happy for you," her mother said. "André is a lovely man."

"I'm not sure he's the one, though, so slow down, Mama."

"Well, you'll have a lovely evening." Delphi picked up a pair of dark green opal earrings. "Mama and Papa Dight gave me these." She examined them. "Genuine Australian opals. Papa Dight said they were to remind me of George. As if I would ever forget! But that was a long time ago, and I'm so lucky to have you and to have found Rainier."

Delphi had just finished arranging her scarf around Flora's shoulders when a car entered the courtyard below. Mother and daughter looked at each other, Flora with panic in her eyes and Delphi with a smile.

"You look fabulous. Like a million *francs*," Delphi said. "Go with confidence that you'll be among the best looking."

Flora descended the stairs. As she entered the living room, Luca was there. His gaze was appraising, and his intake of breath was audible as he opened his eyes wider than usual. Then a knock at the door drew her attention away from him and she glanced at her mother, who gave her shoulder a little pat. Rainier opened it, since Luca seemed rooted to the floor.

"Come in, André," he said, shaking the mayor by the hand. Luca stepped forward and did likewise. André presented Delphi with a small posy of winter jasmine and gave Flora a buttonhole. A tiny delicate sprig of conifer, some red berries and an ivy leaf were bound together with thin brown sisal and a wisp of fine lace.

"This is so beautiful, and very ingenious at this time of year," Flora said. "Thank you so much." She kissed him on each cheek as a greeting and an expression of gratitude.

The top of his head was close to her face while he fastened the posy to her coat. When he looked up, their noses were almost touching. There was a pause when nobody moved. Then he stepped back, and the moment passed, leaving Flora's heart thumping and her legs weak.

Luca became loud and unlike himself. "Well, you two, have a lovely evening. Now, if you'll excuse me, I have work to do." He disappeared through the door and his footsteps could be heard mounting the stairs.

I'm not sure what work he has to do upstairs in his room, Flora thought.

"Have a wonderful evening," her mother said.

Rainier opened the door for them, and André stepped aside to let her pass.

Outside, he put his hand under her elbow and guided her to the car. Opening her side, he helped her to settle before moving around to take his own seat next to her. The leather squeaked as she settled back and tried to appear relaxed. Glancing at the house, she saw a shadow at the landing window. So, Luca was watching.

In the close confines of the vehicle, she was tongue-tied.

CHAPTER 34

From the outside, the restaurant looked like any other, except that it lay inside one of the many caves in the area. The sign above the glass door had a flourishing style. *La Grotte de la Reine* was announced by fine and flowing gold letters against a cream background, and above the letter 'i' there was a stylized crown. The façade was carved from the rock, but in this light it looked more grey than white. The doors were in the French style, but chiffon drapes afforded only a misted glimpse of the interior.

Inside, the style was Art Nouveau; the opulence was staggering. Flora's feet sank into the rich red pile, but she was occupied by the ceiling, which was domed glass and wrought ironwork at the far end. Stained with images of branches and leaves in delicate colours, the overall impression was of a spring evening, so although it was January, it felt warm and fresh. If the lights were off, Flora imagined that stars would penetrate the leaves. At the far end, the glow from wall lights with Lalique shades cascaded downwards, ensuring an intimate atmosphere for the diners in that area. The wall panels beneath, each in its own arch, were decorated with spring flowers and country meadows. Tall palms softened the columns, and the lighting above these was soft and mellow.

The *maître d'hôtel* greeted them with a deferential smile while someone took their coats. They followed their waiter, who walked to the far end, pulled out a chair for Flora and spread a white linen serviette on her lap. She glanced at André, who smiled. Then she looked up and saw stars peeping through the painted foliage.

"This is smart, is it not?"

"Yes, most beautiful," Flora whispered with simplicity.

A different waiter arrived and gave André the wine menu, while a third brought a tray of tiny savouries.

"This is all making me quite tongue-tied," Flora whispered across the table.

"They're friendly here. We shall have some champagne before our meal." André put the wine menu to one side and picked up that for the food.

Flora opened hers and started to study it, relieved at having something to occupy her. There were no prices written, but otherwise she assumed it was the same as André's.

"I think we should start with oysters. It's the right season for them. When I had them here once before, they were delicious."

"Oh no, André, not for me," Flora said hastily. "They would be too rich."

"Oh. Oh, right. Well, maybe some scallops or a terrine?"

"Scallops would be lovely, thank you."

They each settled on a filet mignon steak for the main course. After the waiter had taken their order and left, they both sampled the champagne.

"This is delicious," André said.

"Yes, it is, not too dry. A good choice, André." Flora was tempted to take a couple of gulps to steady her nerves, but she managed to refrain and sipped instead. André looked at her across the table, and the candlelight glowed in his eyes. She began to relax.

"Is this all suitable for you?" He sounded so formal, and it flashed through Flora's mind that Luca would be highly amused by all this.

"It is indeed. You sound as if you've been here several times before."

"Only once, in fact," he answered.

Looking around the room, Flora took in the candlelight that flickered off the glassware and the silver. A few other diners were seated and more entered, so the room was filling. The ladies wore bright colours and jewels, leaning forward as they whispered to companions seated opposite, fluttering eyes and using expressive hands. Light tinkling laughter and deeper male utterances surrounded them.

Flora became aware of being watched and as she returned her attention to André, she recognised his appraising gaze. It confused her. Aware of the warmth creeping up her neck, she was certain that her colour was heightened. She was relieved when their first course arrived. André amused her with his chatter, becoming less pompous as he relaxed with the champagne.

The waiter cleared their empty plates, but before their next course arrived, a man in grey uniform approached their table. André stood, throwing his serviette onto the chair as he did so. He stood with his heels together, as if to attention. "*Herr Major*," he said.

The officer stood very straight and nodded a greeting. "Duclos," he said. "You have a beautiful companion this evening. *Mademoiselle.*" He nodded at Flora, and then took her hand from where it rested on the white cloth. He raised it to his lips. "*Major* Weber at your service, *mademoiselle.*"

"*Major*," she said, imitating André's greeting but having little idea what the German insignia on his uniform meant.

"The information you sent regarding the radio transmitter reached my desk. I hope you still have your ear to the ground, Duclos."

"Oh, yes, indeed, *Herr Major*," André said, clearing his throat and looking uncomfortable.

"Forgive me, *mademoiselle*," the officer said to Flora in his strangely accented French. "This is not the place for business. Enjoy your evening." Turning to André, he said, "We shall be in touch."

He returned to a table some distance away, where he joined three other officers in similar uniforms. As he sat, laughter drifted over. One of the men glanced across at their table, leaving Flora in little doubt about the subject of their mirth. She grew hot and her skin prickled.

The wine waiter arrived. Showing the label of the bottle he carried, he began the ceremony of uncorking and allowing André to sample the wine before pouring it for Flora. He left the bottle on a silver stand at the end of their table. André did not mention the visitor, but Flora noticed him glancing across the room more than once. After a while, the waiter brought their main course and André waved him away as he offered to pour more wine for them both. André did those honours himself. It was a deep, rich red that tingled the tip of Flora's tongue before it slid down her throat, where she tasted the full roundness that complemented the meal.

"This is delicious. It's a long time since I ate red meat like this," Flora said. The exterior was salty and slightly crisp, but the centre perfectly *saignant* as she had requested: tender, juicy and pink.

"Yes, there are some advantages to my position, although at times it doesn't seem like that." André glanced across again at the German officers.

The noise in the room rose as people became uninhibited with the atmosphere, good food and the wine. One lady at a table nearby wore a huge fox fur around her shoulders and laughed raucously. The Germans turned to her. Smiling, she raised her glass to them. Flora knew she didn't like the woman.

In fact, she wasn't enjoying her evening as she should. The whole place had a falseness to which she was unused and, she decided, not suited. It was brash and insensitive when so much hardship and trouble crept across the world.

"Is everything to your liking?" André wore a worried expression.

"Yes, indeed," Flora said. "I'm a little unused to all this opulence."

"Me, too, to tell the truth," said André. He put his head down and avoided her eyes. Then, after a moment, he continued, "I think it was showing off, to bring you here. I wanted to impress you."

Flora was immediately contrite. "André." She reached across the table and touched the back of his hand. "It's such a kind gesture, and this food is absolutely wonderful. I'm very grateful. Truly, I am. It's an amazing experience." His smile lit his face with a radiance she had not seen before. She withdrew her hand and picked up her knife. "Just look at all these people. It's lovely to see such enjoyment." She spoke with artificial brightness.

Despite her resolve to drink little, by the time she had sipped champagne, wine with the meal, and a delicious cherry liqueur, Flora was smiling and mellow by the time they left the restaurant. The moon was almost full, so the evening was bright. André tucked her hand under his arm as they walked back to the car. "I don't want you to slip if it's frosty," he said.

She looked up at him and smiled. *How considerate, and what a gentleman.*

"This is one of the best evenings I've had in a long, long time," he said.

"It has been different for me. I can't remember when I was last taken out like this."

"You must have had many admirers where you lived before. Was there no one special?"

"Not really." She smiled. "I did have offers, and one I thought might have been the right one, but it turned out not to be so. And then we came here. I've been busy helping at home, and now it's lovely to have a job again. One that I can really enjoy."

"I'm so pleased about that. It was a good day when you came to my office. I fear it will not get easier but with you there, I shall manage to make some good decisions and help to keep our corner of France safe."

With the warmth of the blanket over her knees, the rocking motion of the car and the hum of its engine, Flora's thoughts moved on. How would Luca have reacted to the slippery path? Would he have taken her hand like that and been protective? She doubted it. Her mind continued to pursue its own way, and Luca wheedled his way in again. She knew he wanted her to find out information, but she liked this man next to her. She couldn't betray his trust like that. Surely she owed her boss some allegiance. Life was so complicated.

The living room light was still on. Flora could see slivers around the shutters, which were closed against the chill winter air.

Mama will be up, and Rainier too. I wonder if Luca is there, or whether he has made some excuse and gone to bed.

Turning to André, she said, "Thank you for a wonderful evening, and for your generosity."

"It has been my absolute pleasure, Flora." He leaned towards her and she experienced a moment of panic.

She presented her cheek and then the other. He cleared his throat, turning his head away for a moment, and then returned to his own space. Then, as she turned towards the car door, he leaped out and ran around to open it for her and to help her out. He grabbed her gloved hand and held it. She felt awkward.

"Thank you, dear Flora." Releasing her, he hastened back to his own side of the car and watched as she made her way across the courtyard.

She gave a wave before going into the house. As she closed the door behind her, she heard the car pull away, then only had a few seconds to gather her breath before the family rose from their seats and descended upon her with their questions.

CHAPTER 35

Delphi came with arms outstretched and enfolded her. Over her shoulder, Flora's eyes met Luca's as he remained in his chair at the table. "Take her coat, Rainier. Tell me everything, darling. How did it go?" Delphi took her hand and pulled her to a chair at the table and then put the pan of water on the stove. She lifted the bottle of brown liquid made from roast chicory root and ground acorns they now had to use in place of coffee and poured some into the pan. "What did you eat? Tell me what it was like inside. I've only seen the outside. Did it smell dank inside a cave? How did André behave?" She saved her most important question until last, Flora guessed.

She did her best to describe the sumptuousness of the décor and the abundance of people wearing their finery, but she could not get halfway. It all seemed surreal now she sat back in the familiarity of home. "To be honest, I felt uncomfortable. German soldiers dine there, and half the people seemed so friendly with them. There was one ghastly woman slathered in make-up and furs. André was a gentleman, though, and I'm not sure how comfortable he felt. He confessed he wanted to impress me … and it was impressive," she added hastily. "It was very, very kind of him."

"How did he react with these Germans?" Luca spoke for the first time. He sat slouched back in his chair and played with a spoon left on the table, avoiding all eye contact.

"He had to speak to them because one of them came over to our table, but he looked uneasy," Flora said and recounted the conversation. "He was polite and courteous, this officer. But it all seemed awkward."

"Huh! Right, I'm off to bed. Work to be done in the morning." Luca got up with no further words to anyone.

After he'd gone, Flora said, "He can still be so rude sometimes."

"He's confused and upset by your outing, that's all," Rainier offered.

"I don't see why."

"He thinks you like André. It worries him because of his position as mayor in our current political climate."

"Perhaps he's a tiny bit jealous," Delphi added.

"André's a work colleague, that's all. As for jealousy, that's plain ridiculous." Flora said, jutting her chin out.

Flora intercepted a glance between Delphi and Rainier. One of those husband and wife looks where nothing needed to be said.

"But did you have a good time?" Delphi sounded like she still needed some reassurance.

"Yes. Yes, I did," Flora said as she stood to go upstairs.

Flora had the weekend to recover before meeting André again. The question of how to handle things whirled in her mind. When Monday morning came, she was no wiser, but tired and grumpy.

Luca didn't help when he saw her leaving for work and called across the courtyard in a sarcastic tone, "Greetings to lover-boy."

"Grow up," she muttered back as she got on her bicycle and wobbled away.

Her feet pumped the pedals. *Grow up, grow up, grow up.* Her journey into Thorelière passed quickly, and she was propping her bicycle against the wall in no time at all. She took off her headscarf as she entered the building and hung that and her coat on the stand in the corner of her office. André came through from outside. She had a moment of agitation, but there was no need.

"Morning," he said over his shoulder as he hurried into his office and closed the door.

Just then, the telephone rang. *Major* Weber requested to speak with M *le Maire* Duclos. "Is that *la jeune femme* that I met at La Grotte de la Reine on Friday evening?"

"Yes, *Herr Major*," Flora answered.

"You are very beautiful, *mademoiselle*. Perhaps we shall meet again. I do hope so."

After mumbling her thanks, Flora put the call through to André. She flopped back in her chair. It wasn't the first time she had taken calls from German officers and transferred them. It was the first time she had received such a compliment from a Nazi, and to say she felt uneasy was a huge understatement.

Perhaps André expected the call and that's why he was in such a hurry this morning, she thought, remembering her first day, when he'd rushed through her office into his like a tornado. Then she wondered if he was uneasy about their parting the other evening. The more she thought, the more confused she became.

Later that morning, André asked her to get the *gendarmerie* on the line for him. He looked troubled, fearful, she thought. *Something's going on, but I can't imagine what it might be.*

She wondered all day, but he gave nothing away. Nor did he mention their evening out, and by the time she'd put her coat and scarf on to go home, Flora was in a tizzy. To give André a chance to speak to her before she left, she decided to say goodnight. Having knocked, she opened his door a crack, but the words died before she uttered them.

He closed a brown folder and sat with his head in his hands.

"Are you alright?" she asked tentatively, coming further into the room.

He looked up at her. "Yes, I'll be fine. I find myself in a dilemma, but I'm afraid I cannot share it. I must decide on my own what to do." He smiled half-heartedly.

"Is it to do with the phone calls this morning?"

"Yes." He said no more.

"Is there anything I can get you before I go?"

"No. Have a pleasant evening and I'll see you tomorrow."

Flora walked to her bicycle, feeling troubled. What on earth was going on for him to be so distracted? Had the *Herr Major* told him something? Maybe he'd demanded some information. When she'd gone in to say goodnight, M Duclos had quickly closed that folder on his desk. Was she imagining that? *He hasn't asked me to type anything during the afternoon. I wonder if something in that folder would tell me what's going on.* She'd glimpsed photographs inside, but she hadn't been able to see what they'd depicted.

On her way home, Flora tried to decide whether to recount this incident or not. Should she tell only Rainier, or should she inform Luca as well? It did seem odd.

Perhaps I will say nothing and wait. Tomorrow he will show me or ask me to prepare a document. That's the normal way of things. Yes, that's what I will do. After all, there are bound to be confidential things that even I can't be told about.

She owed the mayor some loyalty. He had been most caring and generous the other night, and clearly not any more at ease in the company there than she had been.

The next evening, Flora sat at the table twiddling the stem of her wine glass and pushing the food around her plate with her fork. She ate little and spoke less.

"You're quiet, my love," Delphi said. She received no response and glanced across at Rainier. He shrugged in that French way that she had come to understand and love. It meant so much more than it appeared to on the surface.

The soft touch on Flora's arm brought her attention to her mother, who smiled at her gently.

Flora glanced across the table at Luca. Finding his eyes on her, she looked down with haste. When she raised her head again, she found Rainier smiling at her. He had always been her father, if not by blood. She debated with herself now whether she should share her anxieties. These had returned at first light, when her resolve of the night before had faded. Surely Rainier would give good advice. Something was going on, and it was highly unusual. All day she had waited for André to indicate what was troubling him. She'd expected the brown file to arrive with letters for her to type at the least, but she'd waited in vain. During the afternoon, she'd given him several opportunities to share what was going on. He'd told her nothing, and again he'd tucked the file away with haste when she'd entered his office. The frown creasing his brow had remained.

Flora came to a decision. She needed to talk with Rainier alone. No way would she share anything with Luca. He was too unpredictable.

CHAPTER 36

The moon hid behind thick clouds, and it was cold as Luca and his friends made their way in silence towards the great bulk of the château. It wasn't possible to work out the outline of the turreted towers or the ornate dormer windows, but the long line of the gallery roof spanning the river was discernible even in this gloom.

"*Merde!*" Antoine cursed as he tripped over a winding bramble shoot and it tore at his trouser leg.

"Shh. Even on this side of the river we must be careful," Luca remonstrated.

"I can hardly see my hand in front of my face," Thibault said. "Are we nearly there? This seems a bloody long way in the dark." The younger lad had been eager at the start of the journey, joking and talking with bravado. Now he had been silent for a couple of miles.

The fourth member of their little party, Hubert, trudged along stoically but answered the lad. "Not far now. You can see the outline of the château as easily as we can. Remember, this was your idea."

"Yes, and a good one too," Luca said, pacifying them all. "Look, we must skirt around to the south, but the wood there will shield us. We still need to be quiet. Sound will travel even with this northerly breeze."

"What if the old guy hasn't left the doors unlocked?" Thibault sounded worried.

"Then we won't be going anywhere," Luca answered. "Now hush."

They made their way through the rough undergrowth, but it had not been maintained particularly well in the last few years, making their passage difficult. Previously coppiced trees were sending thick branches shooting skyward, and there were tangles of ground ivy and brambles. All the leaves were underfoot.

"These piles of leaves are so noisy at this time of year," Hubert muttered. "My imagination is working overtime, making me think we're waking all of *Indre-et-Loire* and the other regions beyond with our footsteps."

"I know. I'm worried about the same," Antoine whispered over his shoulder.

"I wish you'd given me more warning for this evening. I'd have worn something warmer. It's bloody cold." Hubert shivered.

Luca's heart thumped as they slid along the wall of the château at last. He stood at the foot of the steps leading to the oak door and took deep breaths to steady his nerves. Here was safe enough, but as soon as they entered and found their way into the long gallery, they were in serious danger. He put his foot on the first step.

The door had opened smoothly. Someone had oiled the hinges. Luca was aware of treading lightly on the steps. Like most of the rest of the building, the tufa rock from which it was built was strong, although each step had an indent from years of footfalls and there were no rush carpets to deaden the sound. They climbed and found their way up to the gallery. Lifting the latch on yet another heavy door, Luca pushed it open with care, ready to flee if needed. Looking back over his shoulder, he realised the others were poised for flight too. Thibault, bringing up the rear, was already half turned.

The chalk- and slate-tiled floor looked expansive. Sixty metres of chequered emptiness. Luca stood inside the door and the others joined him. Their ears strained. Silence. A door slamming, muffled in the distance. Footsteps. They shrank further back against the wall. Shadows. Waiting. More silence.

Luca took a single step forward. Looking over his shoulder, he jerked his head. They crept on. Instinct took them around the edge. They passed one window in its round-arched recess. There were seventeen more to negotiate. Sidling up to the next, Luca peered around the side and almost cried out as a tall shape greeted him. He sank back against the wall, his heart in overdrive. A conical tree in a pot. He put his hand to his chest, blew out and then breathed deeply. He stepped smartly across to the next window. It was impossible to see out. He hoped no one could see in either. Fifteen more to pass. In five minutes, the real danger came: exiting the door on the other side and re-entering the cold fresh night.

Flora was restless. Her ears were attuned to the noises of the house now, and she'd heard Luca leaving, although he was trying to be surreptitious about it. Peeping around the edge of the curtain, she had witnessed him scooting across the courtyard. She thought she saw three other shadowy figures huddled at the gateway, but it was hard to tell. The night was cold and dark, with heavy clouds tumbling across the sky from the north. Hearing noises from the kitchen, she wrapped her dressing gown around her and stepped lightly down the stairs.

When she pushed open the door, as she expected, Rainier was there, making a fresh pan of coffee. She nodded as he indicated it to her.

Seated at the table with cups in front of them on the oil cloth cover, she asked, "So where is he off to now? Can he be trusted? He's always sloping off somewhere. Just when I wondered if he was accepting me here and as much against the Nazis as we are, he seems to be secretive and … oh, I don't know." She shrugged.

"Which question shall I answer first?" Rainier smiled at her. "Believe me when I tell you he is trustworthy. He is doing more than any of us to fight this regime and annoy our so-called protectors."

"So, what's he up to tonight?"

"Safer if you don't know. That's why your mother's gone to bed."

"Oh, come on, Rainier. He's obviously up to something. Just tell me, please." She gave him the wheedling look she'd used as a child.

"You needn't look at me like that. It's for your own safety."

"Then I'll stay up until he returns and ask him myself."

"Oh, Flora! You are exasperating sometimes." He huffed.

She smiled. "So tell me."

"They've gone into the Occupied Zone. They've got plans to cause some disruption by cutting telephone wires."

"Is that via the château? The gallery crosses the border because it spans the river. Everyone knows that."

"Yes, that's it."

"People say there aren't that many guards on the other side," Flora said.

"Let's hope that's true. It won't last long, though, if they make many forays like this."

There was silence between them for several minutes, each appearing lost in their own thoughts.

"Rainier, can I tell you something? You must promise not to tell anyone this."

"Unless your mother needs to know, I shan't say a word."

"It's about something at work. I was going to wait and see what happens, but since we're sharing things tonight… It's just that I gave my assurances about confidentiality when I started there."

"Do you think me having this information will affect someone else badly?"

"No, I don't believe that," Flora said.

"Then I shall keep it to myself and no one will be the wiser."

Flora shared her concerns about the folder and André's odd attitude. "I can't help feeling something is going on, and he's clearly not happy about it. He hasn't shared anything with me at all, which is unusual."

"Mmm, it's hard to say without seeing what's in the folder. Would it be possible to find that out? Without getting yourself into hot water, of course. The last thing you want to do is be asked to leave this job. Or worse," he added.

Flora hugged herself and, puffing out her cheeks, blew out a great breath.

"Let's have another coffee. You don't need to decide anything this minute. It might only be if an opportunity arose that you couldn't resist using, anyway. Or maybe it'll all come out if you give it a day or two. Problems are often like that. They resolve themselves, given a bit of time." Rainier filled the pan with water, placed it on the cooker again, and reached for the bottle of coffee-flavoured liquid that passed for the real thing these days.

They sat sipping their drinks. Flora glanced at the clock above the fireplace several times. Its loud tick, usually unnoticed, impinged upon her consciousness tonight.

"Are you not going to bed?" she asked.

"Not yet," he answered. "You?"

"No, not yet."

A log slipped in the burner as the ashes died down. Flora opened her eyes. Raising her chin from her chest, she regarded Rainier, who smiled at her.

"I must have dozed off." She rubbed her face and stretched her back.

There was a crunch on the gravel outside. She and Rainier watched as the door opened. A cold draught blew in.

Flora jumped up and went to the stove to reheat the coffee. Taking a loaf from the bread drawer in the table, she hacked off a piece and slathered it in butter. Here in the country, there was no shortage of that. She placed the bread and a cup of the hot liquid in front of Luca, who had slumped in the chair she had vacated. She watched him rub his hands across his scalp and over his face, then he picked up the bread and put it to his mouth, taking a bite as if he had to think how to do it. He swallowed as both Flora and Rainier watched and waited. He looked at them watching him and started to laugh. He laughed until he could laugh no more, so he put his head in his hands and sighed.

Rainier stood and went to put his hand on Luca's shoulder. "Tell us, lad. Get it out of your system."

"The journey home was almost worse than the rest of the evening." He almost laughed again. "We were all so tired by then."

"Are the others safe?" Rainier returned to his seat.

There was a long silence before Luca spoke again. "Yes. We all got back. We nearly got caught, though."

Flora gasped. "What on earth happened?"

"Antoine and I shinned up a couple of telegraph poles each. We were doing quite well. We had to get the other two to bunk us up, but after that there were metal angles to climb up. We were so lucky. Once Antoine was on the ground again, he sneezed as a soldier was coming close. The others must have heard him coming. I was still up the telegraph post, so I couldn't do a thing but stay still and hope for the best. My knees were knocking. I was sure the old boy would hear them against the wood."

"He didn't look up, then?" Rainier asked.

"No. I stayed as still as a rock. Well, as still as I could. *Merde*, I was frightened, I can tell you. Antoine began acting like he was drunk, rolling around and laughing a lot. The soldier was elderly, apparently. Antoine said afterwards he thought that was the safest option, a diversion. The soldier told Antoine he shouldn't be out and to get off home. Said he was an ignorant French boy who should behave better and show respect for his country as he himself did for the Fatherland. He cuffed Antoine on the shoulder with the butt of his rifle and said if it happened again, he'd arrest him. He must respect the curfew."

"Where were the other two?"

"Hiding in a ditch. They slithered down the bank and lay there with their heads down in the weeds when they heard the soldier coming. Thank goodness it was such a dark night. They got soaking wet, but it was the only place." He smiled.

"So, what did Antoine do?" Flora leaned forward, placing both hands flat on the table.

"He rolled off down the road, but as soon as the old guy had passed on, he doubled back. By that time, I'd climbed down the pole. We moved fast after that, I can tell you, and came home."

"So, you cut some wires? They'll gather what happened in the morning, if not sooner. When they realise it's where Antoine was seen, they'll put two and two together easily enough," Rainier said.

"It's too dangerous for you to go back," Flora said to Luca.

Luca shrugged. He seemed to have regained his equilibrium. "We have to fight these people any way we can. If there was something we could do on this side of the border, we would do that too."

Flora and Rainier exchanged glances.

Luca looked from one to the other. "What is it?" he asked.

Rainier sighed. "Flora is pretty sure something is going on, but she doesn't know what. There is a folder, the contents of which André doesn't seem to want her to see."

"He's clearly not at all happy about something," Flora added.

"You have to get in there to see it. We need to know what it is."

"It's not that easy. He doesn't go out that often," Flora said. "Anyway, he's my boss. He's obviously uncomfortable with whatever it is, so it may all blow over if I wait."

"Yes, and it may not. It may be something we could usefully work on. You must like him a lot if you trust him that much."

"That's not fair," Flora said. "He's a decent man in difficult circumstances. He's doing his best to protect everyone."

"By helping the Boche? Get real, Flora, and open your eyes."

"Steady, now," Rainier said. "It's late. We're all tired. Flora will do what she believes to be the right thing at the right time."

Luca kicked his chair back as he stood. "I'm going to bed."

CHAPTER 37

Flora awoke with a headache. She'd had little sleep. Luca's last words had kept replaying in her mind.

There was no sign of Luca when she finally made it to the kitchen for breakfast.

At least I'm spared more of his bad temper, she thought.

"Morning, darling," Delphi said. "Goodness, that was a late night."

Her mother always looked radiant and elegant, even this morning, wearing her old cotton work dress which seemed to cling in all the right places. Her hair was tied up in a scarf. Her long neck still had taught skin and her rich hair had only a smattering of grey here and there. Her green eyes always held a spark. She was simply one of those people to whom others responded positively. She pulled her long cardigan closer around her. It was a chilly morning, despite the log burner.

"For some reason, the fire burned too low last night. I had to relight it when I got up," she said, shivering. "Rainier gave me the gist of Luca's adventures last night. They were very fortunate. He is so brave."

"Mmm," was all that Flora could manage.

"Are you alright?"

"I have a headache, that's all," Flora answered. "A glass of water and a coffee will sort me out."

"Luca is determined to fight in any way he can," Delphi said as she cut bread for Flora. "I think we are blessed to have young men like him around."

Flora tutted under her breath. The last thing she needed was to say something to her mother she would regret. They'd always had a special closeness. This was probably because they had spent many years in Australia together with only her grandparents for company when she was a child. She drifted away as she remembered those carefree days of riding for miles in the hot sun. She didn't remember the dust and the flies and the heavy rain when it came, although she knew it must have been like that.

Delphi put her hands on Flora's shoulders and bent to kiss the top of her head. "I can see you're out of sorts this morning. Anything I can help with? Is it this thing at work?"

Flora glanced up at her.

"Now, don't be cross. Rainier told me about that too. You normally share those things with me, but I understand why you told him."

Tears came to Flora's eyes. "It's because we were here together last night, and it was late. I needed to share it. Times are so complicated now. Then Luca was mean because I said I wasn't sure whether I should spy on André. Why does he have to be so horrid at times? One minute he's pleased I'm working there, and the next he's nasty to me. He didn't like me going out with André, did he?"

"No, he didn't like that," her mother said. "He wasn't happy about that at all."

"Which is odd, if he wants me to get closer and find stuff for him."

"Maybe," Delphi said, with an air of mystery. "Emotions are complicated, as you just said."

Flora looked up sharply but discerned nothing more.

As she pushed her bicycle out of the yard, Luca came around the corner, making her jump. She'd thought he was still in bed. She glanced across at him, but he steadfastly made no eye contact.

She had plenty to consider as she pedalled along the lanes towards Thorelière. Should she look for the folder and find out its contents if the opportunity arose? It would be risky. She had told Luca there were few times when André left her alone, but that wasn't true. There were many times he went out to the *gendarmerie* to speak with the higher-level officers, or even for his lunch, leaving her alone in the office.

In a moment of clear honesty with herself, Luca's words had stung. One minute she was attracted to her step-cousin, and the next she could gladly throttle him. Did she trust André so much? How much was he helping the Germans and how much was he protecting the French citizens, as *Maréchal* Pétain kept on saying in this part of France now called Vichy?

She was no nearer deciding what to do as she parked her bike, entered her office and hung up her coat.

"Good morning, Flora," André said as he breezed through to his own room, five minutes later. He was frowning and the door banged shut behind him. Flora watched blankly, full of indecision.

PART 3: ACTIVE SERVICE

CHAPTER 38

The morning was tedious, and time passed slowly. Nothing was going smoothly. Flora was constantly reaching for the typewriter eraser, but then she would rub too hard and a hole would appear, and her typing became a mess. More than once she pulled the sheets with brute force from the rollers of the machine. Screwing them into tight balls, she dumped them into the wooden wastepaper basket at her side.

Her headache returned, and she threw a couple of aspirins down her throat and gulped as much water as she could manage. Slumping back in her chair, she took a deep breath.

At half past eleven, André came out of his office and said, "I have to go out. Here's some more typing, I'm afraid." He gave no further explanation, but still the frown wrinkled his forehead. "I'll be back straight after lunch." He paused. "Are you alright? You seem a bit tired this morning. Take a proper break. Don't forget your own lunch."

She nodded. He was kind and considerate, even when he had much on his mind. Now seemed to be her opportunity to look for the confidential folder, but should she? Spying on her boss seemed wrong. This wasn't spying on him, though, so much as spying on the enemy. The Boche almost employed André their influence in his appointment was so strong, so he had to be doing their bidding, and Luca needed to find out what that involved. But André was her friend, and he had been generous to her. Her mind kept returning to that point. He'd given her this job when she'd sorely needed it. The night out had been luxurious, and he'd taken her into his confidence regarding his dead wife and child. He was vulnerable. Flora's mind wandered on. He was gentle, but he was working with the Nazis, who were dangerous.

Right that's it. Family first.

She slid over to the door that led to the hallway. Cracking it open, she strained to hear any nearby sounds. A door banged but it was distant, and no footsteps approached. Her heart steadied. So far, she had done nothing wrong.

Returning to her desk, she picked up a folder and moved towards André's office. Stopping at the door, she took a deep breath and turned the handle quietly.

This is ridiculous, she thought. *There's no one here but me. If anyone comes, I'm simply returning a folder of typing to M le Maire's desk for his approval and signature.*

She entered the room, and a moment of indecision halted her on the threshold. Should she close the door behind her? Safer not to be in full view, but more suspicious to be inside his office with the door closed, surely.

She pushed it but didn't close it fully. Now, where to search? She looked around. It was all familiar: the coat stand; the large, heavy desk with papers in a neat pile; the cabinet in the far corner.

Should she look in that first? Perhaps, but if it was current work, wouldn't it be among the pile on the desk?

Flora advanced. Putting the folder in her hands down, she leaned over and started to rifle carefully through the pile, listening all the while for any exterior sounds advancing. Nothing.

She felt a swooping disappointment. Having made the decision to search, she desperately wanted results.

She moved around to the other side of the desk and tried the drawers. The top one slid open easily. Pens, paperclips. Nothing else. The next one down opened smoothly enough. A pair of bicycle clips, a single glove, a glass, and a half empty bottle of calvados. The other top drawer held labels and other office detritus.

I don't want to search the filing cabinet. It could take forever. One more drawer. Flora gripped the handle and pulled gently, but it wouldn't open as the others had. She pulled harder. It wouldn't budge. It had the same keyhole as the others, but they weren't locked. *What if he has the keys on him?*

She felt deflated. Where did people keep keys for a desk? In a pot somewhere? In the filing cabinet in a tin? She looked around and saw a pot on the window ledge. She looked inside. Nothing but dust. Nothing left but to check the cabinet. That might well be locked, too, like the drawer. Two strides and she was pulling open the top drawer. It slid out easily enough, but with a screech.

Her heart thudded and she stood still. Silence followed, but still she was breathless with nerves.

"Hello, is anyone there?" A disembodied voice sounded from her own office.

What should she do? Stay still and silent, or breeze out to greet the visitor?

"There's no one here. They must have gone for lunch already."

"Do you want to wait? I'm starving." A voice came from slightly further away.

"The door's open to the inner office."

"Yes, but you can't go in there. That'll be *M le Maire's* office. It's his secretary you need to see."

Having remained, it was too late now for Flora to go to see the visitor. They would think it odd of her to have delayed.

"Yes, that stuck-up bitch who got the job instead of me," the voice said.

Flora's eyes popped wide, but she managed to stay still and quiet. No way could she show herself now. She ducked down behind the desk.

"His door's open."

Footsteps advanced quietly and the door gave a squeak.

"Come away. What if you get caught? It could be serious, you daft *salope*," the distant voice said.

"Who're you calling a slut? *Salope* yourself."

"Oh, come on, I'm hungry. Call back tomorrow," the voice outside whined.

The footsteps receded. Flora glanced at her watch. She still had time. Smarting from the remarks she'd overheard, she stood. Creeping quietly across the room, she entered her own office area and closed the door that the two girls had left half open. *Bloody cheek*, she thought.

Having closed the outer door, she became bolder and moved with long strides back into André's office, determined to get the drawer open. Noticing the pot on the window ledge, she picked it up. As she did so, something dropped down and landed at her feet. A small key with a rounded barrel: a desk drawer key. She picked it up and fitted it neatly into the stubborn drawer lock. Success.

Inside the drawer the folder lay on the top of others. Flora recognised it instantly. The label on the front said '*Juifs Dans Votre Region*' and then in German '*Juden*', but it wasn't André's handwriting.

She opened the folder and saw several sheets of paper, each with names and addresses of certain families. Some photographs of individuals and family groups. She read the names Berenbaum, Damrosch, Grinberg, Margolis, Rosenthal, Rubashkin, and Taubman. Some of the men had the Jewish side-locks and many wore the skullcaps that identified their respect and reverence for their God.

Flora turned the pages quickly and copied the names and addresses. Instinctively she knew this list of the local Jewish community was meaningful. Having finished copying, she glanced at her watch. Oh no! Time had flown.

She turned the last page and read with horror, but there was no time for more. She replaced the folder, as far as she could remember, in the same position, locked the drawer and put the key back underneath the pot on the window ledge.

Rapidly folding the sheet of paper upon which she had written all the names and other damning information, she wondered what to do with it. This was potential dynamite, and if caught she had no doubt that she would be taken away too. She rammed the paper down her shirt and into her undergarment. Then, hurrying across the office, she left André's office and crossed to her own chair. As she flung herself down, a distant thud of the great oak front door resounded.

Oh my God, the folder. She ran back into his room and retrieved the folder that she had taken in with her and left on his desk.

As he entered her room, Flora stood at her own filing cabinet with her back to him. Looking briefly over her shoulder, she greeted him with a 'good afternoon' and a smile. Her heart pounded, her voice seemed false to her own ears and her smile was too broad.

"Did you have lunch, my dear?"

"I brought a baguette with me, so I ate that here at my desk." The lie fell easily enough.

"I shall take you out for a proper lunch," he said. "Not tomorrow. Unfortunately, there is something going on already, and I may have to be around for that, but the next day we shall go somewhere nice, *serait-ce bon*?"

"Yes, that would be very good." She nodded, not trusting herself to say more since her throat seemed to be closing.

The afternoon passed with exceeding lethargy on Flora's part. She managed most of the typing that André had given her that morning, but her apathy for work increased as the long hours passed by. All she wanted was to escape and get home to share what she had discovered. Each time she moved, the paper scratched her left breast, reminding her of its incriminating presence. She didn't think its crackling was obvious, but each time André came through to tell her something or she knocked at his office door to give him her work, she was uncomfortably aware of it.

"Do you mind if I get away in good time today? I seem to have had such a headache all day," Flora said at last.

"No, of course, my dear Flora. You should have said sooner. You go, and I hope you're better tomorrow. Don't forget, not tomorrow but the next day we shall have that lunch together." She smiled wanly at him and went to retrieve her coat and headscarf.

As she pedalled, all that was on her mind was getting home as quickly as possible to share her awful discovery. Her stomach sank with dread as she considered what was clearly planned for the very next day. She prayed that the action would not be brought forward.

CHAPTER 39

Flora flung her bicycle down. Leaving the rear wheel spinning, she dragged her scarf from her head and hurried into the kitchen.

"I must speak with Luca," she said to Delphi, who stood at the sink washing some underwear.

"Hello to you too," her mother responded.

Contrite, Flora rushed across and gave Delphi a hug. "I'm so sorry," she said. "Mama, I discovered something terrible today. I must share it with Luca and maybe he can do something to avert a disaster for some of the people in Thorelière."

"Can you tell me?"

"Of course, though I don't know how to say it." She turned around in a circle and then stepped one way before stepping to the other. "André is prepared to let it happen. Luca was right all along. Mama, you know there are Jewish families in the town. Some of them have been here for ages. Some moved here from the Occupied Zone quite recently. All their names and addresses are in a file. I'm sure tomorrow they are to be taken to camps in Paris. Pétain has already prevented them from working. Today I discovered that a *M'sieur* Grinberg has been working as a school teacher in Thorelière for years and years, and since that Jewish Statute before Christmas he's been prevented from doing that."

"I read about the Statute, but I didn't realise it would really affect anyone round here," Delphi said.

"Me too, but in the folder it says they're going to round up these poor people. It called them all kinds of dirty names.

There are children, babies even. They will be separated from each other. Mama, I must find Luca."

"He's probably in the vinification barn."

With that, Flora hurried out and across the courtyard. On the way, she met old François, whose shuffling gait was propelling him slowly towards the house. His blue overalls were ragged at the hems where they constantly dragged at his heels, and his denim jacket, shapeless as ever, made him look like a windblown scarecrow.

"Where is Luca, please, François?" Flora called towards him without slackening her pace.

He had the perennial roll-up hanging from the corner of his lips, so he grunted and tossed his whiskery chin back over his shoulder towards the vinification barn.

"Thank you," Flora said as she hurried past.

When she found Luca, he was in conversation with one of the hands, a young lad of sixteen, too young to have been away fighting and so spared the ignominy of being held as a prisoner of war.

"Luca, I need to speak to you. It's urgent. Sorry to interrupt," she added as he glanced across at her with a familiar scowl.

"It can wait, surely," he said.

"No, really, it can't."

"What is it, then? You'll have to be quick. I have plenty to do here."

"Can we go outside?"

She waited while he finished his conversation with the lad, tempted to pace and huff but managing to stay where she stood without twitching and shuffling too much.

As they left the building, Flora said, "Luca, I owe you an apology. I should have guessed that André is weak simply by the position he has agreed to take. I found the folder. The one we spoke about last night."

"Well done, Flora. That's excellent. I'm sorry too. I've been grouchy and rude to you when you were trying to see the best in the man. Your optimistic nature makes you who you are."

She glanced at him to ascertain if this was sarcasm, but he stopped walking and took her arm. "It must have been frightening, looking for it. You have been very courageous."

She acknowledged what he said but hurried them on.

"Let's go into the room at the back of the barn. We can talk in private there. No one will overhear what we're saying." He took her arm again and guided her through the barn's detritus towards the room at the back. He sat her down on a straw bale and proceeded to light the candles within their jars. "Here." He passed her a small glass of Pernod from the bottle on the floor. "Medicinal." He laughed. "You look like you could use it. No water, I'm afraid, unless we go back to the kitchen."

"This is fine." Flora sipped the aniseed liquid. She didn't miss the admiration in Luca's eyes, which sparkled in the candlelight.

"So…?"

She told him all that she had found in the folder: the photographs and addresses which identified each family member and the time projected to take them from their homes.

"Five o'clock in the morning gives them little time in which to act. It'll be dangerous and difficult." Luca was anxious.

"Clearly we must warn these people and get them away. To where, I have no idea," Flora said.

"There's down toward the Indre. It's about thirty-five kilometres, but there are caves there, and it might be a stopping off point. After that, I don't think we can do much, but it would save them tomorrow. How do I find them all?"

The Pernod had warmed Flora and given her courage. She delved down her blouse and laughed as Luca raised one eyebrow, his eyes following her hand. She handed over the piece of paper, warm from its proximity to her skin. She felt embarrassed but he made light of it and held it beside the candle to read her scribbles.

"This is amazing. Clever girl. I'll find Antoine. We can warn them and get them away before the early hours and then come back here."

"What if they're watching these houses? You'll be caught. It's dangerous."

"You might have been caught earlier today."

"Yes, that nearly happened." She told him of the two women who had called by the office while she'd hidden in André's office.

"Ah, Flora." He regarded her with admiration as he shook his head. "I didn't want to put you in such danger. I'm so sorry." He stretched his hand out and touched her face.

"We do what we must." Flora was confused and breathless but unable to resist leaning her cheek to his touch.

"I can find Antoine now, but we won't go into the town until it's dark. Hubert's too far away at such short notice. We can avoid the *gendarme* easily. Many years of practice." He winked at her.

She cleared her throat and gave a nervous half laugh. "Can I come? I'd really like to see this through."

"Absolutely not!"

"Why not? Do you think I couldn't cope? Don't you dare say it's because I'm a woman."

"I'm sure you'd cope, and I wouldn't dare say that. On this occasion, there would not be safety in numbers. The fewer the better. We can move more quietly, and we'd be less likely to be spotted."

The two men moved through the shadows, listening intently as they went. They each knew the town intimately and took the shortest, safest route, which they had planned while waiting for nightfall. The first call turned out to be the most difficult. These people were naturally wary and reluctant to come to the window when Luca tapped. Having no one else of the Jewish faith with him, it was hard to persuade the family at this house of his seriousness and that they were in direct and imminent danger. Eventually he managed to convince the man, his wife and son to pack a bag and explained where to meet him later. He asked the man, M Damrosch, to accompany him and Antoine while his wife prepared their belongings.

The evening continued. Luca and Antoine left each family to gather a few belongings, having explained it would be a very long walk to temporary safety. They arranged a meeting place outside the town boundary and moved on to the next house on the list.

All went well until they got to the house of M Rubashkin, a middle-aged man who lived with his wife and young daughter. It took a long time for the three men to raise him from his bed. They tossed pebbles at the windows, they rapped on the door. They even called quietly, and their Jewish companion finally called to him in his native Hebrew, citing a passage from the central reference of Judaism. As he explained after, M Rubashkin would recognise anything from the Torah, but the reference to Exodus seemed to do the trick.

However, the man simply refused to move. He raised both his hands and said what would be would be. It was the will of God. He was tired of moving and he intended to stay put. Nothing would persuade him, and his wife seemed intent on following her husband's will. Even persuasive discussion about his young daughter's safety would not shift him.

"God's will always prevails," was his only response.

"We can spend no more time here," Luca said. "We still have one more to visit. M Taubman has a young family. We must get them ready."

"We'll go and get them," Antoine said, "if you want to stay here and try again." He looked at M Damrosch, who nodded his agreement. "We'll see you later at the meeting place."

"Don't wait too long for me," Luca said. "Get them away in good time. It's a long walk for them. Then get yourself off home without being caught."

After Luca tried one more time to persuade the family and the man shook his head and closed the door, he hunkered down on some rough ground not far away. He could observe the front of the house, but his own presence was sheltered from view by the bushes that had sprung up. Someone had dumped a pile of rubble too, which was helpful.

It was cold. The wind had died, but the air hovered only just above freezing.

I shall have to be careful my breath coming out as a cloud doesn't give me away if anything happens, Luca thought.

The clear night and the lack of lights ensured a heavenly display. As he sat on the hard ground, he looked up and spied several constellations which, as a boy, his father had taught him. There, the big W of Cassiopeia, and the pan and handle of the plough both glimmered down upon him from the north. If he looked hard, he saw the more easterly Pleiades too, but was only able to count six stars instead of seven.

He yawned and his eyes grew heavy. *Merde, I mustn't fall asleep. I might not awake in this cold. Can one freeze to death at two or three degrees? Perhaps not. I wonder how long I should wait here. If no one comes, so much the better and I can go.*

Then he became aware of it — cars speeding. Luca buried his chin in his coat but kept his eyes on the house. Two cars and a lorry with a canvas-covered back pulled up with much skidding and a spray of gravel and dust from the road. Luca witnessed several soldiers in full gear with helmets and guns jumping down from the back of the lorry and others from the cars with officers' caps and long greatcoats. There was much shouting and gesticulating.

As he watched, his heart pounded and his mouth grew dry. *Please Lord, let the house be empty. Let that be the reason why I got no reply when I tried again. Perhaps they left on their own out the back.* But this was a forlorn hope.

The door was hammered with the butt of rifles, and then a soldier arrived with a sledgehammer, making short work of opening it.

There was masculine shouting and then screams from within.

Tears came to Luca's eyes and he dashed them away with his cuff. He could have saved this family. Should he have been more forceful? They wouldn't even follow one who shared their faith.

Next, a soldier came out with a child. She was squealing and wriggling, but he had a firm hold. She wore a nightdress and had no shoes.

"*Maman, Maman,*" she cried out before the soldier cuffed her and almost threw her into the back of the lorry. A woman carrying coats was hurried out, her upper arm in the vice-like grip of an overweight soldier.

Lastly came the man. M Rubashkin. This family had a name. They weren't faceless aliens. A short time before, they would have been asleep, dreaming, hoping.

An officer waved his arm and then M Rubashkin, who had been trying to do his best for his family, was shoved towards the lorry.

Luca had seen too much. He clasped his hands around his knees and put his head down. Sometime later, he realised his knees were wet and he rocked back and forth. His throat was sore, and he was drained. All was silent as the grave. He stood slowly and hobbled away.

CHAPTER 40

When Luca entered the courtyard, a shadow disengaged from the wall and Antoine came towards him. Luca raised his hands from his sides and shook his head.

"*Ah, mon ami.*" Antoine put his hand on Luca's shoulder. "The others got away. That's what I came to tell you. They will have a long walk ahead of them, but let's hope they are saved. Their lives will be difficult, but at least they will be a little longer because of your work tonight."

"You better get home," Luca said. "We'll talk soon. We need help here." He shook his head and shrugged. "We're just scratching the surface with our petty activities."

"We could do with that English girl. Edith, or Colette, was it? Or some of her saboteur friends. Take heart, my friend." Antoine shook hands with Luca and squeezed his shoulder before he left.

Luca stood still, not knowing what to do or where to go. His arms hung limply by his sides as Flora approached from the house. She'd witnessed the brief exchange from her bedroom window.

"I watched for your return," she said. "I'm so pleased to see you. I've been so…"

She took in his immobility, his head hung low. Then his shoulders heaved as he gulped some air and sniffed, and she realised he was crying.

"Oh, come," she said and enfolded him in her arms. "You're tired. Two nights with no sleep and too much anxiety." She held him while he fought to control his emotions.

"I'm so sorry…" he began.

"Shh." She took his face in her hands. The roughness of his cheeks reminded her of the early hour of the morning. Placing one hand behind his head, she drew him down and kissed him, tasting the salt from his tears.

"Flora," he said, finding her mouth with his, tentative at first. His lips were gentle and uncertain, but she returned his kiss. He became more insistent and the tip of his tongue searched for hers until he pulled away abruptly. "I'm sorry."

"I'm not." She put her hand back behind his neck and kissed him lightly once more. "That's enough for tonight, though. Go to bed and sleep."

"We got them all away except for one family."

"That's a whole lot better than I feared."

"I hid and watched what happened to them, the ones who refused to leave. There was a child."

"You have saved many. Focus on that, Luca, and deal with the rest when you have slept." She kissed his cheek once more and taking his hand, she led him towards the house.

Flora, too, had had little sleep for two nights in a row. She was very reluctant to speak with André the next day. She would have liked to relinquish her work, even with the money and freedom it brought her. She had spoken of it with her mother and stepfather over breakfast. There had been no sign of Luca.

"I can hardly bear to go into work this morning," she'd blurted. "André is weak and as good as a collaborator. How can I speak to him after this?"

"But you have proved that your position there is useful, my child," Rainier had said.

"You must do what is right and what you are able to do, darling," her mother had added.

In the harsh light of the morning, she had time to consider her position as she pedalled along the lanes to Thorelière.

She had been in a place to discover useful information that had helped to save several families, or at least give them a chance. There may well be more knowledge she might glean. If only Edith were here. Together they might hatch a plan. This was more serious than their childish schemes at school, though. She was risking her life.

As she entered her office, Flora realised André had arrived already. She walked quietly across to her desk, wishing to delay the moment when he would become aware of her presence and emerge from his office. She shivered in the chilly room, and barely had time to arrange her expression before he came out to speak with her.

"How are you today, Flora? Better, I hope." He smiled and rubbed his hands together. "It's a bit nippy this morning, *n'est-ce pas?*"

"It is, and thank you, I'm much better. I had a good night's rest." The lie came easily, she discovered, now that she knew what he was. "You seem brighter too. You have been distracted for the last few days."

"Yes, I apologise for that. There was something, a job, that had to be done, but it is over for the moment and so I am better for that."

"Oh," Flora said. "Is it anything I could have helped with?" she probed, knowing the answer.

"No, no. All was undertaken last night apparently and, I imagine, with German precision and success. I have not been told the details yet."

Minimal success, Flora thought but smiled at him with as much warmth as she could muster.

"I am expecting a visitor this morning. I had a message telling me that *Herr Major* is coming to our humble office. He is going to the *gendarmerie* first. I expect he will be sharing the events of last night with me. I had to play my small part to protect the citizens of our little town."

The visitor arrived halfway through the morning. He clicked his heels at Flora and saluted with that vile hand and straight arm raised above his head. She rose from her seat, tapped on André's door, and showed the *Major* through to his office. When she sat back down, she strained her ears to catch any snippet of the conversation. She discerned nothing but deep murmuring voices, and so she moved across the room with a file in her hand. As she approached the door, she was startled by a raised voice and the sound of what may have been a glove slapping the furniture. She discerned a German swearword, and then leapt back to her desk. Opening the folder, she made as if to begin typing.

Five minutes later André's door opened, and the officer came striding out. With a curt nod at Flora, he left. André followed a few moments after, looking flustered.

"*Un café*, I think, Flora. A strong one."

"Yes, straight away." She hurried down the corridor to make him his drink. A smile played around her lips as she returned. Placing the drink carefully on his desk, she lingered. "Is there anything else?"

"Not all success last night, it would seem," André said. He took a deep breath and sipped his coffee. "There was a suggestion that the people involved received a warning and were therefore not available. I reassured Major Weber that these folk are slippery customers and that they are not liked or supported by any of our local people."

"So, he's happy with you and this office?"

"Yes, yes. He comprehends, from previous experience, that I shall be helpful in protecting our people, just as *Maréchal* Pétain has encouraged. He is a good and compassionate leader with the safety of his French citizens at the heart of his policies."

Flora returned to her own desk, hardening her resolve to continue working here. She would find out as much as she could and convey it to the resistance.

A couple of weeks passed with nothing of note presenting itself to Flora. She had gritted her teeth and gone for lunch with André, managing to persuade him to take her a little further afield than Thorelière for the purposes of decorum. That seemed to keep him happy. He was attentive and kind to her. If only this other business had not occurred, she would like him more. So far, he had not suggested another evening venture, so for now Flora considered herself safe.

The intimate moment she had shared with Luca had not been repeated either. She knew he had wanted to kiss her, but had it simply been the circumstances of the night and his need for comfort? Perhaps he felt nothing more for her than that. Did he regret the action?

She determined this must not continue and decided to corner him when she had a chance. She would ask him why he was avoiding her.

That evening, Flora saw Luca from where she worked at the kitchen sink. He crossed the courtyard before entering the barn opposite. Drying her hands on a cloth, she pulled off her apron and hurried towards the outbuilding. She pulled open the door and entered. The windows were high and covered in dust and cobwebs, so the interior was dim. She stood for a moment to let her eyes adjust after the early spring sunshine outside. She heard Luca moving about in the small room they had used for meetings, so she called his name and advanced. They met in the doorway.

"Flora." He stopped and looked awkward.

"Luca," she said at the same moment. "I must speak with you." *Here we go*, she thought. They both opened their mouths but said nothing. "Look at us. When we weren't bickering, we were always easy with each other. Now we're standing here tongue-tied."

"I need to apologise for the other night. It must have been the circumstances. I'm so sorry. I shouldn't have done that." Luca's forehead wrinkled.

"That's why I came to speak with you now. You have nothing to apologise for." Flora looked away. "I liked it," she whispered.

He ignored that, or perhaps he hadn't heard her. "You've driven me mad at times. After being insanely jealous of you coming here when you were young, and fearing I'd lose control of my home, I realise I've been rude and insufferable."

"There were moments when I believed you to be lazy and worse because I wasn't certain why you kept disappearing. I even wondered if you were collaborating." She grimaced and chuckled nervously. "I've crept around you for years." She paused and lowered her gaze before meeting his eyes again. "Now I'm confident you are a hard worker and that your duty to our country comes first."

"And I know you are strong and courageous," he said. Taking her hand, he looked at it with wonder, before turning it and raising it to his lips. He planted a gentle kiss in her palm and closed her fingers around it.

And so, at last, they became easier with each other.

CHAPTER 41

It was evening and Flora collected the eggs and ensured the chickens were closed in. She was sure she'd heard a fox calling the previous night. The last thing they needed was an intruder of that kind. She'd witnessed it once some years ago. The predator had managed to scrabble its way under the wire and in the early hours of the morning had gone on a rampage, killing most of the hens and leaving their bloody bodies strewn across the ground. She'd awoken with the racket and rushed outside, but she'd been too late to save all but three of the birds, and one of those had been mauled. Rainier had despatched it with speed.

Flora shivered and hurried towards the kitchen and the warmth of the log burner. She had her hand on the large black doorknob when she heard her name being called. Turning, she was startled to see Edith coming into the courtyard. With a very broad smile, her friend ran the last few paces. "Surprise! It's your cousin Colette. I've come from the south to see you." Edith put down a small suitcase and bag and enfolded Flora.

"Edith! What…? I can't believe it," Flora managed to mumble into Edith's hair. She had recently written to her but hadn't expected a response.

After the greeting and some laughter, Edith continued. "You must call me Colette now. It's imperative you don't forget, because it's for your own safety as well as mine."

"Right. Come in." Flora pushed the door. "Look who's here. Cousin Colette's come to visit."

There were gasps. Everyone got up to greet Colette in the time-honoured way, with three kisses on alternate cheeks and hugs.

"If you don't want me here, or if things have changed, I understand, and I shall go. To put you in danger is the last thing I want."

"Of course you must stay," Rainier said.

"We were saying we needed you just a few days ago," Luca added. "There are things we're doing, but we need help."

"Before all that, let ... Colette get her coat off and sit down," Delphi said. She crossed to the stove and heated a pan of coffee. "Not our usual standard, I'm afraid." She nodded at the bottle of brown liquid she was adding to the water. "But it's passable."

"Back in the UK, even tea is rationed to between two and four ounces a week. As for coffee, it's unheard of. I gather some people are using ground acorns to make something called coffee." Colette pulled a face. "Not sure if that's true."

"This isn't quite that bad yet but it's not what we normally call 'coffee'."

"Mind you, at 'home' further south —" Collette emphasised her words with a nod — "things are the same as here."

"Please, sit down. Let me get this straight," Delphi said. "Your father died? And my sister, your mother, is where? We need to have the story right, and we all need to give the same version."

"Absolutely. Yes, my French father died, and your sister moved to America. It's a bit random, but we wanted her out of the way, and if we'd used 'she re-joined her family in the UK', that would throw suspicion onto me. Hopefully the subject won't arise anywhere. Your French citizenship is useful too,

Delphi. I'm living in the Allier region, according to my cover story. It's a small village near Montluçon called Bédorgues."

"How long are you here for?" Luca leaned forward.

"I'm here for as long as it takes, this time," Colette answered.

"How did you get here? I suppose it was an aeroplane again. I remember you told us about the Lysander, which can land in a field. I thought it could only be at certain times of the month, though, when the moon is right," Flora said.

"Actually, I've been in France for some time. I was brought over and landed by an MGB. That's a Motor Gun Boat. In fact, they dropped me off at a tiny coastal village in Holland. It was no more than a jetty, where the boat tied up. One of the seamen, his name was Cyril, but they called him Sid, Sid Connew, said his ancestors were French. He told me to keep my head down until he gave me the nod. He was such a kind lad, very young. I bet he signed up earlier than was regulation. I hope he makes it." She stared into space for a moment. "Anyway, about eight commandos sneaked ashore and created a bit of havoc, firing their guns and causing an explosion and so on, and me and another two operatives slipped off into the night during the confusion. It's not an unusual method. I've done some supporting of saboteurs in that region and now I've come this way."

"We need to do more. Cutting the occasional wire is stupid and almost pointless. It's like spitting into the ocean, no more than a mild irritant to the Boche. It's certainly not going to put out any fires quickly. What's going on elsewhere?" asked Luca.

"There's talk of a new weapon the Nazis are working on. As long ago as 1941 there were reports from Polish field units regarding some kind of secret tests being carried out by the Germans on the island of Usedom in the Baltic Sea, some place called Peenemünde. It's all to do with an unmanned flying bomb. They've started to build ramps in northern France, all facing the south of England."

"Oh, my Lord! What does that mean?" Delphi looked shocked.

"It's not good. In typical fashion, the operation is highly organised." Colette took a deep swig of the coffee that Delphi had placed in front of her. "The design of the buildings on sites is remarkably standard. For example, the 'assembly' huts are easily recognisable. They all have two doors, five square windows, then another door, and finally three more windows."

"That's so typically regimented," Luca said.

"They arrive in kit form on lorries and they just put them together. A bit like the Meccano kit my brother had when he was young. There are several other buildings and a water reservoir, all the same at each site. The Germans seem to be choosing the positions very carefully, too. Several of these places have the major buildings hidden in woods and forests. The launching ramp itself seems to be the only object which projects into a clearer area. Others are being placed in or near a village or farm and camouflaged as much as possible, to look like part of the local landscape. A way of finding them is to search for concrete roadways we've discovered. One of my counterparts has got himself a job at a site. He's sending back information about where the buildings and development are up to. We've been feeding information about the locations of as many construction sites as we're able back to the UK."

"That's brave. There's such a lot going on, and we're doing nothing compared to all that." Luca was disconsolate. "We have no resources, but then all the action seems to be in the Pas de Calais where those V1 ramps are. There's not much around here to sabotage."

"What we need here is to develop the escape route for evaders — downed airman and others, like escapees from camps. There's a bit of a route, but as more air raids take place on these installations, for example, there will inevitably be further need for safe houses and guides to get airmen back to the UK. One such way is through Spain and Gibraltar, or even from the coast near Marseille."

"Some time ago we got several Jewish families away." Luca described how Flora had discovered the relevant information and how the people had been warned and smuggled away.

"So, you have indeed turned into the spy you wanted to be at school." Colette laughed.

"Not quite in your league, though," Flora said.

As usual, Delphi was aware of empty stomachs and set about organising food. All talk of war matters ceased. "Tomorrow is soon enough to make plans," she said, and they all agreed.

Conversation turned to more mundane matters, and Flora and Colette had the opportunity to reminisce.

"19.45 hours," Colette said, having glanced at her watch several times during the last half hour. "I need to make a transmission to tell them I'm here and have made contact." She crossed the room to the small suitcase she had brought with her, leaving the bag on the floor in the corner. "May I take it up to your bedroom, Flora? I can trail the aerial out of the top window."

"Yes, of course."

"Do you want to come and see?" Colette addressed all of them.

They trooped upstairs.

"That's significantly smaller than that old thing in our barn," Luca said. "We haven't used it really."

"So I was told," Colette said.

Luca and Rainier exchanged glances.

"London or wherever is aware of us?" Rainier asked.

"Yes. You've been on their radar because they thought you might be useful. And so you are going to be. Look, this is my transmitter, and this is the receiver below. It has its antennae here."

"How long is that?" Flora touched it with one finger.

"It's eighteen metres. This is a spares box with all these things in, and a Morse key. It can operate from a mains plug or from a six-volt DC battery. It's like the old one in many ways, but much lighter for travelling, especially in this cardboard suitcase. I'm expecting a drop next week, though. They'll send me another one, a container version in a metal waterproof case. More practical for hiding now I'm going to be more stationary."

"Are you on your own here? You spoke of 'we' when you landed," Luca said.

"I am until next week. Some others will be dropped in when they drop more equipment." Colette didn't look up as she assembled the parts she would need to make her transmission.

Silence descended as they watched her find the correct frequency and place the antennae wire and slide the Morse key into position. Then she found a piece of paper in her pocket and, with a pencil, began to make a list of letters and numbers on a second sheet.

"This is my poem code," she said. "I chose Emily Dickinson — 'I died for Beauty, but was scarce'. Lots of people tend to go for Kipling or Wilfred Owen. I also have a key word. I must use all three things together, or Blighty may think I've been compromised in some way. It's all for safety. Have you seen anything that might be a detector van around?"

"Someone pointed one out to me in Thorelière," Luca said.

"I better be quick, then." Colette looked at her watch. "Here goes." With a series of taps and clicks, she sent her message and repacked her equipment efficiently.

"That all looks very impressive," Luca said.

"I'm here to train you; you and those other men. Antoine, was it?" Colette looked at Flora. "I remember him. Who were the others?"

"Hubert is a good bloke, and then there's Thibault. He insists on being involved, but we only tell him limited stuff."

Flora grinned at Colette's reference to Antoine. He was as big a flirt as ever, although he didn't trouble her any longer.

"Tomorrow is soon enough to start your training, I think," Delphi said.

"Yes, I'm really tired." Colette nodded and rubbed her eyes.

That night, squashed into Flora's bed again, they chatted long into the early hours of the morning.

"Tomorrow I can tell you about the escape route and what we might do," Colette said. "Now you must tell me about Luca and you."

CHAPTER 42

Thank goodness for the weekend, Flora thought as she opened her eyes and rubbed her face. *I don't have to meet André and I can spend time with Colette.*

As Flora had begun to mention Luca the previous night, Colette had fallen asleep, so she'd not been able to share anything with her. Now she turned her head to watch her friend sleeping. As Flora regarded her lightly freckled face and brown hair mussed on the pillow, Colette opened her eyes, smiled and stretched in luxurious warmth.

"That was one of my better nights," she said. "I've slept in some strange places. Some cold and damp ones, some barns and some boarding houses but this … this felt like home. Let's go into Thorelière this morning. I can begin to get the lie of the land."

"Is that safe?"

"Yes. I'm your cousin from Bédorgues who's come to stay with you, remember? What would be more natural?"

Later, Colette borrowed Delphi's bicycle and together she and Flora cycled the few kilometres into the little town.

"Let's have a coffee first," Flora said. "I'll show you the best place. It's called Le Café De La Poste. Then I must get the things Mama asked for."

"There's a café called Le Café Du Coin. Maybe we should go there?"

"Okay." Flora looked sideways at her friend, knowing her well enough to suspect she had an ulterior motive. "How did you hear about that place? It's not new and not very upmarket either."

"There are a couple of people I could do with meeting who might be there."

"You're joking!" Flora said.

"No, Flora. No, I'm not joking. I have to start work straight away."

"Ah, I see. Would you rather I lose myself?"

"If you stay and meet them, it would be a good idea and very helpful, but only if you want to. There will always be an element of danger in all my activities, although this morning there really is very little risk."

"Then I'll stay with you. We want to be part of anything that will be useful. We've already demonstrated that with the small things we've achieved so far."

"Yes, you have." Colette blew her a kiss and laughed, which lightened the mood.

Several people were sitting outside, preferring the weak sunshine and enjoying the breeze which had warmed over the last few days. Colette led the way indoors. The interior seemed gloomy by comparison and there was a fug of tobacco smoke. It was comfortable, with the smell of both stale beer and coffee.

Behind the bar was a woman with very red lipstick on her cigarette-crimped mouth. Her hair was pulled sharply back into a plait, and she wore a flowered overall which covered her ample frame. She was pouring a beer. Two old and whiskery men in blue denims had propped themselves against the countertop and an older lady, still wearing her headscarf and overcoat, sat with a small dog on her lap. Her chair had a bright red plastic seat and the table was covered in a matching oilcloth with flowers.

At least it lends an air of gaiety, Flora thought. *It's grim otherwise.*

Colette hesitated and appeared to cast her eye around. Seeing two men seated near the back of the café, she moved forward. Nodding a greeting to the other occupants, she finally shook hands with each of them and sat down. Flora followed her lead. Introductions were made.

"Flora, this is Jean-Pierre and Pascal," she said. Speaking in an undertone, Colette explained to Flora that Pascal had come to this place via the same route as herself, but that Jean-Pierre lived several kilometres to the south in the direction of Loches and knew others in the region who had a similar outlook.

"My cousin, Luca, will be keen to meet you," Flora said to Jean-Pierre.

"Yes," Colette said. "He has a route across from the Occupied Zone. He's used it already for some sabotage work. Local knowledge is a real asset."

"It wasn't him who sent those Jewish families our way, was it? We helped them onwards, but they said they'd been warned about the raids by someone round here."

"It was Flora here who dug out the original information which saved them." Colette gave them a shortened version of events, which spared Flora the embarrassment of seeming to brag about her endeavours.

"There used to be a really good escape route virtually all the way from the Netherlands to the south coast and Spain. It was set up by a Belgian who took on the persona of a French Canadian and called himself Pat O'Leary. His line was excellent until a couple of years ago, when it was infiltrated by a real criminal guy and several valuable operatives were rounded up. The man had obviously turned for some rich pickings. We need to help make a similar idea work again. There are quite a few escapees and evaders who rely on us. Are you in, Flora? Will your family help?" Jean-Pierre took a tobacco tin from his pocket and proceeded to roll a thin smoke, pulling the loose strands from the ends before lighting it.

The bell above the door pinged.

"Don't look, any of you. We have company," Pascal said, picking up a discarded paper lying on the next table.

"Laugh," Jean-Pierre said to Colette. "We're four friends having a flirt and a drink."

Colette responded with ease and picked up her drink, saying, "*Salut, mon ami.*"

Flora raised her eyes to see a man in a *gendarme* uniform leaning on the bar to buy something. The woman in the headscarf left her table and, taking her dog in her arms, headed for the door.

The two old men stopped talking and paused before resuming their conversation. Suddenly, the atmosphere had altered.

Flora's mouth was dry and her knees were shaking. *All we're doing is meeting friends and having a drink*, she reasoned with herself.

"I'm going for a piss," Pascal said. He stood to head out to the back alley, which most men used for that purpose.

That takes his face from the scene, Flora thought.

While he was gone, the *gendarme* left and there was a collective exhalation and shoulders relaxed, or so it seemed to Flora.

"All back to normal, I see," Pascal said as he sat down again. "I've checked out the dead letterbox," he added after a moment.

Flora frowned and glanced at Colette.

"It's the name we use for making contact without meeting anyone else. It's for messages or exchange of small items. This here, us seeing each other face to face, is a live drop."

Pascal glanced around, but no one was listening or even close enough to their table to hear. "There's an old brick on the high window ledge to the left of the back door," he said. "If you find some information that would be useful, Flora, you leave it there and one of us will collect it. If we want you to look for something in that office of yours, we'll ask via that too."

"You can access the alley from the street; you don't have to go through here," Jean-Pierre said.

"Where does it lead to at the other end?" Pascal asked.

"It takes you to the edge of the town. There's a wall, not too high, which you could vault over to make a getaway across the fields, or there's a dirt track that turns and runs along behind this row of shops. It's like a rural service road."

"Useful indeed," Pascal said.

"That's why I chose to put the dead letterbox there." Jean-Pierre tutted, shook his head and muttered under his breath, "*Idiot Anglais*." There was an awkward silence. "We think of all possibilities at all times. Safety is our first consideration. Those of us who have been doing this for so long have this as second nature. You need to learn quickly."

"Jean-Pierre, you and I have these things, but these two are new, and what's more they are volunteers. They will learn and you must be more patient."

He shrugged.

"I must go," Pascal said and rose to leave. He shook hands with each of them and shrugging on his denim work jacket, he made for the door.

"I would like to meet your cousin." Jean-Pierre changed the subject.

"We are a busy and productive vineyard, but if you come one evening Luca will be there if I warn him. Shall we say Tuesday?"

"I'll come at about twenty-one hundred. The curfew won't be on then, but it'll be dusk."

"Fine," Flora said. She did not like this man and was not disposed to be more fulsome than that. She gave him the address. "I'm sure you'll find your way."

"Of course," he said as he stood.

"Don't mind him," Colette said after he had gone. "He lives on his nerves most of the time, but he's a brilliant and brave man."

"I'm not sure how Luca will get on with him. He's strong-willed too. The last thing we need is fireworks between them if they are to be working together."

Having queued at two different shops, they managed to buy most of the items Delphi had requested. With a bulging shopping bag, they headed back to their bicycles. As they passed the *mairie* they nearly fell over Thibault, who rushed from the building, looking left and right but not straight in front of him. He came to a halt and, trying hard to look composed, he followed convention and stopped to greet them. Flora introduced her cousin Colette.

"I'm not sure you met her when she last visited," she said.

"No. Pleased to make your acquaintance." He looked around, as if wanting an excuse to leave with continued speed.

"Is M Duclos at work today? I'm surprised if he is," Flora said.

"Yes, well, yes. I had an appointment," the young lad said with importance.

"Oh, he didn't say." Flora was puzzled.

"Conversation of a confidential nature. I imagine his secretary had no need to know," he said.

She could have cheerfully slapped him at that point, but she managed to refrain.

The girls wished him a good weekend and without further exchange, took their leave.

CHAPTER 43

"Why on earth was he so secretive?" Flora asked Luca. "Sanctimonious idiot. I wanted to box his ears."

"*Il a le cervau d'un sandwich au fromage. Stupide.*"

Colette burst out laughing. "His brain is more like a lump of lard than a cheese sandwich."

"It's probably nothing, but he likes to creep around those he thinks have some power. It makes him dangerous. What about this other bloke you were just telling me about?"

Colette filled him in. "Jean-Pierre has been in *La Résistance* for a very long time. It's playing with his head a bit. Several trains came to grief, and he sabotaged a large fuel dump near Paris recently. He travels far and wide, but he's here now and wants to meet up with you and your group. He spoke about rebuilding a line for escapees and evaders to travel to the south or into Spain. They're more likely to be able to get across to Gibraltar or catch a passage on a ship from there."

"I can round up the others and we can meet here in the back of the barn. I'll contact Hubert and Antoine. We won't include Thibault with this one, though. He's been over when we've cut wires, but that's about it."

"No trouble?" Colette raised her eyebrows and tilted her head.

"Only the first time we crossed over, but it wasn't serious. We've let him come but not given him any warning at all, so he's not been able to pass any information on beforehand. Hubert and Antoine came then too, but the last couple of times Hubert wasn't able to get away, so the three of us made ad hoc decisions to go."

"Can you get Antoine and Hubert here on Tuesday, then? I'll send a message to Jean-Pierre. He'll probably bring Pascal too. That'll be seven of us with Flora and me."

Two nights later, the candles glowed in their jars and they all sat around on the bales of straw.

"This is prickly." Colette wriggled.

Antoine took off his jacket and made a great play of giving it to her to sit on. "She needs some pastis, Luca. It'll toughen her up and put hairs on her chest." He laughed.

"Enough of that," she said and flashed her smile at him. "Leave my chest out of this." She swiped at him playfully.

His eyes sparkled in response.

"We need to concentrate." Luca sounded grim. "So, Jean-Pierre, what's the plan?"

Late one Sunday night a week later, Luca whispered to Antoine as they stumbled along the lane behind Jean-Pierre on their way to the Château of Chenonceau. "Can't say I'm taking to this guy," Even though they were now familiar with the route, the night was dark, and the surface was pitted with puddles and tufted with clumps of coarse grass. "He's surly and downright rude."

"Seems to know what's what. I wonder where Hubert got to? I understood he was coming."

"Me too. We couldn't have waited any longer. It's not as if we actively need him this time, though, not just to see a couple of airmen over. In fact, the fewer the better."

"You say 'just', but it's still a big deal. I have to say, every time we go over, I want to shit myself. After that first time, when we were nearly caught red-handed, it's got far more risky. There're so many more of the blighters around on guard and on our side too. Pétain's really lost it. He's as much a traitor as the Boche themselves. *Baiseur*!"

"Your vocabulary does you credit, my friend." Luca laughed.

"Hush, you two. We're close," Jean-Pierre snapped.

Luca grinned as Antoine pulled a face behind the older man's back. Antoine always lifted his spirits, even if he was a bit of a wild one sometimes. *At least he'll cover for me*, Luca thought and patted his friend's shoulder.

As before, they approached the looming shadow of the building and slunk around to the door that would ultimately lead to the long gallery, which crossed the river and therefore the border to the Occupied Zone. These days, patrols were just as frequent on either side. Initially, the appeasement by the Vichy government meant fewer troops in the Free Zone, but not so now. Deportations of the Jewish community as well as those who displeased the Germans were taking place, and shootings and beatings were not uncommon on the Free side, either.

Jean-Pierre had told Luca and his companions that escapees and evaders were entitled to lose their uniforms and don local clothing, as long as they could prove that's who they were. They kept their dog tags to do this. Otherwise, they would be shot by the Nazis as traitors or spies. At the very least, they risked being shipped as slave labour either to the North of France to build the many new blockhaus constructions for the flying weapon or worse, to Germany or beyond where they would face mistreatment, malnutrition and torture as prisoners of war, if rumour was only half true.

They crossed the gallery. It didn't have the power to set Luca's heart racing as it had done that first night. However, his breath was still a little shorter than normal. They slid along the walls and stroked the floor with their toes as they stepped across the black and white tiles. There were no distant sounds, and all was as silent as a cemetery, dark and unnerving.

They left the building and ventured forth to collect their first fugitive. By the time they had travelled to the pick-up point, to which Jean-Pierre had guided them, Luca's nerves were jangled again. Every tree became a shelter for a man, each branch the nozzle of a gun, each distant thud a marching army of terror.

I'm not built for this, he thought.

"How does he remain so calm?" Antoine nodded at the back of Jean-Pierre.

"I don't think he is. That's why he's so irascible. Living on his nerves," Luca whispered back.

The man they collected was introduced as Andrew. He was tall and thin, with the moustache of someone barely out of adolescence. His trousers were too short, and his denim jacket had sleeves that showed bony wrists. His hands were cold, despite the mildness of the night. His cap was pulled low over his eyes, so it was impossible in the dark to see his face properly. Luca got the impression of undernourishment, and the lad was jumpy with lack of sleep.

Luca felt old next to him. As they greeted each other, he placed a hand on Andrew's shoulder. "Take heart, my friend. We'll soon have you in a warm barn with good farm food." He mimed eating.

Andrew blew out his cheeks, releasing the air in a rush and nodding violently.

The return journey went well, and they weren't far from home. Luca had begun to relax when Jean-Pierre stopped, and they nearly crashed into his back in the dark. He raised his hand and cocked his head to one side.

They all heard what had caught his attention. As they stood like statues at the edge of the road, they saw the flash of lights through the trees. A patrol.

They flung themselves into the drainage ditch that ran parallel. Luca thought, *Thank the Lord it's dry. If this were winter, it would be full of cold peaty water. It's damp as it is.*

The vehicles — motorbikes, by the sound — crept inexorably closer. Luca lay still and said a silent prayer. As the machines advanced, his heart began thumping so hard that he feared he would pass out. Turning his face, he smelled the pungent odour of the soil. A weed tickled his cheek. He dared not brush it away but willed himself to stay as still as he was able. The noise seemed deafening.

The urge to turn his head and peek was difficult to resist. From the racket and vibrations through the earth, Luca judged that the vehicles were almost upon him. He kept his face averted but opened his eyes. A light swept past, glowing among the trees, and even the grass near his head was illuminated. He imagined it playing across his torso and legs. He waited for something to spear his spine. Then all went dark again, and the commotion receded. Breathing deeply and making a conscious effort to relax. The trees whispered; an owl hooted … the sound of a boot scraped somewhere nearby.

Then Luca realised it was one of his friends moving, and he turned and eased himself from his prone position.

CHAPTER 44

Luca opened the kitchen door and looked in before entering. Andrew followed. Delphi, Rainier, Colette and Flora were all seated around the table, despite the late hour.

"You shouldn't be here." Luca addressed them all. "The less you know, the better."

"I told them that," Rainier said. "None of them listened." He extended a hand to Andrew and spoke in English for his benefit. "Welcome. Sit here."

After shaking hands, Delphi got up and went to the pantry, returning with as much as she could carry on a tray. Rainier returned from the cellar with a bottle and fetched glasses.

"Flora and I have made a bed in the hideaway. It's only blankets over the straw, I'm afraid." Colette smiled at the stranger.

Flora observed the man. He was very young, and his skin was almost grey, he was so tired. His hands shook as he ground them together. There were dark half-moons beneath his eyes, which darted around, not settling for more than a second on anything.

"You'll be safe here until you have recovered and can face the next part of your journey," she said.

He gave a small smile and nodded. "You're English?"

"Yes, but I've lived in France for much of my life. Rainier here is my stepfather, and Luca is my sort-of cousin." She looked in his direction and rose to go and stand beside him as he propped himself against the sink. "You look tired too," she said under her breath. "Was everything alright?"

"Mmm. A patrol on the way back, but that was all." He laughed, but it didn't reach his eyes. "Between you and me, it's bloody nerve-wracking." He shivered. "A goose is on my grave — is that what you say?"

"Something like that." Flora touched his arm and smiled.

After they had eaten a small amount, Andrew tried to smother a yawn, but another followed almost immediately.

"That's catching," Colette said as she, too, opened her mouth wide and hid it behind her hand.

She and Delphi began to tidy up and Rainier damped down the fire.

Flora and Luca escorted Andrew outside to the barn and to the little room at the back.

Luca pulled away the planks to show him the hidden space. Flora had had no idea until recently that it existed.

"We used to build dens in there," Luca said. "I don't know why it was built originally. Some ancestor must have used it, although I can't think why. It will certainly be of use now, that's for sure."

"This is cosy," Andrew said.

"And safe. There's a candle in that jar, and matches, but be careful with those, for goodness' sake. The last thing we want is a fire and you holed up in here."

"Thank you for everything," the young man said.

"Flora will bring you breakfast, but you'll be better staying in here during the day. In the evening after the workers have gone, it should be safe to come out and stretch your legs," Luca explained.

"I'll be happy to sleep all of tomorrow, I think." Andrew collapsed onto the makeshift bed.

"Goodnight, then. We'll have to put the partition back. I hope you're not too claustrophobic. There's a mallet in the corner if you need to break out and the bucket under that cloth for the necessary. Sorry it's not better than that." Luca grimaced.

"Right now, it's a palace."

Having fastened the boards in place and mussed up the straw, Luca and Flora stepped outside into the dark.

"Do you remember that night when I came back from helping the Jewish families?"

She looked directly into his brown eyes. "Yes, I do. I told you then I wasn't sorry, and I'm still not."

He stepped towards her. She raised her face up to his and he leaned down and kissed her. Then he pulled her back into the close confines of the barn, and sinking down to sit side by side on a straw bale, they leaned in to each other. With foreheads touching, he closed his eyes and so did she.

"Thank you," he said. "Oh, Flora."

Then he kissed her again. Not innocently, but with fire and passion. His arms came around her back and across her shoulders. They were bound together. It lasted forever, or so it seemed. She was lost. He kissed her neck. His hands moved. One came around and encased her breast, gently kneading its fullness. He groaned imperceptibly before pulling away. In the dim light, she smiled up at him and saw desire in his eyes. He took her fingers in his.

"I think I knew I loved you, but wouldn't let myself give in."

They embraced again before rising with reluctance. As they stood, Flora was aware of him against the length of her body. She felt each ripple, each movement, every swelling. He pulled away and with fingers entwined they headed back to the house. They shared another long kiss by the door, during which Luca threaded his hands in her hair and pressed Flora to him. Every muscle, every contour of him made her senses reel. Part of her seemed to melt into him.

Disentangling, they entered the kitchen. A small side light was left on for them, but everything was tidy and empty. The others had gone to bed.

Over the next few days, Luca touched Flora's shoulder as he passed when she was sitting, they linked hands briefly when meeting outside, and they made excuses to see each other in the dark before bedtime, when they exchanged murmurings and kisses which gave them an excited warmth but left them both wanting more.

Andrew, who turned out to be a young RAF officer, gained colour in his face. He slept in the daytime or read books that Delphi lent him. She apologised for their content and the romantic nature of them, but he didn't seem to mind.

"It's far better than you know," he said.

In the evening, he joined them in the kitchen for the meal which was taken later than in the winter, since work in the fields continued while it was light. The vines were growing with speed, and it was a constant job to snip off the shoots that insisted on sprouting out beyond the bunches of grapes. This would encourage the fruit to swell with the juice they needed to produce their wine. The elderly François often ate dinner with them at midday but never in the evening, having retired either to the bar or his own humble dwelling.

Luca was in the barn, releasing Andrew from his hiding place, when the sound of spraying gravel in the courtyard was followed by a knock on the kitchen door. Luca froze and Andrew scrambled back into the cubby hole. There was no time for Luca to replace the boards, and anyway, the noise would give them away. As Luca emerged from the back room, André appeared at the barn door.

"Ah, Luca. My apologies. I knocked at the kitchen door, but there was no reply. Is my bicycle in the way there?"

Luca said, "André." He managed not to turn back to look at the place where Andrew had hidden but advanced towards André, guiding him towards the house. He glanced at the bicycle propped against the barn beside the door. "No, it's fine there. Please, come in."

"It's late and I am unannounced."

He's such a prick, thought Luca. *Why does he have to speak like some old-fashioned person from la noblesse? We did away with that class nearly two hundred years ago.*

The family were gathering in the kitchen and there was a delicious odour coming from a pot on the stove.

"Ah, here he is," Rainier said.

"And you have Andr— ah, André with you." Delphi hastily changed what she'd been about to say. "This is a lovely surprise. Please sit down."

"Will you take a glass with us? Pastis or wine?" Rainier fetched the bottles and filled a jug with water.

"I'll be back directly," Luca said. "I just need to finish putting away those tools. Shan't be long."

When he returned, he went to the sink to wash his hands. Flora was speaking. "I didn't realise you were coming, André. This is a surprise. Oh, and may I introduce my cousin, Colette? You have heard me speak of her."

Colette came across the room and shook his hand. "Sorry, I didn't hear we have a visitor. I was upstairs."

"Yes, you said she was staying. *Enchanté, mademoiselle.*" He smiled at Colette. "All the cousins together."

"I thought you were working late tonight?" Flora passed a glass to him and offered the jug of water for his pastis.

"I did quite a bit, but then I got tired. I meant to ask you before you left if you'd accompany me for dinner one night again, Flora. Perhaps Luca and Colette might come too. We could make a party of it."

At that point, Luca turned off the tap and came to the table. "Did someone say my name?"

"André is suggesting that we all go out together one evening." Flora beamed at him with a merry glint in her eye. "That would be fun, wouldn't it? Did you get everything put away?" she asked.

"Yes, always best to tidy up properly and keep things safe."

"Absolutely," Flora agreed.

A silence followed.

"So … what have you been doing since you came, Colette?" André sipped his drink and raised his eyebrows at her.

"Not too much. It's lovely to stay with the family, though."

"I don't remember you visiting before." Was it Luca's imagination or was André watching her closely? "Yet Luca has lived here all his life."

Colette seemed relaxed and breezy in her response. "No, I haven't been for many years. My father was killed just after the last show. My mother needed me."

"But she is not here with you now?" He appeared to be pursuing the facts.

"No, she's in America now, so I am free."

"America? My word!"

"Yes, she has friends there. When things became complicated here, she left to visit and decided to stay."

She's mighty good with the lies tripping off her tongue, Luca thought. *She looks so innocent. No one would guess she has a radio transmitter or that she uses a dead letterbox in Thorelière to communicate with other so-called traitors.*

"When shall we go out? That would be such fun, wouldn't it, Flora? We can't possibly turn down such an invitation. May Antoine join us? And doesn't he have a sister, Luca? Would that be acceptable, *m'sieur*? If we are making a party of it, I mean."

"Er, well, yes, *mademoiselle*," André said.

Arrangements were made, and after some polite conversation they all stood and shook hands as a goodbye. Luca walked André to the door, and behind his back he jerked his head at Flora to accompany him. With great reluctance, she agreed, and as she stood next to them Luca made his farewell remarks and left her to see him out.

Not impressed, she waited at the door while he mounted his bicycle and disappeared.

"I must go and release our friend," Luca said when André had gone. He made to pass her and cross the courtyard. She followed him out.

"How could you leave me to do that? You know how I feel about him. It's bad enough that I have to work with him." Flora marched at his side towards the barn.

They stopped before entering.

"My sweeting," Luca began as he opened the door.

"Don't try that with me," she said.

"We need him to think we're on side. We must have access to what plans are afoot. Darling Flora, you are magnificent when you are fiery." Grabbing her hand, he pulled her inside the barn and against his chest.

"Oh, Luca, you are so … so annoying."

He cut off further words by covering her mouth with his, and her lips parted.

CHAPTER 45

"I heard last night that there are a number of escapees and evaders who are desperately searching for an escape route. We must help more in this area," Colette said.

"Now that Andrew has moved on, we have space here and we could conceal more than one." Flora shifted on the prickly hay bale upon which she sat.

"We have a place too," Antoine said. "We might hide at least three."

"It's feeding them as well, remember." Luca shrugged and spread his arms. "Food shortages are hitting quite hard these days."

"True." Antoine nodded.

"When is the next run to collect people?" Flora knew Luca was keen to get on with it.

"Jean-Pierre will be in touch soon. I'll ensure word reaches you, Antoine."

"I can come next time," Hubert said.

"Too many on the collection is dangerous, but when they arrive you could help relocate to safe houses," Colette encouraged him. "I must move my transmitter. They're combing the area with their direction finders. I need to keep changing its location." Colette looked anxious. "You would be arrested too, if I'm caught."

"I have somewhere," Luca said with a glance at Flora. "I'll show you later."

"Perhaps it would be safer to do it now," Hubert said.

"I have an idea too," Antoine added.

"If we do it now, we'll definitely be alright," Hubert persisted. "We don't want you or your family harmed, Luca."

"Tonight will be soon enough," Luca said. "I'll do it under cover of dark."

"What time? I'll help," Hubert said.

"The fewer who come, the safer for each of us. You included, Hubert," Luca said. "None of this goes to Thibault either. He's too young."

Flora sat at her desk, daydreaming. She was tempted to write Luca's name and frame it, as she might have done had she been a schoolgirl. At times, she felt as giddy as an adolescent now they had admitted their love for each other. She was pondering her situation when a tap at the door distracted her. She was surprised to see who was there.

"Hubert."

"I was wondering if M Duclos was available." With white-knuckled fingers, Hubert twirled his cap around in his hands.

"If you wait here, I'll go and find out. I won't be a minute."

She tapped on André's door, and at his command she entered. Closing it behind her, she made her request.

André looked at his watch and tutted. "I'm not sure I'm able to meet him now with no appointment. I have a meeting in twenty minutes, and I must get over to the *gendarmerie*. See if he can return at two o'clock. Better still, perhaps you could deal with it…? It's probably nothing much."

Returning to Hubert, Flora thought he looked ill at ease. He was shuffling from one foot to the other and still pulling at his cap.

She relayed the message, then asked, "Is it anything I might help with, Hubert?"

"No, no, not at all. I need to speak with *M le Maire* and seek his advice. It's in confidence, Flora."

"Very well. Come back at two and he will see you then."

Looking everywhere but at her, he thanked her and left.

That's odd, she thought.

At ten minutes before two o'clock that afternoon, Hubert reappeared and Flora knocked on André's door once more. "M Hubert Girard is here."

"Show him in." André nodded at her.

"Please go through, Hubert," Flora said.

"I don't want to be overheard," he said to André before he shut the door.

Flora frowned and stood still, straining her ears, but she could discern nothing above a vague murmuring.

He must be talking very quietly, she thought. *What's going on?*

Hubert was closeted behind the closed door for more than thirty minutes, which seemed a long time for the usual query regarding local citizen's issues. Normally these involved a minor dispute with a neighbour or some question about land or rights.

Finally, the door opened. "Is everything alright?"

Again, Hubert avoided eye contact. "Yes, see you soon."

That evening, Flora walked with Luca as he took a round through the vines. He often did at this time. It was good way to wind down, and after the heat of a summer's day or as the birds were bedding down in spring or autumn it was a pleasant thing to do. This evening it was quite early. Their fingers were intertwined and every so often they stopped to admire the changes in the sky, or to admire each other when a kiss was given and received.

"Luca, Hubert visited André today," Flora said. She proceeded to tell him of his restless demeanour and shifty gaze. Shaking her head, she said, "I'm becoming overly sensitive to everything."

"I think you must be. He's alright, is Hubert. I've known him for ages. His father fought during the last show and died in the war for his troubles. Hubert's been on several wire-cutting missions with us too. Now, if it was Thibault, I would understand your concern. He's definitely not to be trusted." Concerns disappeared for a while as Luca took her face in his hands and gently kissed her, first on her forehead and then on her lips. "I've found here a woman who is strong and courageous, but sensitive too."

He kissed her again. His fingers explored her back and then moved around until he managed to undo her top two buttons. He caressed her inside her blouse. Her hands rode up inside his shirt and they were as close as they could be under the circumstances. As they broke away, she listened to a blackbird singing, broadcasting its happiness all around her.

"That's such an iconic spring sound," she whispered into his chest. She felt their hearts pumping.

Colette said that evening, "I have to go away for a few days. Please don't ask me why or where."

"Will you be gone for long?" Flora frowned. "I shall miss you."

"Hopefully not for too long. Perhaps you would tell anyone who asks that I've returned to Bédorgues for a short visit to ensure everything is as it should be at my home."

"Stay safe." Flora gave her best friend a hug. "When will you go?"

Colette laughed. "I said don't ask me why or where, so you ask me when. I shall go tomorrow evening, after we've been out with the others to eat, if that's alright with you all?" She turned to look at Delphi and Rainier. "I shall need to take my suitcase with me, Luca. Would you mind coming that far to help me retrieve it after the meal tomorrow? Then I'll be out of your hair for a bit and you'll all be safer."

"I think I should come with you on your travels," Luca said. "I would be of assistance in many ways."

"No, you're needed here, and it would seem odd for you to accompany me. André for one would wonder why, and he would likely communicate that to the Germans. No, it would be useful to have another person, but your suggestion is not possible."

No one spoke for a moment.

"What about me?" Rainier glanced at Delphi.

Involuntarily, she gasped, "*Mais non*, Rainier."

He went to put his arms around her.

"I could go," Flora said into the silence. "What would be more normal than two cousins on a journey? I'd learn and be so much more useful."

"You can't take such a risk, Flora." Delphi came and put her arm around Flora's shoulders.

"In truth, Delphi, it won't be that risky this time," Colette said. "It would be less risky for two of us than me on my own, which does seem a bit odd. It's not really the done thing, is it, for a single girl to be pedalling about the countryside?"

"What about your job with André in Thorelière? He will miss you." Delphi was catching at every reason against her daughter going on this mission.

"You must telephone and say I am sick, Mama. No, better still, I'll ask him for a few days off and tell him I wish to accompany Colette to her home. That would be natural. How long will we be gone?" Flora turned to Colette.

"Less than a week. Maybe five days at the most."

"There you are, then. Perfect!"

"Oh, Flora, please take care," Delphi said.

The argument was won.

CHAPTER 46

All the friends and André Duclos met at the *Auberge de la Ferme* in a small village a couple of kilometres from Thorelière. It was a respectable place, where the farmer's wife provided a good three-course meal and included a carafe of wine and a bottle of fruit-flavoured liqueur for an *apéritif*.

As they each arrived, they leaned their bicycles against the fence. The girls removed headscarves and shook out their hair. Antoine's sister, who was a buxom dark-haired lass, said, "I hope I don't look too much of a fright. I hardly ever go anywhere, so this is a real outing."

They exchanged kisses and handshakes, and then together they climbed the few steps and headed for a table on the terrace. The evenings were longer and warmer now. The new season was fully here. The leaves on the trees were turning to a darker green. If spring was a child laughing and skipping among a cloud of drifting almond blossom petals and bright flowers, then summer was a bride arriving sedately and treading softly with a borrowed bouquet amid the blue from above.

The table at which they sat lay beneath a straw awning. Lights were strung around the edge, but only every other bulb glowed faintly — a sign of the times. However, the cloth was pristinely white with a sky-blue overcover and matching napkins. Once settled, André took charge of the bottle in the centre of the table and poured for each of them. They sipped the sweet alcohol while nibbling the little pastries and dipped the crusty bread pieces in the flavoured oil. This was an opportunity to make small talk and get the politics of the group sorted out.

"Flora, your glass is empty," André said, and without waiting he refilled it.

She smiled. Glancing at Luca, she saw a frown flit across his face before a mask slid down and he smiled too.

Colette entered the fray. "Antoine, *s'il t'plaît.*" She held a glass across with a cheeky smile, and he picked up the bottle and served. Flora saw him return the grin with one of his own that made a dimple deepen, and he gave a wink that left his thoughts undisguised.

Just then, Flora became aware of Luca's knee against hers under the shelter of the long tablecloth. Heat rose up her neck and she was tempted to giggle. With the fever of her thoughts, she became tongue-tied and when André addressed her, she was forced to say, "Sorry, André, I didn't catch that."

"I was just saying we are so lucky to be able to sit here and enjoy ourselves on such an evening. We thank Marshal Pétain and out Protectors for this."

Silence followed his remark, until Colette said, "Well said, *m'sieur.*" She smiled and raised her glass while the others rallied and copied her example.

"Ah yes, *mademoiselle*, Colette. Flora's cousin? You agree with my comment?"

"*Bien sûr, m'sieur.* Where would we be without such a protectorate? There are troubles and troublesome people from whom we need to be kept safe."

"And how long do we keep the pleasure of your company?" André raised his glass to his lips, keeping his eyes firmly on her face.

"A while longer," she said. "There is much to interest me here." She exchanged a glance with Antoine and smiled.

"Although I was going to pop home for a few days. I was hoping Flora would come with me. Might she, M Duclos, André?" She gave him her best smile.

"Ah, you find our little community tedious?"

"Oh, no. My village near Montluçon is small, and here I have family."

"Whom you don't see much."

"That's right. It's so good to catch up again," Colette said. "After all this time, we still have a lot in common. Do we not, cousin Flora?"

"Yes, we certainly do. It's lovely to meet you here again. Although I understand you need to go home occasionally to make sure all is well. Would I be able to take a few days off work, André? Colette would like to leave tomorrow."

"Well, it is always busy and that's short notice. I do believe something is on the horizon, but if it's just for a while, I'm sure I can manage."

The rest of the meal passed without further political comment. The food was good, considering the shortages that were beginning to bite. The rabbit was tender, and a sauce made it tasty. Vegetables were local and easy to come by. Baked apples were enlivened with a jam that was sweet and formed a juicy dessert.

By the time little cups of strong black coffee had come, it was late in the evening. Darkness had crept upon them and the hostess had lit candles around the terrace that were attracting moths and other insects but kept them away from the company.

"I shall go and settle the bill," André said with a proprietary air.

"No, we'll pay our way." Luca pushed his chair back and stood.

Flora regarded his expression and recognised the line between his brows. Antoine must have seen it too. He arose, and putting his hand on Luca's arm, he said, "Come, my friend, we shall split it three ways." With that, they followed André with speed. Whatever happened indoors, they all emerged together, and no blows had been dealt.

Colette looked at her watch and stifled a gasp. She glanced at André's back before she spoke. "I must get home, or I'll miss my sked," she whispered to Flora.

"Your what?"

"My scheduled transmission, I hadn't realised it was so late. I've a date with a headset. I mustn't be late, or I'll miss my slot for transmission."

They each made the *au revoir* by waving, blowing kisses and saying *tout le monde*.

"Maybe we'll meet again soon," Antoine said to Colette.

"I'm sure we shall, if you come to visit Luca." She smiled up at him.

"Mmm, I meant you and me," he said.

Flora listened to her enigmatic reply. "We shall see." But she also noticed her friend cock her head to one side and wink at him.

"Flora, my dear, this has been such a pleasant evening." André claimed her attention as they reached the bicycles piled against the shed. "I shall see you at work after your little holiday. There is some new information that I must attend to, so I shall be in early and it will keep me busy until you return. We must hurry now and be home before curfew. It's for our safety, after all."

"Yes, indeed, André. Thank you for such a lovely evening," she managed to say with a smile.

They each prepared to go their separate ways. André cycled off towards his village. Antoine kissed Colette's fingers in mock gallantry.

"Remember I said I will be going home for a few days, to Bédorgues."

"I heard you say, but why so soon?"

"Needs must in these uncertain times."

"*Au revoir, mon ange.* Hurry back." Antoine blew her a kiss.

"I'm certainly no angel. More a little devil," Colette said, winking and grinning again.

"Colette! Time to go, I think." Flora nodded and smiled. "You two are as bad as each other."

Luca took Flora safely home and then he and Colette turned their bicycles around and headed out of the courtyard, returning thirty minutes later with her small suitcase.

"Did you get your messages sent?" Flora asked upon their return.

"Yes. Now we must collect our bags and leave. At least we have very full stomachs. We've a way to cycle, and on the back roads it will take a little longer. I'll be in touch via Jean-Pierre, and he may make contact via the dead letterbox. You've had that information about where, Luca."

As they went outside to go, Luca accompanied them. Colette gave them a minute as she waited by the entrance.

Luca wrapped his arms around Flora. "I'm so proud of you, but I shall be heart-torn if anything happens to you. Take no risks at all. I should have been firmer and accompanied Colette myself."

"No, that would look terribly wrong. It's better this way," Flora said as she lost herself in his hug. "I love you."

"And I you, dearest one."

CHAPTER 47

As they pedalled, they listened until they were well away from habitation.

"I can't believe I'm doing this," Flora whispered. "It's surreal. It's bizarre. You better tell me some of our mission now, don't you think?"

"The next stage of the escape line was blown. We must mend the web, join the bloodied strands, reset things in motion. I have a contact near Loches."

"What happened to the previous people?"

"Something small, no doubt. Locals sell their produce to Germans. Sometimes women sleep with them. Mousetraps are set and a watch maintained if a live or dead letterbox is suspected. Informants are all around, and agents have learned to their cost that no one can be trusted. Detection vans are becoming swifter and more deadly all the time. Transmissions must be short and to the point, and radio transmitters must be moved frequently these days."

"I see."

"Things are much better co-ordinated now, though. Hitler really blew it when he took on Russia. They were supposed to be allies. Now all the communists in France are up in arms, literally. Pétain's gone overboard with his mass round-up of the Jews, and this *Milice* under Joseph Darnand is shooting people without trial. People have had enough, and the Vichy government have let down even their most ardent supporters. It's getting easier in another respect too. Georges Bégué's messaging system via *Radio Londres* is more efficient and more widely used."

"I thought he was a prisoner."

"He was, over here, but he escaped and he's back in England now."

"We did listen in and hear some weird messages. We assumed they were some sort of code."

"Exactly. If you hear 'Pierre is well', it would mean a drop is to be expected, but if you hear 'Pierre sends greetings', the drop will be off for whatever reason. It's much safer to get that from a radio at home than from a transmission like the ones I make."

"You mean a drop of equipment?"

"Yes, or personnel, like me. Although I came by boat, of course. Either way can be used."

"So, what exactly are we going to do next?" Flora was more and more curious and tingled with nervous excitement. At last, she was being truly useful.

"Two things. We're going to meet a garage owner in Loches. It's been a live letterbox, but we need to set up something else. His wife's become very jumpy about it and we need to be quick in case the Germans are watching it. It won't take long before it's blown. The Boche already set a mousetrap, that's a watch, on a café and took three agents. They all had instructions to contact this man Frédéric at the café, but when they phoned the number someone closely resembling him in looks and voice gave them false instructions. Of course, that someone was a Nazi sympathiser. All three walked into the trap."

"I'm thinking this mission is considerably more dangerous than we all thought when we were back at home," Flora said.

"Now is the safest time to go."

"How come?"

"They've just picked up and cleared out the cell, or so they believe. If we get in there and get it back up and running, we can skedaddle quickly, and all will be well."

"I can't believe I'm in this situation." Flora shook her head. "What's the second thing?"

"There's to be a drop of equipment. I need to tell someone about it. You were born for this," Colette said. "Remember the spying scrape you performed at school?"

Flora chuckled and then sobered. "But I was caught, and I got into a terrible lot of trouble over it. I hope that's not a forewarning I'm ignoring here."

"It's a good thing you're doing. Remember some of the dreadful things that have happened to innocent people. We must combat all that's going on in any way we can."

"Yes, of course," Flora said.

They cycled on in silence for a while. They had to travel just under twenty-five kilometres, which wasn't far, but as they neared the town they had to travel with extreme care. They couldn't afford to be caught out beyond the hours of the curfew.

"I think we better get off and push in case we need to dive down an alley or hide in a doorway," Colette said in an undertone. "If that's the case, leave your bike propped against a wall. Don't just drop it and run. That would be highly suspicious, especially if a wheel is still turning."

In the silence their footfalls sounded like a marching army, despite the fact that they tried to step quietly.

Of course, it was too much to hope that they would reach the garage without incident.

"What's that noise?" Colette stopped to listen, and Flora nearly bumped into her. "Patrol."

They left their bikes against a wall. Colette unhooked her case and bag, and Flora did the same. There was nowhere to go.

"What shall we do?" Flora's voice was tinged with panic.

"Leave the bicycles. Back this way. Quick," Colette said. "There was an alley around the corner."

"I didn't see one," Flora said. Her breath came in agitated puffs.

"I've been keeping a lookout all the way for just this kind of thing. Keep to the wall and follow me."

They ran as if their lives depended upon it. Flora thought they probably did.

The sounds of motors roared louder as the vehicles rounded the corner and lights swept the road. They dived up the tiny back street that Colette had seen.

"Turn to the wall and stay still," Colette said.

For Flora, the temptation to turn her head and peek was intoxicating. She almost felt a light sweep across her inert form, but it could not have penetrated far into the alley. She shuddered and her breath escaped in a rasp.

"Give it a minute or two," Colette whispered. It was impossible to see her, even when Flora opened her eyes. Her heart was pounding in her ears and her thoughts swam until she was faint. Leaning her forehead on the wall, Flora concentrated on not being sick.

"Okay, let's go," murmured Colette.

How can she be so calm? Somehow Flora wobbled to the entrance of the little cut and peered around the corner. She was convinced she would see a soldier marching in her direction. What if they knew where the two were hiding and were waiting for them to emerge? All was quiet, and no one was to be seen. She scuttled after her friend.

"It's not far now," Colette said, and to Flora's relief it wasn't. They knocked on a door with peeling paint. Flora craned her neck back, peered at the faded sign above the entrance of the building next door, and could barely make out the word 'Garage'. She had no time to see more, as the door in front of which they stood slid open a crack and the occupant, upon seeing the two young women, waggled his hand with vigour to indicate they should enter quickly.

They each struggled with their bicycles up the three steps and parked them in a dingy hallway. The bulb hanging from the ceiling had no shade and was barely alight. The paint was a shade of tobacco-brown and shiny. The old cabbage smell would have turned Flora's stomach in normal circumstances, but she was too tired to mind.

M'sieur, le garagiste, for such he turned out to be, beckoned them forward into an equally dull, dim and grubby kitchen, where his wife was drying her hands on a rectangle of striped cotton with ragged edges. He indicated they should sit. The oil cloth on the table was sticky, so after one touch Flora kept her hands in her lap.

"*Café, mesdames?*" he mumbled at them through the wet cigarette that dangled from the corner of his mouth.

"Thank you," Colette had the presence of mind to answer.

Flora would have declined, but she didn't want to offend and she was parched. Coffee would be safer than a glass of untreated water, she was sure. The garage man's wife obliged and set a cup before each of them, and sugar cubes in a cracked bowl in the centre of the table. As Flora raised her cup, there was a crackling sound as it unstuck from the oilcloth beneath. She gulped down the lukewarm liquid.

"At seven in the morning, Gilles will be here. It's to him you must speak. After your visit, we're having nothing more to do with this foolhardy business. Leave us out of it. We've seen what they can do," said the man.

His wife nodded in the background and rubbed her knuckles together feverishly. "Come," she said and tossed her head at the door to the hallway from which they had come. She was a woman of few words and fewer niceties.

They followed her up a sturdy old staircase, devoid of matting. She showed them into a room with a double bed. As soon as she had gone, Flora grimaced.

"It's better than a hedge, believe you me," Colette said.

They kept their clothes on but removed their coats, using them as covers. They both slept fitfully. Flora awoke to every small, unfamiliar creak of the old building, and every footfall on the landing had her visualising the door being beaten in or the *garagiste* peering through the keyhole.

CHAPTER 48

"That was a grim night," Colette said as dawn turned the sky from black to grey.

As they emerged into the kitchen-cum-living room again, there was no offer of water in which to wash, but both women gladly accepted the cup of coffee and piece of bread and dripping that was offered for breakfast.

At seven on the dot, a man arrived and was introduced as Gilles. He looked to be in his mid-twenties and wore the uniform of blue cotton overalls and a jacket. His cap was at a jaunty angle and his roll-up cigarette was fresh. He flashed them a smile and said, "Good night, girls? I bet you slept soundly." He chuckled. "If you've finished your breakfast, we'll make tracks. It's not far. There are some people I can introduce you to. Do you want to come?" Gilles turned to the *garagiste*.

"Be on your way," the old man said. "I'll wish you *bonne chance*, but don't come this way again in a hurry."

His wife avoided their eyes and mumbled.

They each shook hands and took their leave. Gilles helped them down the steps with their bicycles, and bags were stowed on the rear carriers again.

"We better have a story. You are my sister, come to visit," he said to Colette. "We are the most alike in colouring anyway. You, Flora, are my sister's friend, accompanying her for safety. It's not so far from the truth."

They met two other men and a woman in a café. They were already seated but stood as they entered. Each kissed the other like old friends and all took their seats. Once coffee was ordered for Colette and Flora, and Gilles had a beer in front of him, quiet introductions were made. Flora said little, but Colette told them to expect an equipment drop that very night.

"It's a harvest moon and the wind is light. Perfect conditions. You've done this before, I gather." She looked around at the men in the group, who nodded at her with grim faces.

"Much has changed in the last two years since Henri Fiocca was betrayed, tortured and shot over the Marseille escape lines. We're all much better co-ordinated," one of the men growled.

"There should be a new radio coming, and some weapons and explosives. Bury the parachutes as quickly as possible."

"We do know that."

"Yes, of course, I'm sorry. I'm wound up. I wired Baker Street to send more money too, so one of the packages should contain enough *francs* for you to keep going."

"About time too. We've been financing ourselves for weeks." This man spoke French, but his accent was not local. Flora suspected he was English, but no one volunteered this kind of information.

Flora had time to study the woman who, until now, had also sat silently. She was about Flora's age, with blond hair twisted up onto the top of her head in a knot. Her limbs, from what Flora could see, were long, and she sat straight-backed. It was her eyes that were so arresting, though. They were a brilliant blue and flashed around the company, making her seem lively.

"Marie, you must take the briefing documents that will be in the packet with the money. Take them to Hector. You know where to find him?" Colette addressed the young woman.

"Yes, I'll be there at the drop. After that is fine, where to go, and so on."

"Now, Rhoda and I will go to the safe house and stay there until it's time for the drop." Colette nodded at Flora. It seemed she had gained a new name. Rhoda was fine. Colette knew the story of the rhododendron wood in 1916 and how she, Flora, had been conceived.

"This is the place that we can use for evaders and escapees from now on, yes?"

"Yes, and the dead drop is close to here too. I'll show you on the way to the house. Although if you speak to the lass behind the bar, she'll contact me, Gilles said."

Business completed for the time being, they bade their farewells. They would all meet up again for the drop when it got dark.

Having sorted themselves out in their lodgings, Flora and Colette headed to a *bistrot* which was cramped and cosy. The tobacco and rich gravy smells were comforting. The menu, such as it was, was chalked on a blackboard propped on a chair. They found a small round table in a corner and waited for the overworked waitress to come.

"I wondered about telephoning home," Flora said. "Just to say we're alright and that we're making good time. There's a payphone over there."

"That would be natural enough. Remember, we're on our way to my home. Don't mention any place names. If you say something wrong and someone's listening in, it would be catastrophic. Just tell them we've completed the first leg of our journey or something. Have you got the right change?"

"Yes." Flora pushed back her chair. "I'll eat whatever you're having if she comes before I'm back." She nodded towards the waitress.

"I don't think there's any choice." Colette smiled at her.

Flora found the slot for her coins on the top of the box and she lifted the heavy black receiver off its hook. She dialled the number and waited, tracing the word 'Taxiphone' on the front of the box with her finger. It seemed like an age until she heard her mother's voice.

"We've reached our first stopping off point," she said. "Everything's fine. Is Luca there?"

"He's at my elbow," Delphi said. "Here he is. Love you."

"My love, is everything alright with you?"

"Yes, we're fine. Having a right adventure, the two of us."

"I miss you already," Flora heard him say.

"We got talking to some people and they're organising a birthday party and gift for Colette tonight. Isn't that kind? It's a little early, but she'll be so pleased. She's excited about it, of course."

"That's wonderful," Luca said, but she could hear the concern in his voice.

Flora so wanted to share what was really happening. "Yes, we met these people at the Café Flavian, and they offered to do that. Such a lovely gesture. Money's running out. Love you," she said before they were cut off.

The food had arrived when she returned to Colette and relayed her conversation.

The moon had risen and was high by the time they met with their co-conspirators again. It was a mild night, but Flora shivered as they all greeted each other. A morbid thought came: *I hope that's not a goose walking over my grave.*

This was a point of no return. She had joined the insurgents, as the Vichy government called them, or the terrorists, as the Nazis referred to them.

Some of the team skirted the field and headed for the woods on the far side as Flora and the rest ducked down amongst the *maïs*. The plants were well above their heads and the cobs of seeds were beginning to form.

All was quiet except the dry rustling of the leaves in the breeze. Flora felt a tickle and brushed some insect from her cheek. She shivered again.

"You'd think a dark night would be safer," she whispered to Colette.

"They have to fly low to avoid German radar. The pilot needs a good moon by which to see the landmarks."

"If it's that low, does the parachute have time to open?"

"It'll be fine. They use a static cord, so it opens almost immediately."

"Will it just be odd bundles of stuff?" Flora had so many questions buzzing in her mind.

"I imagine it will be in cylinders. We'll have to load those and bury the parachutes," Colette said.

They crouched in silence for some time longer. Flora shifted her weight. She was getting a cramp.

"Listen!" Colette's whisper was urgent.

Flora strained her ears. Yes, a low rumbling sound. As she listened, a shape ran out into the field like a wraith, silent and dark. Then a beam of light blinked upwards — four short dots of light and a pause. Then it was repeated. The aeroplane was close now but not yet in view.

"Sounds like a Stirling," one of the men nearby said.

Then it appeared over the trees. The sound of its four engines was terrifying, and Flora was sure it would wake every German for miles around. She wanted to lie flat to avoid the noise. *As if that would help*, she thought bitterly. As she watched, parachutes floated out of its rear, and then there was mayhem as they all charged from their hiding places and headed across the field to track the precious cargo. All thoughts of the lonely pilot were gone as Flora ran towards one of the cylinders. Copying the others, she hauled it towards the cover of the trees. It was not as heavy as she'd expected. All the while, her ears were straining for sounds of motors, for only Germans had use of them these days.

Finally, after what seemed like hours but was only minutes, all the cylinders were loaded onto the cart and one of the men set the horse off at a trot. Some of them stayed to bury the detritus of the drop in the woods but Flora, Colette and Marie were to mount their bicycles and pedal into the night. They had arranged to meet up at a barn belonging to one of the men in an hour's time.

Flora watched as Marie tucked a small bundle of papers into her coat. The young woman caught her gaze. "This is the most dangerous time of all, Rhoda."

For a moment, Flora forgot her codename.

"I'll sew these into my coat lining tonight to take them onwards tomorrow. We may not meet again. I shan't be at the rendezvous now. I must get home and do this." Marie patted her pocket.

She peeled off at a crossroads lined with woods on both sides and disappeared into the shadows. The other two pedalled onwards.

"When we get to the edge of the village, we must be watchful. It's well after curfew, of course, and we must be wary of being seen. It might be better to get off and walk beside the walls."

"Right-o," Flora agreed.

Dismounting in good time, they hugged the treeline and walked towards the sign at the edge of the village. As they neared it, two figures stepped out from the shadows.

CHAPTER 49

Flora thought her heart would jump out of her mouth and Colette gave a muffled moan. This was so unfair. Everything had gone without a hitch, and they were all but at the *rendezvous*.

"We nearly missed you," a voice in the dark said.

"Antoine? Is that you?" Colette dropped her bicycle against her own advice and ran towards him. He kissed her warmly on both cheeks and then gave her a hug.

"Flora!" Luca covered the few steps and enfolded her.

Tears came to her eyes. "What on earth are you doing here?" She snapped at him because she was so relieved. "You scared us half to death. The Nazis need do nothing with you around."

"Hey!"

"Sorry," she said. "That was a terrible thing to say. You really frightened me."

He chuckled and said, "It's me who's sorry, my love. Come here." He hugged her to him again and she revelled in the warmth of his body and his strong arms as they encircled her. "Needs must, however. We have news and it's disturbing."

She pulled away and peered up at him, straining to read his expression.

"Thibault is a collaborator, and this route you're re-establishing is still not safe. We had to come and warn you. There may well be a trap and it could be imminent."

"I remember André said he was working on something. How did you find out?"

"Hubert mentioned it. He told me Thibault went to see André; he didn't say about what, but apparently the boy saw a paper while he was there. Then Hubert closed up, but I pressed him. He wanted me to tell him about where you had gone. I didn't let him know it was here, of course. He asked if I knew this place. It was enough to give me the frights for you, my love, so here we are."

"We can't stand here and talk. It's too dangerous." Colette had come to her senses and picked up her bicycle. "We're also expected at that barn, Flora. Luca, tell us everything when we get there. It's not far at all from here."

When they arrived, a gruff voice asked from the darkness, "Who's this with you?"

"It's alright. He's part of the team further north."

"We're not supposed to meet each other. If one of us gets caught, the whole line would be compromised." The voice continued, sounding far from happy.

"He has news and it's disturbing. Gilles needs to hear it," Colette said. She sounded authoritative and the man stepped aside. He huffed and tutted.

They entered the barn, bringing their bicycles along to keep them out of sight. The sweet smell of hay filled their nostrils. The air was dusty but warm. The team were ahead of them, but only just. One was taking the harness off the horse, which stamped and steamed, while the others were unloading the wagon and removing the equipment into a back room. Flora surmised there might be a similar hidden place partitioned off, as they had in their barn at home.

Gilles approached, frowning. "What's going on?"

Colette stepped forward. "Please listen: this is critical. I know all the rules, but this is Rhoda's step-cousin. He has information."

Luca came up. "To cut a long story short, a young lad in our area is probably a collaborator. This youth is speaking to the town mayor, who is in the pay of the Nazis. A friend of mine told me the lad was bragging about a piece of paper with this location named. I don't think he knows exactly what's being set up here, but he's curious. Searches might well be planned. The friend who told me this wanted me to say who you were and where you're based so he could come and tell you himself, but I didn't know of you at that time and certainly didn't have all the information about where you were operating. This threat needs to be taken seriously."

"All this equipment must be scattered around and hidden in different places, preferably tonight," Colette said. "Too much investment has been made in getting it here. It can't be wasted now, and your team is in danger."

Gilles was galvanised into action. The group of friends from near Thorelière stood together and watched.

"You mentioned the Café Flavian, Flora," Luca said.

Flora glanced at Colette, remembering her friend had warned her not to mention any names when she'd telephoned home. Maybe on this occasion she would be forgiven, but Flora understood it was critical to be more careful in future. *My God, I'm an amateur at this*, she thought.

"Any rumour must be taken seriously," Colette said. "Are you talking about the lad, Thibault?"

"Yes, the boy we saw coming out of the *mairie* the other week. Do you remember I told you about it, Luca? He was really secretive," Flora said.

"He's never been reliable. We've not included him as a result," Luca reminded them. "I thought he was just trying to impress since he's young, without a father to guide him. I did believe he'd be vindictive if he was crossed."

They stood and watched as each of the men went into the back room and came out one by one with arms full of equipment. Some of the canisters hadn't even been opened yet.

"Take them and hide them well. If you must bury anything, make sure its waterproof. Be careful. We're all in danger if any one of you is caught. Colette," Gilles turned to her. "I was going to talk with you about the timescale for sending us escapees to the new safe house. We better lie low for a while. Can you hang on to anyone for a bit longer? I'll contact you with an address."

Luca glanced at Antoine and they both nodded.

"It won't be too long," Gilles said. "Just until we're certain we're not compromised. You better get going. Will you get to the safe house now and gather your things?"

"Yes, we'll collect our stuff and head for home," Colette said. "It won't be the first time we've had to evade the Nazis at night. Things must pick up soon," she added as they left. "It's been one disaster after another recently."

"I imagine this is particularly important," Luca said.

"It's always crucial, but right now the French Section is in crisis," Colette said as they got on their way. "A major player, Prosper, and his wireless operator, codenamed Archambaud, are both in Gestapo headquarters in Paris. Prosper's empire has covered twelve *départements*. It's all a bit dire." She laughed but with no mirth. "If they can't resist talking, we've all had it."

"Are you safe?" Flora asked.

"None of us is safe. Well, you should be alright so long as you aren't caught out here after curfew. It could be tricky to talk our way out of it. I've done alright so far. My chances are limited anyway." She stopped and turned to them. "Look, I was offered a cyanide pill before I left. An L pill, it's called. We all are. I handed it back, so we best not get trapped."

Flora was shocked. "To end your own life?"

"Yes. Some of the interrogation is … hard to resist, shall we say. Not revealing information is vital. Not that I have much to reveal. That's why all the cells are normally independent of each other. It's just that now things are limited, and with the breakdown of the line I had to come and try to make a connection again. I have something here, though, that will help if we have a problem." Flora frowned as she watched Colette's hand slide down her leg and pat her thigh. "It's a .32 Colt." Colette lifted her skirt quickly. The gun nestled in its holster against her stockings, well hidden by the fullness of her clothing and the light coat that she wore to keep out the night's chills.

"Are you serious?" Flora was shocked.

"What's that?" Antoine peered back at the two women.

"She's got a gun," Flora whispered.

"Whoa, great girl," Antoine said.

"Let's hope we don't need it," Luca said and came to put his arm around Flora. He kissed her hair and she leaned into him, gaining comfort.

Flora and Colette managed to collect their belongings, and all four were on their way out of the village without incident. As they pedalled, Flora strained her ears for sounds and scanned the sky for reflections of lights. Occasional scuffling had her turning her head sharply, and an owl's cry made her jump and her bicycle wobbled. The sound of a horse snorting in a field should have been comforting, but her overactive imagination meant it wasn't. She remembered Luca's tale of the patrol that had passed them as they'd returned from the Château of Chenonceau. He had told her how he'd lain in the ditch and experienced true, debilitating fear. She understood better now. Hadn't she felt that in the alley, so recently? She'd barely been able to walk and could so easily have emptied the contents of her stomach.

They hadn't gone far. The trees on either side were dense, dark and menacing. Then they heard an unfamiliar sound and saw the outline of a man on the road in front.

CHAPTER 50

He stood still like a stocky statue, his loose trousers and worker's jacket adding weight to his form, but Flora realised he had a rifle resting across his arms. The long barrel stuck out to his left. Not tall in build, but with legs planted firmly apart, he was immoveable. It wasn't until they got closer that they recognised his features. Even in the fading starlight, his red hair glowed.

"Hubert." Luca laid his bike on the ground and ran to his friend but stopped when he saw, with surprise, the fierce expression on Hubert's face. It looked like hate. "What are you doing here?"

"I followed you. I lost you, but I guessed you'd be back this way at some point. I was prepared to wait as long as it took. You wouldn't tell me where you were going; where this other cell operates from."

"I didn't know at the time we spoke. Hey! It's good to meet you, though." He stepped forward and clapped Hubert on the shoulder. "We managed to save the day. We're just on our way back home. It's lucky we talked before I left. Can't have our plans betrayed and ruined now, can we?"

"Betrayed? Ruined?" Hubert grunted. "You have no idea."

"What do you mean? We've averted danger for now. But we must get home without getting caught. Come on. Where's your bicycle?"

"Huh, you imagine you're so clever." Hubert stood his ground.

"Hubert, we need to get going," Antoine said.

Flora frowned. Something was wrong. Hubert's scowl was unnerving. "Hubert," she said, "are you coming? I'm sorry you didn't find us in time, but we managed to save everything, so all is good. We do need to go, though."

"You superior bitch," he snarled.

Flora gasped.

"Hey, watch your tone. What's the matter with you?" Antoine stepped forward.

The sky began to grey. Dawn would arrive soon.

"We must leave or hide in the woods," Colette said. "Hubert, I don't understand your problem, but we all need to get off this road soon, before daylight comes. Nazis may well come this way once the sun is up."

"Then I'll hand you over like the traitors you are," Hubert said and pointed his rifle at Luca.

"What are you saying?" Luca frowned.

"I'm saying that I've had enough of your superior attitude. The French killed my father in the last show. His own people. He wasn't a coward or a traitor, but the officers had it in for him. His face never fitted properly."

"I don't understand," Flora said. "He was shot at Chemin des Dames. We all know that. Hundreds, no, thousands of Frenchmen died there."

"Huh, so much for a road built for the *demoiselles* of the king. They said he was a traitor, a mutineer. He wasn't." Hubert waved the barrel of his rifle at her, and Luca stepped in with both his palms up in front of him.

"Steady, my friend," he said.

"Friend? Friend?" Hubert's voice rose. "You've always been condescending. You, the owner of a vineyard, and me, the son of a good honest Frenchman, shot by his own side for telling the truth. You belong to them, the rulers who think they're better than us."

"Where is this coming from? We're friends."

"Yeah, right." Hubert wiped his nose on the back of his hand.

"We're all Frenchmen here. Loyal and patriotic." Antoine took a step towards Hubert, but all he got for his trouble was the barrel of the gun pointed at him.

"You're no better. Fawning around him all the time." Hubert nodded at Luca.

"Look, Hubert. We're in this together, against the Germans."

"No, we're not. We're not 'in this together'." His voice shook with a mimicking lilt and his head waggled from side to side. "I might be French, but now I'm ashamed of it. They weren't loyal to my father. He was shot. Didn't you listen to me? They shot him at dawn for telling the truth when they were so disorganised they couldn't even feed their own troops or evacuate the wounded. Have you any idea what he put up with? And now this time. Our leaders, giving in at the first sign of difficulties. Pétain and his puppet government. Can't keep his own people safe. Rubbish, the lot of them. I believed he did the right thing at first, along with everyone else. Now he's just going with the next new idea. Give me a people who can be strong. A country that can build up fortune and resources from next to nothing and protect their own."

"You can't mean that," Luca said.

"All these years you've been strutting around, organising us, telling us what to do. I've listened to you and…"

Understanding crossed Luca's face. "You mean it's you, not Thibault, who's been collaborating. You're the traitor."

"I understand who's in the right here. Don't you *dare* call me traitor." Hubert's voice rose.

Luca stepped towards him. A click sounded as Hubert pulled the bolt on the right-hand side of the stock of his rifle, preparing to shoot.

"Don't!" Flora shouted.

"That's an army issue Lebel rifle. Where the hell did you get that?"

"Get back. I swear I'll shoot. Heil H—"

"Don't you say that!" A shout and a crash came from the left. A lanky figure flashed out of the trees, startling them all. Thibault shot forward.

Hubert swung around, and there was a sound so loud it split the air, took Flora's breath away. She was vaguely aware of Luca rushing forward and crashing to the ground as Thibault shrieked. Hubert, too, fell as Antoine barrelled into him.

"Go!" Luca shouted from his prone position. "Flora, Colette, go!"

"No." Flora's breath escaped in one great lungful, leaving her shaky and feeble as she tottered towards him.

"Please, Colette, take her. Ride fast then hide well."

"Are you hurt?" Flora tried to move to Luca, who lay on the ground.

"Please, darling girl, go. We'll catch you up. I'll be fine."

"Come, Flora. Quickly. We'll put them in more danger. That was enough noise to bring a whole battalion here. Get your bike. NOW!"

Shocked at her friend's tone but coming to her senses, Flora turned and got back on her bicycle. Looking over her shoulder, she wobbled after Colette down the long, straight road, gathering speed until they both rode like demons.

As they pedalled, the sound of another shot followed them, quieter than the first.

"Oh!" Flora braked hard and her wheels skidded.

"Flora, come on. It's getting light. We need to find somewhere to hide through these early hours until it's sensible to travel onwards," Colette said. "If we're spotted now, there'll be too many difficult questions."

"But…"

"We'll find out in time. Come on. You're not helping anyone, and certainly not Luca, by putting us in danger."

Leaving the road and manoeuvring their bicycles across the ditch that bordered it, they disappeared from the immediate danger into the forest. An uncanny silence lay heavy and pressing under the canopy, and its darkness shrouded them. The thickness of the conifer needle mat beneath their feet dulled all sound. All the birds were silent in the denseness. No animals were to be heard or seen. Foxes, deer and wild boar had all had their time during the night and now would be settling in thickets, hiding from the light.

This is what we must do too, thought Flora, *but what of Luca? How did Thibault come to be there?* Had he saved Luca and been hit, or had her love been hit by Hubert's stray bullet? Tears of worry and exhaustion brimmed.

She stopped pushing her bike and halted. Now out of imminent danger, a heavy cloak of despair wrapped itself around her, suffocating her senses and making her whole body leaden. The cloying odour of the pine sap, so strong in these summer months, made her retch. She gulped.

Something in the air must have alerted Colette, because at that moment she turned to see Flora drop her bicycle and sink to the ground. "It's alright. This is all new to you. You've had a shock, you're tired, but you've done magnificently with no training at all," Colette said as she stroked the damp hair from Flora's face.

"We'll stay where we are for a couple of hours. We're quite safe in here. When it's a decent hour, we'll begin cycling towards home. There should be no problem answering questions then. We're simply returning from a visit to friends, or we can say from my village when we are closer to Thorelière. We're a little in the wrong direction for that here."

"Colette, you're always full of calm and good sense," Flora said. "I'm so worried, though. What if Luca caught a bullet? What will they do with Hubert?"

"Before we left, I gave my gun to Antoine."

"What are you saying?" Flora's voice rose in panic.

"I'm not saying anything," Colette said, still the voice of reason. "They'll be alright, that's all."

CHAPTER 51

Flora and Colette arrived back at the vineyard without further mishap. With great relief, they put their bicycles in the barn. Colette took her suitcase with the radio transmitter and hid it behind the panels of the secret room where they had harboured the English pilot, Andrew. Flora stood immobile, her mind spinning. Then they headed for the solace of the kitchen and Delphi's arms.

"Oh, thank goodness you're back. I thought you might be gone longer." Delphi skipped around the table and embraced first Flora, then Colette.

Flora needed the comforting natural perfume of her mother, and she breathed it in deeply. Rainier came and enfolded her too, his strong arms a haven.

"Darling, I can see things aren't right. Tell me all about it."

Her mother's gentle tones brought the tears that Flora had tried so hard to withhold. Now they fell in a torrent that she couldn't control. Great shuddering sobs shook her shoulders. Delphi put her arms around her daughter again and Flora sunk her head into the reassuring shoulder. Gradually, her weeping turned to sniffles. Delphi guided her to a chair and pulling another up close, she continued to wrap her arms around her child. Eventually, Flora blew her nose and sat up.

Delphi waited until Flora spoke. The story emerged.

"So, I have no idea whether Luca was shot or not. I can't understand how Hubert, who we believed to be a friend, could do this."

"Tell me his reasons again," Rainier said.

Colette took up the story. "He said his father had been shot as a mutineer by his own officers when serving in the French army during the Great War. He said he wanted to respect a country that was strong and supported its citizens, not one like Pétain's France."

"Many soldiers mutinied on the Chemin des Dames in the spring of 1917. Nearly seven hundred men were sentenced to death, but only about thirty were shot in the end. They were the ones who had shot at their superiors. Conditions were atrocious. We found out all about it when I was on the northern end of the Western Front. In fact, Pétain asked for clemency when he took over the situation from General Nivelle. He was a general himself, by then."

"It sounds as if Hubert only has half the story," Colette said. "He certainly is no fan of Pétain or any French he perceives as being in a responsible position."

"I expect either his mother or someone else in the family filled his head when he was too young to understand." Delphi got up to make coffee and cut bread for the returning pair.

"Whatever, it doesn't help." Flora began to weep again. "How can we find out what's happened?"

"We will know soon enough. Luca will return, you'll see," Rainier said. "He, Antoine, or Thibault will bring us news. In the meantime, we must carry on. If we lose faith now, the authorities will be here scouring the place."

The following morning, the idea of returning to work was horrendous, but Flora had to do it. André had proved, months ago, where his loyalties lay when he'd aided the round-up of the Jewish community.

The dread remained as Flora cycled to work and entered the office. André, there before her, came in from his room.

"Flora." He beamed at her. Her stomach turned. "How wonderful to have you back. I did miss you, my dear." He leaned in to kiss her cheeks. "How was your trip? Uneventful, I hope."

What did he mean by that? Flora's heart raced.

"And how is your cousin and her home?"

"Everything is in order. We had a quiet few days."

"And your parents? They are well?"

"Yes, everything is as normal."

"Good, good. How is Luca?"

"Yes, fine." Flora moved behind her desk to look as if she meant to get on.

"I had a friend of his in here the other day. M Hubert Girard." André left the statement hanging.

"Oh?"

"Yes, I expected him to return and tell me some things, but he hasn't been back yet. It's rather strange, that."

Flora bent to retrieve some inconsequential thing from a drawer to hide her face and give herself thinking time. "Perhaps he changed his mind," she said from her bent position.

"It seems unlikely, from what we discussed. Has he visited Luca at all?"

"I'm sorry, I don't know. He hasn't mentioned it, but I hardly saw him last night, and I didn't see him this morning at all."

"Oh, right. He is at home, though?"

"He was, as I say, last night." Flora's heart pounded so hard her legs felt weak. Her muscles trembled and she had to sit, or she would collapse.

Somehow, she got through the rest of the day. She watched the clock, and, on the dot, she covered her typewriter, straightened her desk and headed for the door.

Flora sat at the kitchen table with a cup of coffee. She was recounting her day and the awkward conversation with André to Delphi and Colette when there was a tap on the door. It was propped open because the day was so hot. Delphi went to see who it was. André stood there.

"How lovely to see you," Delphi said with innocence. She flashed her best smile at him; the one she knew from long years of experience usually worked its magic. He smiled back. "We were so busy gossiping we didn't realise you'd arrived, did we, girls?" She turned to the others and with a wave of her arm, she invited him into the room.

"I heard your girlish chatter," he said.

How condescending, Flora thought.

"I wasn't aware of what you said, of course, but I sense how young ladies like to talk of fashion and cooking." He smiled and Flora could cheerfully have swung her fist in his face. How could she have once been sorry for him, even liked him? He was a pompous, patronising and traitorous idiot. She couldn't bring herself to smile at him, so she turned to the stove and raising the pan, she said, "Coffee? It's freshly made, such as it is, of course, with what we now have available."

"Thank you. I wondered if I might have a word with Luca. You said he was here, Flora."

"He was last night, but I haven't seen him today," she said with more confidence than she'd had earlier, when his questioning had caught her off guard.

"Oh, André," Delphi said with such a sorrowful expression that even Colette was taken in. "He was here this morning, but he had to go and meet a merchant earlier. I'm afraid your journey has been wasted."

"Ah," he said.

"Can I help at all? Rainier should be in from the vines soon. Perhaps he might be of assistance. Is it some wine you'd like to buy, or something else?"

"No. It's no matter. It's Luca I need to talk to. I hoped he might verify something for me, but he seems to be elusive suddenly." He finished his small cup of coffee and stood to leave. The women followed him to the door. "I'll see you tomorrow, Flora. You look tired. After your journey, no doubt. I hope you have a peaceful night. Perhaps I'll call tomorrow and catch Luca then." He turned. "Ah, Rainier."

Rainier had entered the courtyard and approached the guest. Delphi pushed between the girls, skipped towards Rainier and linked her arm through his. "Darling! André is here. Isn't that lovely? He came to talk with Luca, but we explained about him going to see the merchant earlier."

"Yes, a shame you missed him," Rainier said without a blink and looking into André's eyes. "He had to go and find M Mannier. He has plenty of potassium metabisulphite, but he found we are short of potassium sorbate. We can't have our white wines turning brown, now, can we?"

André gave a feeble chuckle. "No, indeed not," he said. He shook Rainier's hand. "I'll be off then."

The family watched and waved in silence as he mounted his bicycle and rounded the corner into the lane.

"What was all that about?" Colette smiled. "Meta—whatever."

"We use it in the fermentation process to stop enzymatic browning, but it's much earlier in the year than this. Let's hope he doesn't have too much knowledge about wine production. Any news?" A frown creased Rainier's handsome face and he kissed his wife's hair.

"No, nothing yet," Colette answered.

Flora shook her head before heading up to her room, where she sat on the bed with her head in her hands.

Colette found her a few moments later. "Take heart. Until we know different, let's be sure that all is well." She put her arm around Flora's shoulders.

"I keep hearing that shot. It was so loud, and then that second one. Why have they not returned here? I fear something is very wrong."

"But we don't *know* that. Have faith. In the meantime, I think I need to take my radio somewhere else. I don't like this nosing around that André is doing. His tone didn't sound normal to me. He may return as he suggested, and he may not be alone."

CHAPTER 52

Luca dived to try and tackle Hubert down, but he was just out of reach. Thibault had rushed out of the forest, taking them all by surprise, but he was too far away to help. Antoine, a little closer, completed the job.

The gunshot deafened them all. All Luca could think of was getting Flora away from this new danger.

He shouted at her, not sure of what he said. Then, he begged, "Please, Colette, take her. Ride fast, then hide well." Luca watched as Flora wobbled away and then caught up with Colette. At least she would be safer.

Luca became aware of screaming and stumbled to his feet. He understood Thibault had raced towards Hubert as the gun had fired. Blood oozed between Thibault's fingers. The shrieking stopped, but the boy lay on the ground, moaning and clutching his thigh. Hubert's bullet had missed Luca but hit the youth. Luca floundered across to him.

He vaguely heard a click-click. Another shot rang out, different in tone to the first. Tinny, but nevertheless noisy at this close range.

He turned to take in the scene. Antoine stood with a small pistol in his hand, looking at the short barrel as if puzzled.

"He was going to shoot that thing again," he said to Luca. "Didn't you recognise the click of the bolt? It can hold eight bullets."

"What the hell have you got there?" Luca indicated the gun in Antoine's fist as he bent over the boy.

"Colette shoved it at me as she left. He would have killed you, Luca, I'm sure of it." Antoine's voice had risen in panic.

"I pulled the trigger. He would have killed you. I didn't even think, I just did it. Oh, my God, what do we do now?"

Luca was cold with fear. "Get him into the woods. We must hurry."

Antoine stood immobile.

"Antoine! Get his legs. Stay still, Thibault. Breathe deeply. Hang on." He thought clearly at last.

Luca placed the rifle on Hubert's body and together they managed to manhandle his lifeless form across the ditch and into the wood. He was heavy, but they staggered far enough in to be safely away from the track.

As they returned, Luca asked, "Where's that handgun now?"

"I threw it down, I think. I'm not sure."

Luca let his breath out in a rush.

As they neared the road again, Thibault rolled over, still clutching his thigh. Luca sat him up, and together they managed to carry him into the forest, propping him against a tree. A lot of blood seeped out of the wound, and the boy cried out in pain. Luca took a wad of cloth from his pocket and thrust it at Thibault. "Press this on it. We'll be back. Hang on. I'm going to see what we've left."

"The bicycles," Thibault muttered.

"Antoine, come with me. Hurry."

Retrieving their transport was easy. Luca had a quick search for the gun, but he was aware of the racket they had all created and he was wary. He found it in the ditch and tucked it into his trouser belt. The hour was very early, and it was unlikely soldiers would be about yet, but a stray patrol was always a possibility.

Luca turned to Thibault who, although quieter now, still held his leg and moaned. "I'm going to tear the bottom off your shirt and try and bind this up. I've no idea what I'm doing, but it might help. We need to find somewhere to get it cleaned, but we'll have to take care wherever we go. No one is safe to trust."

That done, Luca and Antoine stood and looked down at the man with whom they had been friends. How bitter he had become.

"I wonder how long he's been siding with our enemies," Luca said. "The bitterness must have been building up in him. He can hardly have known his father if he was shot in the last war. When would he have found out that information? If he has only heard it recently, that might explain his change of heart and allegiance."

"What are we going to do?" A note of agitation reappeared in Antoine's voice.

"We'll have to bury him here. Find a branch to use as a digging tool."

The task of Thibault's leg done, Luca turned to help Antoine with the macabre work they had allotted themselves. More than an hour passed without respite. They scrabbled at the earth, which was thankfully soft, but they only managed a shallow trench. When they put their jackets back on and dusted themselves off, each looked at the other with a solemn gaze.

Luca and Antoine abandoned the bicycles and with the lad between them, they began to stagger through the woods. The going was worryingly slow. Thibault, faint with pain and shock, was a dead weight. It was very dark beneath the conifers. Every now and again, a tangle of brambles meant they had to detour. They travelled no distance at all.

"This is going to take forever," Antoine said.

"We certainly won't make it home for a couple of days. Thibault needs proper help before that."

Thibault moaned and his legs gave. They sat him down.

"This is hopeless. We might be wandering in circles too," Antoine said.

"You two better lay up here, or somewhere I can find you again. I'll go back, pick up a bicycle and try and get some help," Luca said.

"I think that would be best." Antoine and Thibault sank down.

Luca put his hand to his waist and felt the pistol at his belt. He wasn't certain he would ever be able to use it, but it held a kind of comfort.

He found the bicycles without difficulty, but spent some minutes wheeling one behind a thicket of brambles. No point in making it easy for anyone to stumble upon it. Then, having reached the road, his watch told him it was a reasonable hour to be abroad, especially looking like a poor farm worker. He listened as he pedalled.

He hadn't gone far when an engine, probably a motorcycle, came to his ears. It must have been travelling at speed, because the sound quickly grew louder.

What should I do? I could get off and try to find somewhere to hide, but the woods are behind me, and there are only small fields on either side here.

He looked ahead to the next belt of trees, but doubted he would arrive there in time. He slowed his pace, trying to look nonchalant, unhurried. The motorcycle came around the bend. From the shape of the helmet, the occupant was German. Luca took a deep breath and pedalled steadily. The motorcycle approached. It didn't slow. The soldier nodded at him. It roared past.

Luca put his foot to the road and steadied his shaking knees. He listened for several minutes. The tone of the engine didn't change. It must have passed the woodland concealing the others by now. He breathed in deeply, calming his beating heart. He spoke to himself sternly.

Don't seem nervous. Don't make it easy for them by looking guilty. You're a poor farm worker going to his employment. Act naturally and all will appear normal.

He took in is surroundings. Cows. A horse. A farm must be nearby.

Sure enough, an ancient piece of oak board, eaten away at the edges by countless years of sun and rain had '*Le Sablon*' scrawled in black paint. A long sandy road led beyond that with barbed wire stock fences to either side.

Now Luca had a dilemma. Should he sneak up and find eggs and water to steal, or should he approach openly and ask for help? Surely there were more loyal Frenchmen than collaborators and traitors.

He rode his bicycle up towards what he hoped was a homestead. When it appeared, it was a small, poor property. Lichen covered the tiles; the walls were a dingy grey render; the shutters, which had once been bright blue, were now peeling. All lent an air of decay and poverty. A dog, tied up to a ring in the wall of the little courtyard, barked as soon as Luca got off his bicycle and approached.

A wizened woman appeared from the open doorway. She wiped her hands on her flowered overall. Her grey hair was pulled back in a knot and her lips folded into her mouth. It looked as if her teeth were missing. However, when Luca greeted her, she beamed at him.

"*M'sieur*," she said with a questioning inflection. "We get few visitors."

"My friends and I are working in the woods, *madame*. One of us has an injury. Is it possible to have a bottle of water to wash his wound? If you have any clean rags, that would also help."

"I hear no *tronçonneuses*." The old lady looked up at him.

"No, *madame*? The chainsaw stopped when my friend hurt himself and I am here, as you see. If it's possible to have your aid...? I must return," Luca prompted the old woman.

She turned away but beckoned for him to follow. He stooped as he walked through the front doorway and stood clutching his cap, trying to appear servile in the gloom of the living room. She tottered about, fetched some homemade bandages and filled an empty wine bottle with water.

"Is this sufficient?"

"If you have another, I should be most grateful," Luca said.

"You better take this too, then. I have a second." She held a small brown glass bottle towards Luca, and he read the word '*iode*' on the label, which was stained with yellow-brown drops.

"You are too kind, *madame*."

A large, chipped bowl of eggs caught Luca's attention as his eyes became used to the lack of light from the single small window. *Madame* saw him looking.

"Perhaps you better take some of those," she said, nodding at the bowl and then peering up into Luca's eyes. "You're too tall not to eat well. And bread too, no?"

"Thank you, *madame*."

"Though why you have no dinner with you … if you're working in the woods..." She didn't finish. The woman took her time finding brown paper and string with which to make a parcel.

Luca became nervous. Were these delaying tactics while her husband returned from the fields? "I must be getting back, *madame*," he ventured. "My friend needs me."

There was no reaction to his words, but she carried on at her own slow pace. Then, a noise in the courtyard caught his attention. Luca put his hand to his belt in a reassuring move and felt the outline of the weapon concealed there. A bow-legged, grey-haired man stood in the doorway, blocking out most of the light. Old and wizened too, his cap shadowed his face.

"*M'sieur.* Good day." Luca stepped forward with his arm outstretched in greeting.

"Hmm," the man grunted and took his seat at the table.

"My friend is hurt, and your wife is kindly helping us."

"Whatever," he said.

The parcel was finally ready. Luca tucked a bottle of water into each pocket and caught hold of the string loop on the package.

"*Merci beaucoup, mille merci. M'sieur, madame.*"

Luca took his leave but looked around subtly. There were no telephone wires going to the house. Should he wait and see if either of them left the building before he hurried away?

He kept looking over his shoulder then waited down the roadway. He watched the front door. Nobody came out, but what if there was a back way?

This was wasting time. No one followed him. Time to get going and find Thibault and Antoine again. He set off down the track. He glanced behind him one last time. The man had left the house and appeared to be pushing a rickety-looking bicycle. Luca sped up and pedalled as fast as he could. He would be able to easily outride the old fellow.

He left the road and found his friends. Thibault gasped as Luca tended the wound in his thigh. It bled profusely, but it seemed that the bullet had skimmed through the flesh without stopping.

"That rifle was from the last war and has a small-calibre bullet. It's unwieldy and heavy to hold and aim. No wonder

Hubert took a wild shot. Goodness only knows where he got it from," Luca said.

"There were many of them around after the armistice," Antoine said. "Just as well we buried it with him. It's too heavy and old-fashioned to be of use. That barrel seemed so long. I have no idea whether it had all eight bullets in the magazine, but that would have been all."

They each gulped water and cracked a raw egg into their mouths. A mean breakfast for heavy work, but better than nothing. Supporting Thibault, they prepared to restart their trek, when the sound of twigs snapping and scuffing noises came to each of them. Were hounds of war at their heels? As Luca turned, the shape of the old man shambled towards them and he carried a rifle.

CHAPTER 53

Flora awoke early. Light poured into her bedroom. The cockerel voiced his joy, but straight away her heart beat faster and her stomach churned. Leaping from her bed without disturbing Colette, she grabbed her dressing gown. Perhaps he was back, and she had slept through his return. She peeped around into Luca's room, but the bed was still unused. Hurrying down the stairs, her bare feet made little sound. The kitchen remained empty, and the sink had no used cups or glasses. She thrust her feet into a pair of *espadrilles* left by the door. The gravelly surface of the courtyard crunched against the rope soles as she crossed to the various outbuildings. Nothing.

Returning to the kitchen, she sat down at the table and put her head in her hands. It was only just past four o'clock. Should she make coffee or return to bed?

Then an almighty racket sent her flying to the door.

Several vehicles entered the courtyard. A large utility truck spewed soldiers from the back, a motorcycle with a sidecar pulled up next to her and a car arrived with a German officer in the back seat. Flora pulled her dressing gown tighter around her as this man came towards her and was met by another from the motorcycle sidecar. They both gave her the Nazi salute. *"Mademoiselle.* You will go inside and sit down. Who else is here?"

This was different to the last time they searched the premises. That had been courteous and half-hearted.

Before Flora mumbled an answer, the other members of the family and Colette joined them.

"What's all this about?" Rainier demanded. "It's the middle of the night."

"Sit. All of you," the officer barked. "We will search your house. We have certain information."

"What information?" Flora saw Rainier was rattled but cross. Delphi put her hand on his arm.

"Where is M Harman, your nephew? He went for further supplies, I understand. Why is he not back?"

Rainier repeated what he told André the previous day, and then informed the officer that he'd stayed over.

So that's where these people have their details, Flora thought. *No one else was told that story. André has completed his betrayal.*

"You will give me that address."

"I'm sorry, I don't know which supplier he uses. There are several."

"Are you trying to be difficult?"

"No, no, it's true, *m'sieur*," Delphi said. "We are simply staying here to help out. Our nephew deals with the business. Can I get you coffee, sir?"

"No, *madame*. This is not a social call. You will wait in here." He beckoned a soldier with his head, who took up a position near the door. Then he left to direct operations outside.

From her place at the table, Flora could see nothing out of the window and guessed it must be the same for the others. She relied on her other senses. Footsteps ran and orders were given. Guessing that all the outbuildings would be searched, she prayed that they would not find the hiding places of either the radio transmitter or of the escapees. While both empty, they would look suspicious. Then a sudden thought speared her mind. She gasped. Had she collected that last coffee cup from the escapee's hideout? Was there still a candle in a jar there, partly burned? What if a book remained under the

330

mattress? The fact of a mattress at all was an indication of something odd. These people didn't need concrete information to seize a family.

Next, the door burst open and three soldiers entered. Without a word, they stamped through to the hallway, followed by the sound of their heavy boots on the stairs. They each looked at one another.

So much for keeping the locals onside. That stopped months ago. "There's no difference between the *Zone Libre* and the Occupied Zone now," Flora said in an undertone.

"Shh!" Delphi shook her head and frowned.

A lot of crashing came from the barn opposite.

"They'll scare the horse," Delphi said.

"I moved him into the back room. It's quieter there," Rainier said. "He has fresh hay hanging on the back wall. He'll be fine." He gave the family a look and they nodded at him in understanding.

At least the secret room should not be discovered, thought Flora. *If the soldiers invade the back room, they should only find the horse.*

The sound of heavy boots on the stairs came again. The men who had violated their privacy returned, glared at them and left, taking the one who had stayed by the door with them. There was no time to exchange more than a glance with each other when the officer entered their living space.

"You will come with me." He indicated that Rainier join him.

"Why?" Delphi stood, panic etched on her face.

"Sit down!"

She did as the German said.

As they left the room to cross the courtyard, the women rose. Peering out of the window, they watched the two men, one in uniform, pass the vehicles and turn towards the vinification barn.

The women breathed a collective sigh of relief and Delphi returned to her chair, sinking down and putting her head in her hands. "I thought they were taking him," she whispered. Tears of relief welled in her eyes.

Flora put her arms around her mother and Colette sat again too. All they could do was wait patiently until Rainier returned.

It must have been nearly half an hour before footsteps approached and the door opened. Delphi got up and ran into the arms of her husband. As Flora watched them, her heart ached. She desperately wanted to be in the arms of Luca. A fresh wave of anxiety and dread washed over her.

"I want to speak with M Luca Harman," the officer said. "If I find you are sheltering him, there will be trouble." With that, he clicked his heels and his arm rose straight up in front. "Heil Hitler," he saluted, then left.

The family stood in silence for several minutes as they listened to the roar of vehicles starting up and leaving the premises.

"What did they want you for?" Delphi raised her head from Rainier's shoulder.

"They searched the vinification room," he said.

"There's nowhere there to hide." Delphi looked up at him.

"They thumped the barrels with their rifle butts and then wanted to taste some of the wine."

"Did they think we'd conceal a man in those? They are more stupid than I thought," Delphi said.

"Stupid they may be, but there is no doubt they are dangerous, and they want Luca."

They sat at the table and Delphi began to heat a pan of water.

Flora was rubbing her tired eyes when the door opened. Her head shot up as she feared that the soldiers had returned. Then she saw who it was. Her chair toppled over as she flew at Luca, who stood blinking in the bright light.

His arms came around her, holding her tightly. He sunk his face into her sweet-smelling hair. She imagined him like a drowning man, gasping for survival.

"Son, we've all been so worried," Rainier said and enfolded the two of them as best he could before allowing the young couple to resume their embrace.

Delphi clapped her hands before clasping them together beneath her chin. Colette stood.

"Come, sit down," Delphi said.

Still holding hands, Flora and Luca sat side by side. She couldn't pull her eyes from his face, trying to discern if he was alright. Physically, he seemed fine, if exhausted.

"Luca, my dear boy, you can't stay here. It's become too dangerous," Rainier said.

"I saw the troops leave. Are you all alright?"

"You saw them? Where were you?" Flora asked.

"I must have arrived just after they did. I lay low and watched. My heart raced and when that officer came out with you, Rainier, I was really scared. I thought he was going to take you away."

"That's what we were frightened of. It was awful." Delphi came to her husband again for comfort.

"What happened there in the forest? I saw you go down. I thought you'd been shot," Flora said.

Luca stroked her cheek with the back of his hand, and she leaned into the caress. "I was lucky, but Thibault was hit when he ran in front of Hubert to save me. How wrong we've been. Yes, he's young and arrogant. He's desperate to be a part of things, but he saved my life. Hubert lost his way. Now he's paid the ultimate price for his betrayal. Antoine saw to that."

Colette nodded, but Delphi gasped and put her hand to her mouth. "He's … dead?" she asked.

"Yes. He aimed to shoot again. Both my friends have rescued me in their different ways."

"What of Thibault?" Colette asked.

"We were going to carry him between us, Antoine and me, but it was impossible. I found an ancient couple at a smallholding." Luca explained how he had got medical supplies. "We were setting off again when the old guy came upon us. He'd followed me. I tell you, I imagined that was it. He appeared in the woods as we were leaving again, after I'd bound Thibault's leg as best I could. He had a rifle too. Turns out he wanted to offer us help. His wife and he clearly hadn't believed my story about wood-cutting and an accident. They've got Thibault at their place until he recovers. I've been to the lad's house and told his mother already. He'll be alright in a week or two."

"Luca, the Nazis want you. It's you they searched for," Rainier said. "There's no safety here."

Tears appeared in Flora's eyes, but she managed to say nothing. She knew her stepfather was right. "Where will you go?"

"I'll go south and join the resistance down there. I returned and met up with the men you dealt with, Colette. They told me Free French forces are all operating under de Gaulle now. They're rallying in North Africa since the successes of the Allies there. With Henri Giraud, the Free French are becoming a huge fighting force."

"He's had a lot of experience in Africa. He spent time in Morocco during our show," Rainier said. "He made that daring escape from prison too in 1942. Do you remember?"

"Yes, and Laval tried to send him back to Germany, the traitor. Giraud and de Gaulle don't get on at all, apparently, but it's all going to kick off down there. I need to be part of it if I can't be here," Luca said. "With so many resistance fighters joining, we're soldiers without uniform. The fight against the Axis powers is gaining ground all the time."

"When must you go?" Flora could think of little else.

"Darling girl, he must leave soon. He's not safe here." Delphi came and put her arm around Flora's shoulders.

"And neither will you be, because of me," Luca said. "I'll gather a change of clothes and be gone."

Flora gasped. Why did the world have to be so awful? She had to be brave. She had to send him away with a smile.

Delphi cut some bread and wrapped a piece of cheese in paper, tying string around it. She placed that and a bottle of watered wine in a bag.

When Luca returned, Delphi and Rainier hugged and kissed him. "We're going back to bed. God speed, son. Take care, and don't be reckless. We'll ensure all is safe here for you."

Colette, too, took her leave, aware that Luca and Flora needed time alone.

The early morning was clear and mild as they crossed the courtyard.

"Let's walk," he said, taking her hand and holding it to his lips before moving forward again.

They made their way slowly to the rows of vines and stood among them, gazing down the fields and across the valley to the slopes beyond.

"This is my favourite view in all the world," he said.

"It will stay just like this until you return. I'll be here too," Flora said and put her arms around him. "Rainier will make sure the vines are healthy and the yields are good." She paused. "Luca, my heart will be with you. Come back safely with it."

He turned towards her then and took her face in both his hands. His fingers caressed her cheeks before one hand moved to the back of her head and entwined in her hair, pulling her to him in the sweetest of kisses. "Oh, my love," he said. "My brave, dearest girl." And he held her in his arms.

At his tender words, the tears rolled down her face. She couldn't prevent them, but she cried silently until his shirt was sodden and her eyes were sore. As he held her closely, she felt how much he wanted her, and she yearned to give herself to him, to present him with something for which to survive. Their kisses became passionate. A brief remembered story raced through her mind of another previous giving when she, Flora, had been conceived. That too had been a time of horrifying war and endless bloodshed. Did history always repeat itself with the protagonists learning nothing?

His thumb caressed her cheek and gathered up her tears. The tip of his tongue explored hers. His hands, his fingers. His...

The sound of a distant motor came to them on the still morning air and brought them to their senses.

"Oh, they're still about. You must go."

CHAPTER 54

Flora vowed not to feel sorry for herself. There was work to be done. Escapees and evaders, fearing for their lives, needed her assistance and comfort. She would be busy and brave, and the months would pass. In the end, surely good would prevail and the enemy would be defeated. Luca would return and she would be here with a smile.

This is how her life progressed. Colette left and returned, sometimes with an escapee or an evader to hide in the little back room. Food shortages, always a worry, were overcome with cunning and dexterity. Soldiers returned for Luca, but the family were able to say honestly that he wasn't there, and slightly less honestly that they had not seen him since he'd left to visit the merchant.

Flora gritted her teeth and managed to keep working in the offices of *M le Maire*, because occasionally she gleaned information of use. André accepted her distant demeanour and no longer pressed her to accompany him to a restaurant or café.

The autumn came and went and winter ground on. Flora received a couple of postcards from Luca, which she squirrelled away and frequently re-read. He told her he loved her, but she was beset with fear for his safety and dread that he might find someone else. Sometimes, exhausted, she would go to the fields, remember the last time they'd stood together and looked across the valley, and cry quietly before rallying herself once more.

1944 was a quiet New Year with no celebration. Colette had returned to the UK a few weeks before. No visitors resided in the room at the back of the barn. The community found little for which to be grateful except that they were still alive. Flora had heard so many stories of snatchings in the night or reprisals for secretly working against the enemy. Snippets of information came to them occasionally, of fighting in North Africa or elsewhere.

Then, almost ten months after Flora had last seen Luca, news of momentous proportions began to filter through. On Tuesday 6th June 1944, the family heard tell of major Allied landings in Normandy. For weeks there had been rumours that something was going to happen. Some said the British, Americans and Canadians would take the shortest route across the water and land in and around Calais. Others were convinced the Netherlands might be the place, or the south, where Allies would sweep up through Italy and France.

It was a while before the details began to emerge of one of the largest amphibious military assaults in history.

"Surely this must be the beginning of the end," Rainier said some mornings later, when it became clear that Allied troops had gained ground across the long stretch of coastline. "It sounded as if it wasn't going to succeed for the first few days, but now... All those bunkers and landmines Rommel was charged with finishing are not holding them." He rubbed his hands together and gave Delphi a hug.

"Do you really believe this might be it?" Flora could not bring herself to believe, after nearly six years of grinding fear, revulsion, and outrage, that things were nearing an end. "When will we see the south free too?" Her thoughts, never far from Luca, were with him now.

By August, news came of Operation Dragoon. The family clustered around the radio.

"Hindered by total Allied air superiority and a large-scale uprising by French Resistance…" Delphi grabbed Flora's hand. "The weak German forces have retreated along the Rhône valley and are attempting to establish a defence line at Dijon."

One day in late August Flora pedalled the lanes, and for once she had a song in her heart. The sun shone on her bare arms and legs, now a healthy brown colour. Her hair was tied back from her face with a blue and white scarf.

Her stomach sank as she entered the dark and echoing hallway of the *mairie*. It was cool indoors, and she shivered. Another day of pretence awaited her. She sat at her desk, took the cover off her typewriter, rolled in a piece of foolscap paper and looked at the folder which contained her next task. Her eyes strayed to the clock. André had not come out to greet her. Was he coming in late? He hadn't said he would be, and he normally did. Perhaps he was in his room and so occupied he didn't realise she had arrived. She arose, walked across to his office door and tapped. No response. She knocked again. Silence. This was out of character. She opened the door and peeped around. The room was empty.

Guiltily wondering if she should enter, she hovered. Then, with a bold step, she pushed the door wide and walked in. André's desk was bare. She stood still and listened. Apart from a few noises from outside, there was nothing. With a sense of foreboding, she approached the filing cabinet. She pulled the drawer, which slid open with a metallic squeal. It was empty. She opened the next one down. It too was empty.

Flora stood still for a moment to consider. Moving across to the desk, she opened the drawer on the left. The plethora of office bits and pieces lay there. Paper clips, elastic bands, an

339

old pen with no top, pencils and an eraser innocently jumbled. The usually locked drawer on the other side stared back at her. She knew where the key rested, of course. Should she? Would André be coming in? Flora considered, and she guessed the answer to that.

Lifting the pot that still sat on the window ledge, her fingers found what she required. Again, she stood in indecision. Hearing nothing, she inserted the key into the small lock. It wouldn't turn.

Cross with herself for not thinking this through, she pulled the drawer. It hadn't been locked at all. And it was empty. She returned to her own desk, sat down and stared into space.

By lunchtime, she had done little work and there was no sign of André.

I'll stay on for a while in case anyone wants anything, but I'm certainly not staying all afternoon, Flora thought. *I need to tell someone about this. I'll tell Rainier, since Luca's not here.* A searing pain, a physical tightness, made her gasp. She missed him so much.

As she cycled home, Flora thought, *Rainier will know what to do. No way am I going to the gendarmes. He could visit André's house. Perhaps he's ill and worrying unnecessarily. But there's all the missing folders…*

Flora shared her news. Rainier decided to call on the man who had been first deputy mayor before André's appointment. "He and I can go to the house, and then we'll understand more of what we're dealing with." He shrugged on his jacket, kissed his wife and Flora, and hurried out.

As the door shut, Flora looked at her mother. "André's gone, Mama, hasn't he? He's slunk away like the coward he is."

"Local people are no longer sympathetic. Even those who may have been sitting astride the fence with a foot on both sides are realising this is the end."

Upon his return, Rainer confirmed what they'd already guessed. "We discovered a pile of ash in an incinerator in the yard, but the charred edges of some folders and papers remained."

"That's clear evidence of what he did with them, then," Flora said. "No sign of André himself?"

"No, none at all. He's gone. Safest thing for him, I imagine. He'll find no sympathy anywhere if he lets slip his position here."

"What do you think he'll do? I'm angry with him, and he's despicable in many ways. It's just that in different circumstances... He was always kind and gallant with me, although he turned out to be weak." Flora sighed.

"He may find work on the land somewhere a long way from here, where no one has heard of him. There will be a lot of itinerant men around, I suspect. He'll concoct some story. Right, I must finish off in the fields. I've been tasting the grapes. We're very close to harvest."

Flora and Delphi watched him cross the courtyard again.

"At least some things are constant," Delphi said.

"Rainier or the turn of the seasons?" Flora smiled at her mother.

"Both."

Flora's heart swooped. *All I want is what Mama and Rainier have*, she thought. *When will Luca return? Will he come back at all?*

CHAPTER 55

The weeks of the harvest were reassuringly steady. Routines were maintained and hours were long so that at the end of each day, after the communal meal was eaten outside in the courtyard, the family flopped into bed, exhausted.

Flora continued to go into work, and the first deputy came in each day to try and make sense of the things that couldn't wait. He was an elderly man but whiskery, rumpled and kind.

She often roamed out to the vines after dinner. The sky pearled in shades of pink where Venus shone brightly, the evening star. There followed a deep velvet blue, usually pinpricked with all the favourite constellations of her childhood.

There was comfort for her here; remembered times of calm and those moments of passion before Luca had left. Her mind wandered through the events of the last six years. She folded her arms around herself. All those years ago when she'd come, little more than a child, she'd known that this place was going to be of immense importance. She pulled the headscarf that bound her hair and shook it free. It tumbled down onto her shoulders in a wave of rippling chestnut. She stared across the valley as the setting sun created soft shadows and highlights on the vines.

Exhaustion surrounded Luca like a cloud. He wanted to prostrate himself on his beloved *terroir* that bred the vines that were his life. He had dreamed of returning so many times when he'd slept under hedges on the foreign soils of the south, the land there so rocky and unforgiving. The sun had beat down upon him, and there had never seemed to be a moment of calm. And now he was home at last.

Then he saw her.

Flora stood still with her arms folded around her slim body, and tears came to his eyes. As he watched in silence, she took off the scarf that bound her hair and it cascaded down, a shining, soft waterfall, longer than he remembered. The weariness slipped from his shoulders at the realisation that he was indeed home, and Flora was waiting. He breathed deeply. The cool air re-energised him, and he dropped his bag and moved forward.

She must have heard the sound, because she turned and then for a second or two remained statue-like. In that moment, a thought flashed in Luca's mind: *Does she still want me?* But then she started to run, calling his name, and flung herself at him.

He caught her in his arms, and they clung to each other. *She* was his life. Not these vines. Flora, always.

A NOTE TO THE READER

Dear Reader,

Thank you so much for choosing this book. After *Sisters At War* was published a significant number of people wanted to know what happened to Delphi, and as I had become very attached to her, too, it wasn't a difficult decision to write this sequel.

The school in the first part of the story, Kingshaven, is based upon Kingsmoor, which my grandfather founded and of which he became head teacher in 1927. It was housed in the old hunting lodge of the Howard family — Dukes of Norfolk, in Glossop and it's where I was born. It remained as a pioneering private boarding school, with a good reputation until the late 1950s. It moved and the original premises were demolished when the cost of upkeep become too great. Some of the pillars and other ornate stonework were incorporated into the new estate of bungalows that were built in its place — now called Old Hall Close and Park Close.

Until recently, I lived in Northern France, and in one of the larger houses in our village there was a Frenchman who told me the story of how, when he was a boy in 1940, his family were going to drive away in the middle of the night to escape the approaching Nazis. As misfortune would have it, the enemy arrived as the family were halfway down the drive and they sped back to the house. This property was taken over by the invaders, and subsequently used as a planning base for the V1 rocket installations, many of which survive, albeit in ruins. This incident coupled with the germination of other ideas for Delphi and her family, became part of *Resistance of Love*.

In the story, Sid Connew lied about his age to enrol for active service early and join a small ship which runs British secret agents into Europe as part of his work in the Royal Naval Coastal Services. In reality, Sid did this, and also undertook commando training in Scotland, as well as his initial instruction. He continued to serve on Motor Gun Boats and Motor Torpedo Boats, patrolling the North Sea until after the end of the war. He was involved in protecting ships and small craft from German U-boat and E-boat attacks during the D-Day landings. As such, in 2017 he was awarded the rank of Chevalier and a Légion d'Honneur medal from the French President for his brave service. Over the last six years, Sid became a good friend. He died in October 2021at the age of 96. He never did agree that he was a hero.

Another man mentioned in the story is Henri Fioccia. He was one of many involved in escape lines in and around Marseille in the south of France during the second half of WW2. He was a wealthy entrepreneur, a bon-viveur and was married to one of the most famous heroines of the Special Operations Executive, Nancy Wake. The Gestapo became aware of a troublesome and elusive agent who they called The White Mouse. When the network was betrayed Nancy fled Marseille but Fiocca stayed behind and was captured, tortured, and executed in October 1943.

There are many heroes who don't believe they are and many acts of unsung bravery. This book is dedicated to those people.

If you enjoyed reading *Resistance of Love*, you might consider writing a short review on **Amazon** or **Goodreads**. These, from knowledgeable people, are so important for authors' success but also contribute to other readers' choice of a book. If you would like to know more about my writing, my website is **www.rosrendleauthor.co.uk**. You can also **sign up for my**

newsletter. I often give free gifts and there is early access and information about my books. I love to hear from readers, and you are able to connect with me through **Facebook** or via **Twitter**. I hope we'll meet again in the pages of my other novels.

Ros Rendle